Testament of the Stars
Alexandra Beaumont

Testament of the Stars

By Alexandra Beaumont

Published by Gurt Dog Press

Cover artwork by Audrey Golden

Additional cover work by Nem Rowan

Editing by Jordan Ray & Nem Rowan

Proofing by L. B. Shimaira

Chapter header texture by Anna Poguliaeva

Lucien Schoenschrift font by Peter Wiegel

Digital ISBN - 978-91-986729-4-7

Print ISBN - 978-91-986729-5-4

Testament of the Stars

Alexandra Beaumont

"Is it even so? Then I defy you, Stars…"

Romeo & Juliet, William Shakespeare

Chapter One

The Astrologer-Elect oversees the Astrologers, seconded only by the Council and the Guard. All will answer to the Stars.
~ The First Astrologer-Elect

Time crept by for Einya Arden. Locked in the Astrologers' cave for thirty days in preparation for this moment, left blindfolded so that she would learn to feel the fallen Stars without seeing them. They were so close, they felt like her own shadow, but she still didn't feel ready to join the settlement's Star-worshipping cult.

"Initiates, your day has come. Astrologers, enter."

Einya flinched a little as the clear voice rang out, breaking the long silence. Sounds of shuffling leather shoes echoed through the cavern as the established Astrologers sidled in. She twitched as bodies bustled by, knocking against her where she knelt. Soft hands brushed her cheeks before tugging away the blindfold. She couldn't make out the face of the person who'd done it, as cracks of sunshine splintered around the gap in the door that led into the cave, blurring her vision in the sudden light.

Shadows of shapes slowly emerged, her vision settling. What now? Slowly she stumbled to her feet and tried to slow her breaths, watching the other initiates cluster together.

"Over there," a voice boomed behind her. Einya startled and turned to see the face of an Astrologer looming over her. His strong hands jostled her into a line with the other initiates, the press of their bodies surging all around her. Too close, she clumsily stumbled over strangers' feet.

A font etched with Constellations and two carved faces dominated the middle of the Astrologers' cavern. Each initiate ahead of her stepped up to it and lowered their head. What happened then, she couldn't tell in the darkness. Gulping nervously, Einya shuffled forward in the line until she stood before the font, gripping the stone handles.

She looked up, the Astrologer-Elect standing ahead of her with an imperious glare across the cave.

"Drink the Star-blood," he commanded.

Einya's breath hitched, and she looked down to avoid the man's gaze. The Star-blood undulated with translucent colours in the cauldron. What would happen when she drank it? Behind the stone bowl, two pitted fallen stars they called the Star-rocks dominated the chamber and grinned down at her in the flickering torchlight.

Was this really everything her ten-year struggle had led to? The freedoms of rank were all that she'd wanted: to marry and live as she chose. But at what cost? Now she stood between the Stars that had fallen into Gemynd a hundred years ago with disappointment tingling through her. Where were the magnificent glowing beacons of truth the Astrologer-Elect proselytised about? All she saw were dull grey rocks.

The stone floor was slick with frost, her bare feet almost slipping as she took the final step up to the lip of the font. She looked up, longingly glancing at the door to the sunlit courtyard beyond.

Egg-shell whites of all the other Astrologers' eyes reflected the low torchlight, hanging like glowing orbs in the darkness.

The clipped voice of the Astrologer-Elect grated through the cavern again; his deep-gouged wrinkles heavy-set in a frown. "Initiate Arden, mix your blood in and then imbibe the blood of the

Stars. Become one of us. Do not delay your ascension. There is no choice for you now."

Einya dragged in a shuddering breath, bile rising in her throat. Her fingers fumbled with the clasp holding her dagger in place as she tugged it free from the frigid leather. She raked the knife across her palm. Plunging her hand into the cauldron, the liquid seared her flesh as she scooped it up and raised it to her lips.

The heated elixir reeked of eucalyptus and left a blue powder residue clinging to her acorn flesh. The Star-blood stung as it slid down her throat. Staggering away from the cauldron as the next initiate stepped up behind her, she slumped against one of the Star-rocks. The faces of the assembled crowd of Astrologers blurred. Was this normal? A strange euphoria seeped into her mind; manic laughter tumbled from her lips, and long nails dug, claw-like, into her wrists.

A steady trickle of blood pattered to the ground from her hand. Someone clutched her shoulder, muttering some kind of welcome that didn't quite sound coherent. The Star-blood still burned through her veins. Light-headed, she clumsily grabbed at the nearest Astrologer to stop herself crashing to the floor.

"This isn't what I wanted. I didn't know it would be like this," she mumbled, but her words sounded like screams in her ears.

The ashen faces of the crowd blurred entirely then. Feverish and sickly, she found she'd slid to the floor. A pulsing whisper calling her name was the last thing she remembered as a strange sleep tugged at her.

Einya woke much later with the largest of the two Stars at her back, compressing the skin between her shoulder blades against her spine. She pushed herself up and crawled, groggy, toward her coat, which she had dropped to the floor. Her boots were at opposite ends of the cavern somehow, and it seemed that the other Astrologers had similar problems. She dragged herself through the groaning bodies until she'd gathered her belongings, clawing her coat around her shoulders.

Voices babbled through her ears as if someone was speaking just out of her hearing's reach. Staggering to her feet, she hauled herself towards the door.

"Over here, come on sis." Her brother's voice cut through the clamouring crowd, a familiar gentle grip around her shoulders. She gratefully inhaled the muted sandalwood scent he always wore; it took away the damp stench of the cave. He helped her stay upright, and they staggered towards the door.

Einya watched as Bri looked around eagerly as they left. This was the only time he would ever be allowed to see the cavern. All because he had to lead her away in her addled state as was the way with all new Astrologers.

It cheapens the significance of this first night sleeping in the Constellation's cocoon, she thought. *When you have to be carried away in a stupor.*

She tangled one hand into her brother's robes to support herself as they crossed the threshold into the fresh air. It felt freeing to fill her lungs with it, and Einya sighed as she blinked away the haze from her vision. Her other hand clutched the newly given Star-gems, bound in a silken silver pouch, that each Astrologer carried for casting birth-Stars and divining futures. Her memory seemed to fade then.

She experienced the carriage ride back only in short bursts as she fell asleep and woke with a start a few times, winding through the ascending cobbled avenues to the noble quarter atop the hill. She flexed her sliced-open hand, looking down at the thick blanket of bandages tight around it. Bri must have tied it there. When, though? With a start, she realised she was wearing a different outfit too; had they stayed in an inn somewhere? How many hours had she lost? Bri was staring out the carriage window, and Einya shut her eyes again. Maybe it was better not to know.

Her thoughts didn't settle into place until the two of them were sat within the lavish halls of their family home, their bodies each sunk deeply into a comfy leather chair. She felt her brother press a glass of wine into one hand.

A thought clawed its way through the fog lingering in her mind, lighting her eyes. "I'm legally able to marry Tols."

Einya waited, dreading a repeat of his well-known rants about his hatred of the Star-cult that governed the settlement.

Bri just smiled sadly, whispering: "She won't have heard you've become an Astrologer. You know they don't hear our news in Rask. You should go soon and tell her."

Einya nodded, trying to ignore the shadow that flickered through her brother's eyes as she drank deeply. The crystal-blue powder of the Star-blood residue still clung to her fingers and now tarnished the dainty glass in her hands.

She tried not to think about the despair she knew Bri would be feeling at losing her to the Astrologers. What else could she do? She noticed his forced smile as she spoke of her plans, saw that he gripped his wine glass almost tightly enough to snap its stem.

"I'm happy for you, sister," Bri whispered, looking everything but happy.

Einya put her wine down on the granite table, trying to smile. "Speak, Bri, why are you frowning?"

He shook his head. "You don't want to hear it. You know my feelings on the Astrologers' abuse of power, and you know I think you're better than that."

Einya's muted smile fell away, heart plummeting. "You know that I did it so that I can be a ranked spouse for Tollska and give her a life here… not to wield power over her." The last was a murmur, swallowed by the vast hall of their home.

Bri leant forward, matching her low voice. "I know you did, but it's still unjust. People should be able to marry freely without giving over their mind to the Stars."

"You can't say all this." Einya leant forward, spitting her words out urgently. "Someone will hear you and then—"

"Knowing you shouldn't say something and saying it anyway is the bravest breed of honesty," he interjected, chewing on the edge of his fingernail.

"Stars above. You have to be more careful! I don't make the rules, Bri, I just want Tollska to have everything she deserves. That involves her not having a struggling life in Rask. I've worked for this for almost ten years…"

Bri sighed. "There must be a way to help more than just Tollska—there must be."

"If you find it then tell me; you know I've always tried hard to understand your views on this." She shook her head and looked down, noticing he had ink stains on his skin. So, he was still printing anti-Astrologer propaganda. She looked away, pretending she hadn't seen it. "I will always have your back, Bri, even though we have different paths…"

"You will always have me, too, even if we fight. When will you go find Tollska?"

Einya heard him sigh again, feeling relieved at the subject change. She stood. "Now, if you'll forgive me. I want to tell her quickly. I've not been able to visit since the preparations began."

"Get you gone, then." Bri grinned, following it up with a wink. "I look forward to welcoming her to the family. Be careful in Rask, as ever. I'll walk with you down there, and then we can celebrate at the banquet this evening."

She saw his frown as they stood and felt absurdly grateful as he smiled again to hide it from her. He followed her from the hall, making a few light jokes to fill the awkward silence.

Chapter Two

We are blessed by twin Stars. Shine out to all others: show them might, show them glory.
~ The First Astrologer-Elect

Einya had to pause again, her brother was walking so much slower than her. If he sped up, maybe she'd reach Tollska's before her nerves got the better of her.

The streets were empty, the grand folk of Gemynd still in their warm homes. It was too early in the season for snow to settle on the vast, flat-topped hill, but the ground was slippery with the early winter frost. Bri was right to walk slowly, but did he have to take so long?

The only people they saw as they descended the steep hills were Raskians brought up to sweep the last of the autumn leaves from the cobbled streets.

Before descending into the ever-steeper avenues down to the walls, they passed the tall slate tower belonging to the

Astrologer-Elect. Einya paused, rubbing the symbol of a Constellation across her forehead, glancing toward the rough stone walls of the Star-rock cavern below the tower. She ignored Bri's hiss and turned away to continue by her brother's side, down towards Rask.

The bridge towered over their heads as they descended, one of four arching over the Rask district so that Gemynd's nobles could exit the settlement without going through the slums. The alabaster bridges were cleaned to perfection, while the pillars rooted in Rask were covered in moss and sludge in a sickeningly obvious contrast of lifestyles. Einya pushed down a surge of guilt and kept walking.

Einya and Bri weaved their way toward one of several steep spiralling sets of steps cut into the wall that led down into Rask, avoiding the large bridges. At the bottom, Einya lifted a heavy latch on the iron gate into the winding streets. It hadn't been cleaned in years and the rust flaked off the metalwork.

"No guard yet," Bri muttered.

"Too early. They only check permits after midday."

"Yes, and then there's no way to get a cart permit to go up the promontories. It's a mess."

She shrugged. "There are ways to plan ahead."

"One day you'll see past your blindness, I hope."

Einya sighed. "Where are you going, anyway?"

"To see a friend."

"A friend?"

"It's best you don't know."

They'd reached the bottom of the stairs then, and Einya tried not to glare at him reproachfully. How could he be so careless? There had been examples of dissidents made before, and next it could be Bri hanging in the square… She wanted to slap him. They instead shared a quick embrace, before both were on their way in separate directions; Einya heading down the familiar streets to find Tollska, and Bri heading back up the steps towards home.

The Raskian avenue was smeared with grime, vomit and probably worse. Einya tugged her hat low over her brow and stepped brusquely over the cobblestones. It wasn't that the

Gemyndians weren't allowed or expected here, sometimes it was just better to go unnoticed.

Despite all the dilapidation of the settlement, Rask was a lively place. Celebrations always followed the creation of new Astrologers, even in Rask, despite the people never being told who the Astrologers were.

A few drunken waifs splayed across splintered benches in the alleys, paying her little notice. Upon the ragged beamed buildings, colourful words were painted, brightening the otherwise drab wattle and daub with the quick-witted poems or limericks central to Raskian life.

The door she eventually reached was as familiar as it was rickety. Einya knocked, one sharp rap and the door opened almost instantly. She was met by a grinning face as she stepped over the threshold into the small room.

Tollska's black hair tumbled around her shoulders as she gripped Einya tightly.

"Where've you been? It's been so long," Tollska whispered.

Einya held her tighter. "It happened, Tols... I'm an Astrologer at last. I'm sorry I couldn't say before. But finally, you can get away from this horrid place."

"I'm pleased for you." Tollska's smile faded. She pulled away and went to a table by the door.

"What is it?" Einya's stomach lurched when she reached out to clutch Tollska's dress in her hand. "Why aren't you happy?"

Einya's heart trembled at Tollska's expression when she looked back to her, and she gripped the Raskian woman's hand tightly.

"What is it? Tell me what it is."

"I've just accepted rank in the Constellan Council, and they made me take a different Gemyndian sponsor as spouse. I'm to advise the Astrologers. I had to decide there and then..."

She took Tollska by the arms and held her as close as she could manage. "How could you?"

"They made me say yes right there and then if I wanted it."

"Does that mean you've accepted this other offer?" Einya gripped a little tighter, her fingers contrasting with Tollska's pale arms etched with gentle vine-like ink swirls.

9

"It does." Her words barely escaped her lips. "I had to accept it to keep the rank. I couldn't miss my chance to change all this…" She waved her hand vaguely at the threadbare homestead she kept.

Einya held one hand up to Tollska's lips. "You could have waited for me…"

Tollska's frantic words tumbled out. "I didn't know, Einya, I had to make a choice."

Einya felt the sickness from earlier rise again. She could have handled almost anything, but not this. She took Tollska's hand, leading her to sit on the side of the bed. "But you can break it off now. I promised I would change it for you, so I came to ask if you will marry me. Stars above, Tols, you are everything to me. I wanted to ask you more ceremoniously, but there it is."

Silence rattled around the hut as the wind battered the bare stick walls. Tollska's sweet smile slowly returned to her crimson lips. She glanced back at Einya, and they sat together on the edge of the straw mattress, foreheads brushing briefly.

"I'll try to break it off, and then… yes, definitely yes!" Tollska grinned anew, her bright green eyes shining like emeralds.

"Just one more day, and then we'll wrap our hands in silk and find a star-lit glen to be wed. I promise." Einya brushed her lips across Tollska's forehead, her bandaged hand resting in her lover's lap. She had to believe it.

Einya struggled to untangle herself from their tight embrace. "Break it off, and then I'll see you tonight?"

Tollska's nod and smile kindled a fragment of hope in Einya's chest.

"I'll leave you to fix this, Tollska. Know that I love you, always." Einya turned to leave.

As she left the hut, the morning dew had not yet burnt away, and the first of the winter clouds clustered above the spires of Gemynd. Einya walked a few streets and then sagged against a wall, half-hurt yet half-hoping, the burn of tears still lingering in her eyes.

Chapter Three

Words, deeds and outcomes shine brighter than any star.
~ Jesk, The Word-Weaver of Rask

Tollska rushed from the hut as soon as Einya had left, practically running straight to the Temple of Words. The wooden building was nestled between two large oak trees on the bank of a farm irrigation channel. Bright burnt red paints, heavy with acrid scents, mingled with the scent of simmering spices as she entered. The concertina door opened to reveal painted bells hanging in rows like wisteria. In the breeze, each bell plucked its note from the temple's silence.

This place, sacred to Raskians, was the thriving hub of words that guided their plans and ambitions. She'd come here since she was young, always finding guidance in these walls. Tollska knelt in the centre of the narrow hall before a pot of chalk-covered slate shards with words painted onto them—unseen until the chalk was ritually washed away.

The temple was empty. Usually, there were lots of people here seeking guidance on what their lives would hold. After a while, a bald woman with words tattooed down her neck slipped out from behind a curtain to the side of the hall, simply attired in a grey dress that seemed dull against the crimson surroundings.

"Tollska, what's wrong?"

Tollska stood, her eyes flicking around the temple to see if anyone was hiding in the lantern-clad corners of the hall. "Jesk, I need you to break it off... please." Her voice shattered over the syllables as she strode towards the woman.

The Word-Weaver grimaced. "I can't, Tollska. It's all arranged. The seals are set on the agreements, it's done."

"Can't it be broken?" Tollska burst out, heart clenching in her chest.

"I'm sorry. It's too late. You know our needs. It's too good an opportunity to miss."

"This can't be happening..."

Jesk tilted Tollska's face up with one hand, gently lifting her gaze from the wooden floor. "What's changed, don't you want the rank anymore? You agreed to this."

Tollska took a deep breath. "I do. I know why I need it. I thought I was running out of time. But Einya's done it, she's become an Astrologer, and now I'm caught between what I want and what Rask needs."

"I see."

Tollska watched as the Word-Weaver padded, bare foot, across the hall to the wooden coracle at the centre. The lanterns flickered in a whipping gust of wind.

Jesk took a dusty-slate pebble from the coracle, holding it out to Tollska with a grim expression etched on her face. "We've been friends for many years, you know that I'd undo it if I could. You know there are bigger things at stake, it goes beyond the love you and Einya have for each other. I'm sorry for that, but it's the truth."

Tollska sagged to her knees again, clutching the ragged sleeves of her dress. Jesk crouched, wrapping one arm with a gentle tenderness around her shoulders.

"If you marry Einya now, you endanger her. By taking Pearth's offer, you keep her out of it and get us an ear in the military, too."

Tollska bit back an anguished sob of realisation. "I know I shouldn't involve her, but… I just can't believe it's come to this. I've made a route to get to Gemynd that keeps her safe, I guess that's what matters here."

Jesk nodded, sadly smiling. "I think you knew all along that, if you turned against Gemynd, she would be dragged down with you."

Tollska took a deep breath as the other woman's thumb tenderly stroked her spine. "Yes, I suppose I did. Look, I need to go. I need to prepare for this."

"Take this with you, wash it in the river and find the word to guide you." Jesk pressed the chalky slate into Tollska's hand. "Keep it by to remember your purpose in all of this."

"Do you know what it says?"

"I always know, deep down."

"Then my fate is set?"

"It is. I'll make you a legend, Tollska. I'll give your words to those who print words—they'll tell your story. You'll be a saviour to us."

Tollska shook her head. "Jesk, let's be clear, you keep me quiet. I'll be a ghost, not a legend. That's how we win. My story will be saving Rask. Tell my mother. Let me fade from memory."

"That is your choice to make." The word-weaver brushed one gentle hand over Tollska's forehead. "But don't go this alone."

"Alone is all I will be."

Tollska slipped her fur-lined boots on at the temple door and trudged out into the icy fields. The stinging smell of the spices still clung inside her nose as she walked to the river. Kneeling in the frost-clad grass, she gripped the slate pebble in both hands. In Raskian tradition, she brought it to her lips, kissed it, and then plunged it into the biting water. Her rough thumb rubbed against the slate, feeling its grooves as she scrubbed the chalk away.

When she pulled the stone out of the water, her wet hands ached in the brittle wind. She opened her eyes without having realised they'd been closed. One word that would cling to her life, slanted in rough white paint, stood out on the grey slate: *Sacrificial.*

Tollska of Rask knelt by the river until the sun started to fall, its golden hues dappling the leaves. She felt her heart settling like molten steel forged into a blade.

Chapter Four

Rask has forgotten we are one settlement.
~ Sepult Disren, Astrologer-Elect, speaking to the Constellan Council

Bri paused after having ascended only ten of the two hundred steps. He'd dreaded this day for years. He looked back over one shoulder and, when convinced that Einya was gone, turned around to pad back down the staircase. He removed his lavish coat and tucked it away on the lowest step by the gate, revealing a much shabbier one underneath, before heading into the shadowy streets.

In the dilapidated warrens of Rask, he fretfully watched over his shoulder, expecting guards to be following. Until recently, his life hadn't amounted to much: just the illusion of your average nobleman with more time and money than sense. He was happy that way. Only Raskians actually knew him properly. But now his secrets were unravelling.

He weaved his way here and there until he reached the alley he wanted, a small painted sign hanging at the end of it. Its peeling letters read: 'The Dead Mule.' The dilapidated tavern smelt as fetid as its namesake.

Inside it was contrastingly colourful, bright flashes of fraying drapery hanging from every beam and every plank on the wall it could be nailed to.

He walked directly to the bar, remembering many a fond night drowned in cheap liquor in this place. "Luskena here?"

"Out back, you rogue." The barman nudged his head toward the door and smirked.

Bri stepped through the curtain cloaking the door. The back room was a little simpler but with a set of well-worn chairs and cushions as well as a small ladder up to the mezzanine above.

"Where are you, mischievous lady?" he called.

"Up here, troublemaker."

He grinned and clambered up the ladder, striding over to where the woman sat on a stool by a small porthole window. Her curled mouse-brown hair framed her round face, and her broad shoulders were wrapped in a ragged dress.

"Well, well—didn't expect to see you back here." She stood and ran one hand over his chest.

"Needs must, and not like that." He grinned, one hand twisting tenderly in Luskena's hair.

"When you leaving?"

"Tonight, if I can manage it. Listen, I have a favour to ask. My sister is now an Astrologer…"

"At last. Began to think she'd never manage it."

Bri rubbed his soft thumb across the woman's cheek. "Ask them to look after her, please."

"Them?"

"Don't play with me, you know who I mean."

Luskena pierced him with a glance, her eyebrows raised and her lips set in a sardonic smile. "They've brought you misery because you've helped them, and still you trust them?"

"Not as much misery as they live with, and all I have done for them they will revisit upon Einya a hundred-fold. She will be safe."

Luskena gripped his forearms tightly. "I will tell them, then I expect you gone. I'd rather you gone than dead."

"Gemynd wouldn't kill one of their own."

"Maybe they don't see you as one of their own since they discovered your games… same as me."

Bri sighed, the resonance of Luskena's truth bubbling through him. "It matters little. I'm going anyway, so I'm not a hindrance to Einya's life."

"Ah, yes, her ambitions. Must be lovely to have those, and not be stuck down here amongst the pig-swill." Luskena spat on the floor. "Have you told her you're leaving?"

"That's one for this evening."

"Good luck with that, then. I will tell them, as you ask, but they won't do something for nothing. Are you taking Prethi? He's as much caught up in our strife as you these days."

"I'm aware of all that. Listen, one last thing." He dug his hand into the pouch at his hip, drew out a brass key and folded it into her fingers. "Keep printing until the ink blocks are taken or destroyed. Give Rask the truths so they can spread them, so they can turn against despots and injustice. Leave no cobweb undisturbed."

Luskena nodded, wrapped one hand around his upper arm and gently pulled him towards her. "One for the road, then."

Chapter Five

It's very well to have far-reaching objectives, but let's not forget the constitution we built our settlement on. We must focus on our home.
~ Lord Hyther, Constellan Council

The sun spilt through the shuttered windows into the large rooms, blending with the mahogany of the table Einya sat at. Her neat fingernails tapped against the lacquered wooden surface briefly before she sighed at her reflection in the mirror upon the table, picking up a minute clustered lace ruff and pinning it together so that it encased her neck.

She coiled her russet hair up into a twisted style that left the wisps spilling out of her braids loose around her shoulders. Gold paint above her eyes softly blended in with her complexion.

She sighed again, dreading the guests travelling from all across Gemynd to wish her well in her new life as an Astrologer: cousins, aunts and distant relatives no one quite knew the

with anymore. By the time evening arrived, the manor
ig, the final carriages rotating through the square below
·rived.

ya took the final moments to twist small Star-gem clips
ir when there was a knock at the door. Bri came bustling
d, as he usually did.
·s, can I help?" Einya tried to force an affronted frown,
tered too easily into a wide grin.
nya, don't toy with me. Is she coming?"
)elieve so."
nd did you ask? Did she agree?"
le did." Einya shoved away a stab of uncertainty. "She
·r offer, but she's declining it…"
nother offer, really?"
es, but now she knows I'm accepted she can turn the
n."
i clasped his sister's shoulder from behind, smiling at her
e mirror.
hen I hope you'll live in a bright, happy stupor forever
·e wed."
/e've not set a day yet."
lake it soon, for both your sakes."
nya grinned again and turned back to the mirror,
; every inch of her face. Behind her, Bri paced until she
ver to him, concerned.
Vhat's got you fretting, brother?"
saw Pearth in the hall."
ind what did the new Leader of the Constellan Guard

Jot much, some small words. Talk of the Arden dynasty,
drivel of striving for success… what a ranked family we

·xcept you, the wolf in a sheep's family." Einya smirked,
iround to look at Bri properly.
le watched the man sidle round the room, twisting the
lis coat in one hand awkwardly before finally speaking:
'm leaving this evening—silently whilst everyone is at the
I

Einya hauled in a sharp gasp. "What, you can't—wh
would you?"

How could he, on this day of all days? She stood, ange
bubbling in her heart.

"I didn't know how to tell you. It's this or a life in the towe
dungeons, and shadows cast on you, too. I'm going so that I wor
destroy your life and all you've worked for."

Her words took a long time to form. "What have you dor
to make this necessary?"

"You know my views on the persecution of the Raskian
you know I think the Star-worship is an excuse to stamp our powe
over Rask... they're starving, Einya."

"Speak softer! You've never voiced it, not publicly..."

"It's too late to hide it. You see, I wrote a pamphlet with m
views and had it distributed..."

She gripped her hand into a fist, restraining herself fror
slapping him. "How could you? How do they know it was you
How could you be so careless?"

"The Astrologer-Elect found out, and I'll be taken to th
tower in the morning. They let me stay tonight so I don't blemis
the proceedings, but I'm being watched. Pearth was the one to te
me. They're close, the Astrologer-Elect and Pearth."

Einya's nails dug into her skin as she pressed harder. "Yo
know the Elect's words carry weight; you know he is the link to th
Stars. So why take that risk again? I thought you'd learnt from las
time... you know they watch your every move."

Bri ran his hand through his hair, some strands visibl
ripping out as they snagged in his rings. "Listen to me, Einya. It
bigger than just me. It may have begun well, but a deep scar ha
cut through the Stars and at their heart, there is a pitted darknes:
Despite their shine, they are a twisted lie; and because of them, w
are happy to take the food of a starving settlement. And now m
sister will preach their alleged guidance to the people, whilst m
cousin enforces all the petty whims of the Astrologer-Elect. Ho
could I stay silent, when all of that is true? It is better I go."

Einya swiped at her eyes. "I need you here."

"I know, and I am so, so very sorry."

"Why did you pick now, of all the times?"

chewed at the edge of his finger before speaking. "I was

w I was losing you to all of this. I knew you were close

g an Astrologer. They'll mould you, like heat slicing

x. When they are done, I won't recognise you."

on't change." Indignant, and disbelieving, her breath

staccato sputters. "Believe me, please…"

u'll always have my love, but try to stay gentle and

m?"

a tilted her chin upwards, eyes twitching into a squint

her. "I won't try, I will be all of who I am. I won't

u'll see."

was surprised to see Bri smile tenderly then, despite

words, as he whispered. "Listen, I am going to tell you

nd me—and you have to keep it to yourself. Do not

llska."

felt only numb shock.

placed a simple card sleeve, sealed, in her hands. "Hide

er need me, this is where to go. Don't bring your faith

if you come; they are just the illusion of light."

a watched Bri turn toward the door. His eyes seemed

, like they dug into her skin as he spoke.

ya, there's one more thing you need to know about

n I say she's in deep with the Astrologer-Elect. I mean,

s. I think she's doing something for him, I don't know

atch yourself, alright?"

just nodded, numb, as he crossed the room back to her

y squeezed her hand before turning to leave the room.

back through the crack in the door. "I'm going to make

ur sycamore trees, and I hope it will come true."

at wish?" Einya spluttered a little with her words.

tell you it won't come true. Just trust me."

winked and then retreated into the shadows of the stone

tside her chambers. Only then did she let the brief spike

ge out of her eyes before swiping them away again.

ya took one last look at the neatly sealed card, before

nto a small chest under her dresser. She slammed it shut

hands, causing her ears to ring, and strode toward the

er hands bunched into tight knots at her side.

22

Chapter Six

*Marriage may only happen between a ranked Gemyndian and a
ranked Raskian. This is decreed by the Stars.*
~ The First Astrologer-Elect

Einya emerged through the grand doors into the banqueting
hall, her embroidered dress pin-pricked with stars on the dark
velvet that trailed across the floors as she slowly moved towards
the ornately carved top table.

Her heartbeat pattered in her head like heavy rain against a
windowpane at the thought of seeing Tollska. Woven amongst her
excitement remained the constant clinging pang that Bri would be
leaving.

Einya scanned the crowd for Tollska but could not see her
there. Had she not come after all? Einya's mother sat by Briarth at
the table and cousins lined the outer edges. Her cousin Pearth,
Einya noted, was sat at the top table in deep conversation with
Sepult Disren—the Astrologer-Elect. Maybe Bri was right.

She moved to claim her place, but the Astrologer-Elect cut off his conversation and turned, holding out a crumpled hand toward her. "Stars watch you, Sister-Astrologer, and welcome. A long path I hear."

"Yes, Elect."

"Then much deserved. I was pleased to accept you into the Astrologers yesterday."

Sepult Disren daintily took Einya's hand and kissed the back of it, a soft smile gracing his lips with an unaffected politeness, and a welcoming glow you could well imagine from a family greeting. His frosty blue eyes kept a warmth in them that looked like it would melt ice. Einya remembered the man's pushing words, forcing her to drink the elixir or be cast out just the night before. He seemed much politer than the insipid man in the Star cavern.

"And I am pleased to be amongst you, Elect," Einya replied, gently pulling away to reclaim her hand.

The Astrologer-Elect's calm smile still gripped his lips. "Please, call me Sepult. After all, the bonds of the Stars join us together. We'll find their secrets together, you and I."

Einya forced a polite smile. It was hard to deny his warmth and apparent kindness. "Stars guide your path, Elect."

"And yours, dear one."

Moving away, it was impossible not to notice how Pearth watched her closely as she stepped delicately by. Einya ignored her harsh-faced cousin and took her seat near her mother. Customarily distant, the matriarch scowled down the length of her nose with eyes sharp as glass shards as the banquet began.

Platters heavily laden with rich cured meats were carried to every table in the room, chatter and laughter rising in a crescendo. The hall was built out of the traditional pale stone like much of the settlement but adorned with bright banners.

A glimpse of vine-like ink snaking up one arm pinpointed where Tollska sat amongst the guests in the common crowd, and Einya felt a creeping lump in her throat. Tollska should've been with her, not in the place of someone without rank.

Tollska's eyes met with Einya's, their leaf-like colour bright in the darkened hall. A moment of longing stretched thinly across the space between them before Tollska ripped her gaze away.

Einya's mouth hung open, wanting to ask something across that long distance, but instead she sealed her lips shut once more. She turned instead to Bri. "Tols is wearing red, a fine red gown, where did she get it?"

Bri shrugged, offering a sympathetic smile. "How could I know that? I'm sure it's nothing to worry on."

"Maybe." Einya remembered when the woman had barely had rags to clothe her feet, but still ran within the woods surrounding Rask where Einya often walked.

Her fierce intelligence and optimism that she would someday transcend all the hardships had shone brightly. Einya's heart had been lost to that optimism when they'd met in those trees, Tollska's passion burning like wildfire through Einya's own calculated world of marble emotions and the attainment required of nobility.

Even as they'd formed their plans, Tollska had never allowed Einya to gift her items of clothing or tokens from Gemynd. Einya had always been forced to accept that Tollska would make her own fortune, and then have fine clothes bought with her own coin. Yet, here she was, clad in opulent crimson silk.

The steady drone of a gong rang through the room, signifying the beginning of speeches as the dinner commenced. Einya jolted back into focus, snapping free from the memory and back into the room. Einya's mother, as the matriarch of the house, stood and the hall retracted into a miserable silence as propriety stole away the jovial mood.

Krytha Arden opened her lips, the crystal-like quality of the woman's skin glinting in the candlelight of the room. Einya looked at the empty chair next to her, kept customarily free to maintain the illusion their father might one day return, and thought back to when her father had left, angry at the way Rask was treated.

Whether he'd returned to his homeland of Aisren, or still roamed somewhere, no one had ever found out and many preferred the mystery.

"Today, the Arden family celebrates. So, I welcome you all, 'Myndians and Raskians, to our home. Stars shine down on this glorious day. I wish to celebrate the majesty of their benevolence, that they may continue to grant their kindness and radiate the paths of my family."

A gentle rumble of ascent murmured around the hall. Einya looked sideways at Bri, whose eyes were unusually granite-like and unreadable. Across the table, their friend and ward of the Arden family, Prethi, had an anxious look on his pallid face, leaving her wondering what secret the two men knew.

"First, I welcome our shining leader, Sepult Disren, to our halls; may his presence here bring the radiance of the Constellations in his wake."

The Astrologer-Elect raised his hand, inclining his head humbly to the collected audience. "The Stars bless you on this glorious night."

Krytha Arden smiled at the honour, the only time she had looked anything approaching pleased that evening. "Then I would like to raise for the attention of the assembled that my illustrious daughter has ascended into greatness. Her Star-blessed soul is now in the warmest arms of Sepult Disren, who has lifted her into the wise ranks of his Astrologers."

Thundering applause echoed around the large hall, but Einya almost didn't care as she watched Tollska again. Her mother continued.

"Lastly, but not the least of our announcements, I would like to commend to the Stars a match I hope they only see to be proper and beautiful in their shining eyes."

Bri's eyebrows furrowed, looking to his right to glance at Einya, whose lips hung open in clear surprise. The two of them exchanged a glance, and Einya quickly reached one hand to her neck to check her ruff was still in place when the next words her mother spoke shocked her into pausing with her hand still hovering in the air.

"Pearth, my niece, stand."

Einya's cousin stood up next to the Astrologer-Elect, and gestured out to the room, her auburn hair bright against her lavish black coat. The woman's pale-crystal complexion meant she looked more akin to Einya's mother than Einya ever had. A flash of red cloth emerged from the drab browns of the crowds, and in that moment, Einya felt as if her heart had clawed its way out of her chest. Bri's hand gripped her own underneath the large table as if he too had reached the same heart-rending thought that had struck Einya.

Their mother continued. "Pearth Arden, I am delighted to announce your betrothal—as sanctioned by our glorious Astrologer-Elect—to the partner of your choice."

Pearth's usually tightly pinched face brightened in an almost radiant smile as she held one hand toward the woman ascending the raised platform. Tollska's eyes looked only towards Pearth, and Einya's heart plummeted as if torn from the sky, like a soaring bird ripped down by a sharp-taloned falcon.

Pearth's voice grated on Einya's ears while she spoke, keeping a vice-like grip on Tollska's hand. "My spouse to be, Tollska of Rask, is to be on the Constellan Council to advise the Guard and the Astrologers. I am pleased to give her my hand in marriage to secure her rank and raise her from the farmsteads of Rask."

Applause ricocheted around the grand room as Pearth led Tollska from one side of the hall to the other for applause and recognition. Einya's fingers gripped the side of the table, ears ringing and head thrumming. The festivities restarted around her. They made space at the high table for Tollska. Her cousin and lover sat, side by side, seeming mutated and unnatural to Einya.

"Keep your face like stone, sis, and we'll talk later," Bri whispered, his hot breath brushing Einya's ear.

She touched nothing of the food in front of her, Briarth's soft words only distant noises while she counted the moments until she could leave. Bri was a different tale entirely; he twisted a meat knife into the depths of the wooden table until shavings of timber scattered around the plate in front of Einya.

She finally fled her family and strode towards the balcony doors, small heels hammering into the wooden floor. Taking one last glance at the splendid velvet red dress, she turned away with her chin raised determined to look strong and defiant.

Out in the gardens, frost gilded every curved stone surface. Einya's breath stabbed the darkness with misty jets. The music drifted after her, all the sleek marble stones of the balustrades reflecting the Stars. It should have been magical, but each Star cast its shadows across the ground where the trees blocked their glow. This was the only garden in Gemynd with trees, at her insistence. Now, even they offered little solace.

A warm hand found her shoulder. Einya spiralled around, the tail of her dress whipping out as she did, to see the crestfallen face of her brother. Anguish lanced through her again.

"I should have seen it. Tols said she had something to arrange," she spat out.

Bri reached out to her, soft palms brushing over Einya's shoulders. "She's trapped, Einya."

Einya shook her head vigorously. "She knew… she knew I was going to arrange it for her."

Bri frowned. "The Astrologer-Elect, he did this…"

"Why would he? Why would he care?"

"I don't know, I wish I did…"

"I'm sure you're wrong," Einya spat.

"Hm, perhaps."

They walked further away from the grand Arden manor, settling on a stone bench. Einya tugged frantically at the hem of his sleeve, turning Bri to face her. "Will you stay now, please?"

"I can't, but listen, will you come with me?"

"I…"

A shadow emerged from the steps to the manor. Bri rose and stood between the newly arrived woman and Einya. "This is not the time to be here, Tollska."

"I only just managed to get away. Look, I couldn't break the agreement. I'd lose my rank if I didn't go through with it… Einya, please understand," Tollska babbled, flustered.

Einya briefly scrunched her eyes shut, desperate to wrap the woman in her arms despite everything. "Tollska, stop. There are no words for this. I set up everything for you. I secured my rank, so you could get out of Rask. It was all set."

"I didn't know, I hadn't heard… we don't hear when these things happen. I panicked."

Einya tensed her hands, dragging them through her hair. "You should have trusted me. We had this planned for years, Tollska. I'm sorry I didn't become an Astrologer faster, but you knew I had this arranged."

Tollska's lip quivered and the Raskian woman's eyes seemed to spread wide, vulnerable and panicked. "I had so little time, they gave me a day... Einya, the Astrologer-Elect gave me a day to answer Pearth's offer. I was frightened, I didn't want to go back to scratching two coins together to get by. I want what you have: warmth, food, prospects."

Bri hissed, spitting words from between his teeth. "Do you see, do you see? This is what they have done, this is what they do to Raskians."

"Not now." Einya pressed one hand to her brother's shoulder, but he ripped away from her grip and strode off, leaving her alone with Tollska.

A tense silence echoed between them until the notes of Tollska's trembling words sounded again. "Einya, I'll still be close by... we could be together anyway if..."

"No."

"But..."

"I cannot do that, Tollska, it would end everything I've worked for. At least let me have the rank, even if I cannot have you. Just tell me why, why didn't you trust me?"

"Einya, there's more to it. I can't tell you more. I'm sorry."

"Then don't expect me to understand."

Tollska looked back towards the manor and Einya watched the unease in her eyes, pity simmering through her despite the betrayal.

Einya lifted one hand to Tollska's chin and tilted her face back towards her tenderly. "Tell me, please."

"Einya, I'm sorry, but I can't. If I do, and they find out I said anything, it'll be as good as over for me anyway. They knew more than I realised. I'm trapped, Einya."

"They? Who? If there is something else then tell me, let me help you."

A jolt sparked through Einya's heart at Tollska's bitter grimace, the woman's lips twisted into a sardonic half-smile.

"There's no part of me that doesn't want to be yours and share all I am with you, Einya, but both you and Bri are too unsubtle. There's too much at stake. I truly am sorry."

Einya felt a last ebb of disappointment as the final sparks of hope were snuffed out. "Just tell me one last thing: is there any warmth between you? I deserve to know that."

A poisonous look snaked across Tollska's face as she spat out her words. "Do you mean, do I love her? I couldn't, how could I? This is politics, Einya, and I hold none of the cards."

Einya's attempt at turning her heart to stone failed then, all the cold sentiments she'd managed to build up shattered away instantly. She reached up one gloved hand to brush a tear from Tollska's cheek. "I am sorry then that I couldn't give you any of the cards."

The wind battered the trees to fill the silence between them. Einya gently placed a kiss upon her forehead. "Tols, I wish you well. I really do."

"Einya…"

"Goodbye then. If you ever need my help, it will always still be here."

"I'll not forget the joys we had together, not ever." Tollska turned, walking away before anything more could be said between them.

Einya slumped down again on the bench with her fingers propping up her head, hoping that Bri would return from wherever he had slunk to.

The Stars shone their light down upon her as the late autumn leaves scattered from the trees and swamped around her ankles in the fading moonlight. The sun crested the gargoyle-filled roof of the Arden manor, and Einya knew her old life had faded with the previous day.

Chapter Seven

The people of Gemynd have forgotten they were once farmers, just like the Raskians. We used to be one settlement, now it's like we are two.
~ Anonymous, Constellan Council records

Elsewhere in the gardens, Bri circled through the carved stone landscape surrounding the manor, ignoring all the marble figures as he strode through the statue garden. Teeth bared, he huffed out heavy breaths laced with anger as he strode in chaotic loops around the stone plaza. He eventually turned back to find Einya, heading for a small gate on the left that would cut out into the settlement for a quick double-back through to the garden where he'd originally left her.

The guard at the gate did not say anything, but something flashed in the depths of the man's eyes. The guard thrust the butt of his matchlock against Bri's shoulder, which told him all he needed to know.

Pearth stepped out from behind a pillar behind the guard, her ruler-straight hair glistening in the moonlight. "Leaving now, are you?"

Bri sighed, twisting on the heel of his shoe to face her. "Not yet. We agreed the morning, didn't we? Why are you so invested in this, cousin, hmm? The head of the Guard herself coming to stop me walking freely in my own gardens, why is that?"

Pearth's lips twisted in a slight sneer. She shrugged, her scarlet doublet slipping slightly off one shoulder. "I'm trying to keep the peace here. Your words, these pamphlets: they threaten my efforts. Your sympathy with Raskian rebels not only endangers our family, but it endangers the whole settlement. You can't know by how much…"

Bri smothered a musical giggle. Alright, she was a soldier, but she might have learnt to lace a doublet properly. "I did nothing beyond what was decent; Raskians are starving and all we do up here is talk about how they are rightfully lesser than us. How we require them to be beneath us to maintain a so-called peace. Why persecute them?"

Pearth shook her head with a smile sliding up the side of her lips, and she tugged one hand through her hair. "You see shadows where there are none, this was ever your problem. I'm preserving peace, cousin, and stopping you pushing Rask into war against us with your dogma and lies. My aunt must be so relieved that at least one of her children is faithful to the Stars."

"Oh yes, I was ever the burden with all my cavorting; never a serious thought, ridiculous notions, overinflated ego. Must be why I got into politics." Bri grinned icily, eyes bright.

In stark contrast, Pearth's ice-laced eyes glanced over him disdainfully as if he were a slug on her boot.

"Recant all this, cousin, help me find peace, and I'll help you avoid the tower."

He shook his head. "I won't become what I hate."

"Stars damn you then, cousin." She spat and, turning on her heel, strode away.

Bri grinned, sure that the air smelt sweeter without his cousin there. He dallied a little before twisting on his heels back to the manor, seeing the guard watching him from the gate.

Turning back through the longer route under iron arches that branched between stone pillars in the gardens, the rows of gargoyles atop the walls sneered down at him. "I never liked you either," he muttered with a smirk, which quickly died on his lips.

In the distance, Einya sat on the stone bench still, head resting on the tips of her fingers as she stared at the ground. But, in that moment, something else tugged at Bri's attention.

He stopped abruptly, ripping his rapier from its scabbard, adrenaline rising. In the shadows thrown across the entrance to the staircase that curled back toward the manor, a figure rested with their back against the wall, a low hat pulled over their eyes.

Bri raised his blade, setting his shoulders in a strong stance and rolling up onto the balls of his feet. "Not content to arrest me, but rather assassinate me? In my own home?"

As the shadow slunk out of the darkness it manifested into the form of a wiry man with reed-like hair falling around his eyes and a donkey-like grin. "It's just me, you silly sot."

Bri smiled, nerves sliding away easily. "Prethi? How did you know I was leaving?"

"Luskena told me the other day, and then you were gone from the banquet, so I figured."

"You should go back; won't do you well to be seen with me."

"Nah, I'm sick of it here and would happily roam. So, you've no choice. It's about time I did something else other than writing yet more songs about how wonderful the Stars are and the splendour of Gemynd—there's a whole bigger world to write music about."

Bri raised one eyebrow as he slid his blade back into its sheath. "You'd have no idea what to do outside of Gemynd, we both know that."

Prethi circled Bri, plucking his fingers at the bright gold and white doublet he wore. "And you do?"

Bri sighed, grinning, and swatted the other man over the head with the tips of his fingers. How did Prethi always know how to put him at ease? "I need to see Einya first, then find me a way to get out. The guards are watching me, they've already stopped me going out into the streets."

As Bri stepped back close to Einya, he was sure he felt a lonely ache pouring out of her like the cascade of a waterfall. Gently, he lifted her chin as he knelt in front of her. Looking deep into her eyes he tried to brew up a warm smile. "Sis, why don't you leave with me."

"I can't, Bri. I would dearly love to, but don't ask me again in case I agree."

Her words still stung him with disappointment, but what else could he do? He couldn't stay. He kissed the back of her hand, not wanting to let her go.

Bri's heart shattered a little to hear the tears tremble in her voice, and he held tightly onto her slender fingers. "You will be strong, you will be bright. One day, come find me when you need me. Please?"

"Bri, I have lost everything I wanted. I can't lose you. Go quickly, and my life will be brighter for knowing you're safe somewhere."

For all the sadness in his sister's eyes, Bri almost felt that the sun would never rise again in Gemynd. He squeezed Einya's hands tenderly, a fissure of warmth crackling between them before he stood slowly. "Guard my location safely, sis. My world will be empty without your smile."

He watched as Einya trembled a little and stood, the folds of her velvet gown rustling the fallen leaves on the marble slabs.

"How will you leave?" she whispered.

"Through Rask, not over the promontories."

"Go safely, brother." Einya's fleeting smile seemed hollow still, and she turned from him to slowly walk back to the manor. He watched forlornly as she slowly ascended the stone steps, her hands running along the gently curved stone bannister before she faded from his view into the dark shrouds of the stone garden's shadow.

Prethi snatched away his attention quickly, as the smaller man stumbled up carrying a bundle of clothes. "Ready?"

"I suppose."

"Good." Prethi grinned and tugged a low hat over Bri's head, its brim completely blinding him. "Now put this on."

A few minutes later Bri felt like he'd doubled in size, feeling glad they'd stood by the trees, so the guards couldn't see as Prethi rubbed earth over the clothes. "This is some strange plan."

"Quiet down, hold this, and pretend to be drunk."

Bri looked down and saw that, concealed in the bundle, Prethi had been carrying a mandolin. "Pretend?" Bri smirked a little.

"Good point. Let's go."

"Prethi, if any of the Constellan Guard recognise me, you get running, hm?"

"Of course. In two shakes of a song-smith's tail." Prethi grinned, bouncing around Bri whilst they walked. As they approached the guards, he muttered, "Play along."

Prethi grabbed him by the collar of the strange silk coat he'd thrown over Bri's clothes, dragging him toward the guards. "This vagrant sang a song about Lady Arden being keen to take the edge off his pillar, if you get my drift? So here I am, throwing him down to Rask to sober up with the pigs."

Struck by dangerous curiosity, Bri briefly pushed the brim of the hat up, peering toward the guard to see if the lie had stuck. The guard's eyes seemed to pierce through the darkness, and Bri let the hat cover his face again. He slumped against Prethi, trying to seem drunker than he felt.

The guard stepped up, and he even chuckled a little. "They'll never learn, let me see his face though. Just need to be sure of something."

Bri tensed, the guard's hand gripping the edge of the hat. Bri wrapped his spare hand tightly around the hilt of his dagger, ready to whip it out and into the guard's stomach. It was too close for his rapier, the guard's breath hot against his cheek.

The pause as the hat was raised felt interminable, and as the guard realised his identity Bri's dagger flashed out from the heavy layers of clothing. He thrust it forward but saw, next to him, that Prethi had been faster and a small boot knife was lodged in the neck of the soldier.

The guard slumped to the ground with a look of shock frozen onto his dead face. Prethi tugged his blade out and blood cascaded over the cobblestones. "We should move him somewhere."

"No time and nowhere to put him. We've got to go," Bri muttered.

"What next, then?"

"Scratch together what supplies we can and then set our feet to the road."

They headed towards the stairs down to Rask. Bri guided them, pausing often and checking to see if any guards lined the roads or waited nearby. A scattering of small coins bought them both a flask of wine from an inn, which Bri slung over one shoulder. They wove through the smaller streets toward the spiral staircase he always took to get to Rask, doubling back several times to avoid the Constellan Guard.

To Bri's relief, the streets of Rask were easier to travel through with no one looking for them. They walked through the main streets for speed, before heading out through the tracks of the farms. Farmers were still labouring, having begun to feel the snap of winter frost, and were covering the roots of their winter crops with rags to keep the ice away.

Once they were out on the forest path away from the settlement, Prethi lowered the hood of his overcoat and Bri felt him bustle up beside him on the narrow path. "So where are we going, mighty explorer?"

"Parlenta first, and then to Aisren. Warn them both, see if they'll help Rask. I've never been to Parlenta, been to the farms but not through the Parlentan woods beyond."

As the pair wandered onwards, Bri drew his coat tighter around him. As ridiculous as he knew it to be, he always felt strange leaving the stone confines of the settlement and seeing trees. He remembered the song Gemyndian children would sing about entering the fields of Rask, all about catching a parasite from a Raskian bite.

Bri thought back to when he'd wondered about this from a young age, and when at eight years old he had first run from his studies to try to get into Rask. He had not known the way and had walked down the hill as best as he could, finding his way eventually to the rusty gates. His tutor had found him when he'd reached the top of the spiralling stairs and dragged him back to study again, telling his mother what a vagrant her noble son would turn out to be.

Next time, he got more ingenious and waited until the end of his tutoring before sneaking away. That next time, he made it to the bottom of the stairs. A Raskian man saw him and had carried him back up whilst telling him that dressed finely, people would know he was out of place. Curiosity about the wider world dragged at him still, feeling a tremor of excitement at hitting the road.

"Will you miss it?" Prethi's words tugged the tide of his thoughts back to the present as he looked at the scruffy-haired man.

"Not really—not at all, actually. I will miss Einya, but I'll carry her memory with me until I see her again."

Prethi smiled, and Bri was grateful the man made no spiking joke at his expense. "I hope you will," was all he said.

The two men walked until they found the hollowed-out trunk of an old lightning-struck tree. They huddled inside and passed the wine flask between them until the dawn's sun climbed over the horizon.

Chapter Eight

We must look to the ways other settlements worship the Stars and show our leadership.
~ Commander Arden, Constellan Guard

Drab clouds descended as winter stalked the settlement. All colour drifted out of Einya's life; as if the sun on the horizon she'd been running toward for years had now faded away completely. The first week with Tollska living in the Arden manor had been horrid, and Einya had spent most of it within her rooms to avoid everyone. She'd barely eaten and found some small solace in reading her astrological books while drinking a large amount of wine.

Knowing that habit could not continue, she had moved her belongings from the grand halls of the Arden estates after that week and instead settled in a quiet set of rooms close to the Star cavern and the Astrologer-Elect's tower. They were still opulent, though she had furnished them plainly. Her life had lost its frills;

lavish banquets became scant meals as she barely knew how to prepare them.

Einya checked the chest with obsessive frequency in those early days, fearing that someone might stumble upon the note containing Bri's location. No one spoke of his leaving, and whilst that was true, she believed he must be safe. A thought clawed regularly at the back of her mind: was all this nothing to do with the note, but actually to avoid seeing Pearth and Tollska living together in her former home, as was tradition? Of course, she knew the truth, and it gnawed at her constantly.

The wedding was looming, and Einya lost herself in the Star readings and divining that became the life of an Astrologer, to put it from her mind. She hoped to find herself a modest sort of life, away from regular contact with all she had left behind.

Distractions: any she could find would do. She roamed Gemynd, offering guidance and hope from the Stars to any who needed it, assigning the right Constellations to children at their birth and divining the worth of someone's life from the ascending Stars at the time of their death.

In the evenings, Einya would unlock the little door to the cavern each Astrologer had a key to, and wind her way down the tunnel to sit with the Star-rocks. She went to be alone; only a guard stood nearby, at the entrance, and they were not allowed into the cavern itself.

Inside, she would speak to the Star-rocks and let her mind drift. In the shadows with the Stars, she'd let the memories flood through her, aching for Tollska terribly. Her skin reflected the gentle glow of the flames in the wall sconce as she wept softly. How could this be her life now? It felt so hollow. But, when morning came, she would trundle herself out of the cavern a little more healed.

In the month that followed, a steady tension ramped up in the settlement; a growing unease at the pamphlets circulating had led to settlement-wide nervousness about the rising up of the Raskians. The first she really saw of it was when the guidance Gemyndians had asked her for changed.

One morning, she was summoned to a small house near the gates. The homestead was lavish despite its size, as was everything on the top of the hill. Tugging on the brass door-pull, a tolling bell rang within and a Raskian servant opened the door.

"Come in, Astrologer, please."

"What am I called for?"

"Master Thennet needs your blessing, Astrologer. I'll just take you to him. It's best that way."

She stepped into the fire-lit hall, glancing up at the black banners that hung over the mantles. Led through the corridors into a grand master bedroom, a small boy wrapped in heavy fur throws lay shivering on the four-poster bed. Einya chewed her lip; it was always worse when it was the children. She didn't like them particularly, but it was still always worse.

The parents, finely dressed in black silks, rushed to her as she entered.

"Thank the Stars you're here, Astrologer Arden. The Astrologer-Elect said you'd be the best help. He is sick."

"He said that… I—never mind. What sickness does your son have?"

"He's been cursed; the Raskians have taken away his birth-Constellation."

"That's impossible…"

"I know my own child. He is changed by what they have done."

Einya gripped her hands into fists—how could this be? She forced her lips into a reassuring smile. "I'm sure that's not true; it may just be winter-fever. I will see what I can do."

Lady Thennet shook her head. "My spouse is a guard, and the Raskians targeted him. This red-headed witch, she cursed him with a stone painted with a word. She gave it to him, and the next day, my son fell ill."

Einya sighed. "Let me see to the child."

Sitting on the edge of the bed, placing one hand on the child's clammy forehead, she lifted his eyelids with her thumb. The pits of his eyes were grey and vacant, no sign of his pupils. What was this? It was like no winter sickness Einya had ever seen before. But a curse? Surely not…

"Well, what is it?"

Einya sighed thoughtfully. "I'm not sure yet. I will get a tincture for him, try to bring him out of this fever."

The mother nodded. "Go quickly, please."

Speed guided her steps as she left. The apothecary was not far from the house, and she quickly acquired a small bottle with a viscous purple liquid in it. Walking back to the Thennet house, she hoped—prayed—it wasn't true. How could Raskians do this to a child; could they even possess powers like that? Or was it just a convenient Gemyndian belief?

The door to the house was open when she returned. A strange, inhuman wail clawed at her hearing as she crossed inside. Terror clutched her mind and heart as she rushed into a sprint up the stairs into the bedroom.

On the bed, Lady Thennet was clutching her son, who spat blood over the white sheets. "Help him!" she screamed.

Even as Einya got to them, a final spatter of blood shot from the boy's lips. Flecks hit her cheek, but she reached out to the child anyway. How could this be happening?

"Let me help him."

Einya pulled the cork from the bottle with her teeth; she was no healer but what else was there to do? These were the flaws of a society that based all healing on the Stars, she thought, panicking as she tipped the liquid down the child's throat.

The liquid just welled up again out of the boy's mouth; he couldn't swallow. His breathing had stopped, and a brittle silence fell in the room.

After a moment, Einya spoke. "This was poison; it was too quick. Who gives him food?"

Lady Thennet just sobbed, and it was the boy's father who eventually answered: "Our cook is from Rask."

"Fetch them," Einya said to the maid at the door.

The maid hurried out as the sobbing continued. What now? Einya's hands trembled.

The maid rushed back through the door. "She's gone, Astrologer."

"I am sorry for your loss," Einya whispered, still reeling from the speed of it all.

"You should go," Lady Thennet spat through her sobs. "Send another Astrologer to perform the death rites and tell the Astrologer-Elect that Raskians are killing our children."

Einya left the room wordlessly, trying to bury the guilt that stabbed at her. Out on the street, still numb with disbelief, she shuddered. It was obvious now. Something was changing, and no political marriage between Rask and Gemynd would heal the rifts here.

Chapter Nine

*Raskians have long been a curse; we must make sure we cleanse
the pure and rid ourselves of those beyond our saving.*
~ Astrologer-Elect Sepult Disren

It was close to midnight, and the temperature of the cavern
was plummeting but Einya didn't notice, still caught in the fog of
her brooding thoughts. She'd spent three full days in the cavern,
seeking answers. How could she have saved the child? Did
Raskians really poison the boy? Was it actually a curse as the
parents had thought?

A light cracked through the darkness from a door up into
the manor, and the crinkle-skinned face of the Astrologer-Elect
emerged from the shadows.

"Astrologer Arden, do you find yourself so lacking in
occupation that you sit here all night?"

Einya looked up from the floor where she'd cast her Star-gems under the light of a small lantern. "Elect, I come here to think and ask for guidance."

"Which you are welcome to do whenever you wish. Have the Stars answered your questions?"

"I am still awaiting that day."

"What is your birth-Star?"

"The Furnace, Elect."

"Sometimes wisdom is a slow burn thing. Will you come sit by my fire and think with me over some wine, instead of shivering down here?"

Einya nodded, unable to refuse even as a feeling of reluctance crawled over her skin. Warmth, she needed *warmth* more than answers just now.

The pair walked up a spiralling set of stairs through the side of the cavern into the lower levels of Sepult Disren's tower. The room the stairs emerged into was an elaborate wood-panelled sitting room with paintings of old Astrologer-Elects hanging over every wall. The stone-slabbed floor was intricately carved with Constellations, and Sepult guided her over to two pristine leather chairs by a lit fireplace. He poured out and passed her a large glass of wine.

"This is the vintage produced for when I was elected, eight years ago now. How time has passed. Please, sit."

"Thank you."

They settled into the warm leather, the torch-lit hall a cosy juxtaposition to the frosty Star cavern beneath it. The wine was bitter on her tongue, but with a subtle sweet finish, which she swallowed quickly so as not to splutter.

Across from her, the Astrologer-Elect leant forward intently. "So, Einya—if I can call you that? Good. What do you hope to find, sitting with the Stars at night? The guard tells me you have been there often."

She sipped deeply whilst finding her words. What could she say? If she told him about the belief in Raskians attacking Gemyndians, would Tols be safe? She forced a meek smile. "I seek guidance."

"On what, dear one?"

"Direction. I've always been so certain, but now that's gone."

"Is that because you have achieved what you set out to do? It's often this way."

Einya paused, unsure whether to proceed. Sepult leant further forward then with his elbows resting on his knees.

"I had planned to be wed, Elect, but my spouse of choice chose another."

"Ah. Then I am sorry for you. Not even the Stars can mend a bruised heart, dear one."

She smiled, faintly. "I had hoped they might tell me what I should do next."

"Only time can do that."

"I... I know."

A brief pause, and then the Astrologer-Elect placed his glass down and leant back with a casual affectation. "I can help, if you wish. Well, I can keep you occupied, as much as you'll allow me."

His words were slow and precise, one hand twisting the corner of his doublet back and forth repeatedly. "I need someone to take on the mantle of ensuring peace with Rask. The Stars guard our memories and I need access to them. I need someone to see what the Stars remember and tell Raskians that there is no cause for conflict with Gemynd. I want to end a war before it begins."

"A war with Rask? Are you sure?"

"Surely you cannot be oblivious to the growing tension?"

"I have heard some worries from people, but nothing more," Einya murmured, hoping Lady Thennet or the other Astrologer hadn't spoken to him.

"Yes, it is part of a rising disquiet which I hope to end quickly for everyone's sake. There are old books that show previous Astrologers have used memories as weapons. We only found them recently, in an unexpected place. No one has studied them yet. It needs someone of your dedication. You would have to drink of the Star-blood to do it, to speak to the Stars, to tell Rask there's no reason to rebel."

Einya bit her lip slightly, Tollska's words about her subtlety still cascading through her mind, clashing with Bri's repeated warnings. "I'd be honoured to speak to the Stars, but…"

"Excellent, then let's drink to that. I'm very pleased to have one of your calibre among my Astrologers." Sepult raised his glass and she clinked hers against it lightly, momentarily distracted by the swilling colours.

Even so, Einya didn't miss the barely contained excitement that danced in the eyes of Sepult Disren as she downed the rest of her wine. What did he want her to achieve with all of this? A spike of wariness shot through her. Keeping the conversation going a little longer, she forced herself to relax. At last, the fire burnt low in the grate, and she made her excuses. The Astrologer-Elect summoned his Raskian butler and had him bring out a pile of dusty books. They were bound in cracked, crumbling leather with a faint pattern of Stars on each of the spines.

He slid them over the table to her. "Until next time, dear Einya, but I'm glad we spoke. Take these with you, learn what you can."

"Thank you. Good night, Elect."

"Call me Sepult, please. Visit the Stars whenever you wish, find out the secrets of their memories." The man winked. "We will drink fine wines and learn great things together."

She smiled, sure that it would look hollow, and turned quickly towards the narrow door down into the Star chamber. It was almost warm, and she walked the short distance back to her rooms, setting the books to be proudly displayed on a prominent shelf.

The night before Tollska's wedding finally arrived, several weeks after Bri had left Gemynd. Einya settled in the cavern with a thick wool cloak around her and lay at the foot of the Stars, still hoping her dreams would bring some kind of guidance. This would be the last time she tried; it wasn't worth it to live any more of her life in the dark like this.

Reading the books had been hard; the old Constellations mentioned were new to her, and she had not found any reference to reading the memories of the Stars as yet. The books had mentioned the imbibing of something called Astamitra to hear the voices of the Stars. She had later read that it was also known as Star-blood and could be concentrated from liquid into powder. From then on, her ritual had involved drinking from the Star-blood font to try and hear the voices that must be hidden somewhere within the cavern.

She'd settled into a strange routine: greeting the guard at the rickety door into the cave and lugging all the books down into its depths. The last step was to set up a little circle of lanterns and candles, before dipping her hand deep into the Constellation Font at the centre of the cavern and drinking the contents. The swirling viscous liquid, still bitter and peculiar, clung to the surface of her tongue. Einya always swallowed it down quickly, trying to ignore the slimy sensation gripping the inside of her throat. Then, silence. This time was exactly the same as she lay back and shut her eyes.

Fitful sleep quickly grabbed hold of her, and murky dreams soon followed. Einya's skin was melting like wax as she sweated inside her woollen cloak. How, after all her efforts, did no star-voices answer? Instead, blurred scenes of suffering played out in her feverish dreams. People in chains battered their fists against the rocks, greying skin clinging to their gaunt faces in the darkness. Someone was calling to her with a voice she couldn't quite hear, begging for help. It tugged at her painfully until the panic pulled her out of sleep.

She woke with a jolt. The damp cave was oppressive, Einya's eyes still blinded with sleep. Suddenly desperate to leave the cold cavern, she quickly packed her belongings and strode up the passage into the welcome morning sun. The fresh frosty air plunged deep into her lungs. She sighed, exhausted but relieved.

At least the wedding would be done after tonight and she could truly leave her old path behind her.

She'd tried to ignore the loud and constant preparations, but that proved impossible. The gates in the lower quarters of the central settlement had been thrown open. Long feast tables could be seen in the streets of Rask from the towering walls of Gemynd.

All the promontories were laden with carriages bringing nobles from the manors surrounding Gemynd to the wedding, and Raskian citizens were left to look up at the lavish carriages travelling unattainably above them as they stood at the base of the stone pillars.

Amongst the feasting, the music and the dancing, Einya thought no one would notice the wanderings of one grey-clad Astrologer. She hadn't meant to arrive here, but habit had guided her steps. She had drifted through the wide streets of Gemynd and down into the narrow alleyways of Rask. The sun was bright, and the festivities would last the entire day until the ceremony under the Stars after the fall of dusk.

Einya walked through the streets of Rask for the entire day, watching the festivities that should have been for her own wedding. Finally, as dusk fell, she wound her way up familiar cobbled streets until she found Tollska's old door. It had been battered open; someone must be squatting in the now empty rooms.

Her hand hovered, poised to turn the latch, or knock, as the faint tune of a gavotte echoed down the little avenue and the light began to fade from the day. She had one hand resting on the splintered wood when quick footsteps, running up the alley, echoed behind her.

Large hands gripped her shoulders, their pressure digging into her flesh. A rough bag tugged tight over her head from behind cut off her gasp. *Not like this, not now.* Einya struggled, kicking and snarling in vain as her arms were pulled behind her. *Why can't I find the energy to fight?* Her strength gave way and she sagged against the arms that lifted her through the noisy streets.

Chapter Ten

Rask is blessed by the protection of Gemynd. We are one settlement, and all will answer to the Stars. Rask must remember or be shown the backs of our hand.
~ The Testament of the Stars

In an antechamber that abutted the stone-wall gardens, Tollska's last adornments for the wedding were put in place. She felt very much alone amongst the eight Raskian maids who attended her, overseen by the only Gemyndian servants in the Arden household. It was strange; how had she never visited the grand house before the announcement? How out of place she was. She swallowed, distracting herself by toying with the ornate silver hairbrush on the table in front of her. Its opulence didn't help and she looked up into the mirror, sighing.

One maid gently twisted little star gems into her hair, which had been elaborately curled and pinned up. Once this was complete, she stood. Her gown, which she hadn't picked, cascaded around her ankles. White fabric? Not what she'd imagined for this day. The sapphire Constellations stitched down the length of the dress were beautiful but alien to her. The preparations complete, Tollska moved to wait at the door to the courtyard where the Astrologer who was to conduct the ceremony greeted her with a half-bow.

"Tollska, soon to be of House Arden, Stars shine down on you on this happy day. My name is Wiltern Derana. I'll be your Astrologer for the ceremony."

The flat-spirited man seemed like a chain, tethering her to a fortune she didn't want. His eyes a dull grey metal and his pallid scalp reflected the moonlight in the courtyard.

"Thank you, Astrologer Derana." There was no joy in her voice and no light in her eyes as she stared at herself in the looking-glass propped against the stone wall.

"Now, are you familiar with your part in today's ceremony, Lady Tollska?"

"I am."

"Wonderful. Now, just a few things to conclude. As there are different purposes for marriages in Gemynd, I am required to ask that you confirm for me which of the following you are undertaking, as this must match the expectation of your betrothed. Do you understand?"

Tollska bit her lip with vice-like strength to keep any ill-chosen words from tumbling out, but she could feel the sparks of anger stabbing out from within her eyes. She had been told previously, extensively and repeatedly, the form this conversation would take and what she must say.

"I do."

"Excellent, now, is your marriage for the creation of children?"

"No, I am marrying Lady Pearth Arden of the Constellan Guard and we do not intend for children, hence I am able to marry freely."

"Wonderful, and is your marriage for the joining in mutual adoration two star-blessed lovers?"

"Uh. Yes, it is." Her voice trembled a little. She looked down at her feet, tensing when Astrologer Derana placed one hand under her chin and lifted her head to level her eyes with his.

He drawled on, not heeding any of the tension twisting through her body. "And, lastly, do you acknowledge the very great honour bestowed upon you—a Raskian—marrying above Raskian status and forging your right to hold rank by wedding a Gemyndian noble?"

"I understand, much as it means anything."

"Then we may proceed." The man rested one guiding hand on her shoulder, and she flinched at the rubbing of his rough fingers over her skin. How did he think he could just touch her like this? He ushered her out of the antechamber and into the bright moonlight of the gardens where immaculate upturned faces stared into the centre of her soul.

She dithered in the doorway, reluctant and nervous.

"Go." Astrologer Derana prodded her out of the stone doorway ahead of him. "Under the light of our glorious Stars, people of Gemynd, may I present Tollska of Rask."

Polite applause echoed around the courtyard, which, despite being called a garden, was more stonework and carving than any hint of greenery. The marble balustrades and alabaster statues reflected the blue glow of the moon, and Tollska walked slowly down the lantern-lit archway between the guests until she reached the small podium where Pearth awaited her.

Tollska gripped Pearth's sandpaper-rough hand, allowing herself to be helped up the steps as the train of her gown dragged behind her and snagged around her ankles.

Pearth's tight-fitting doublet was studded with sapphire Stars, as was the elaborate feather-adorned hat she wore. The ceremony was brief, filled with speeches about the adoration and blessings of the Constellations. Tollska let the bland words wash over her; no point in listening when your fate is sealed.

No recognisable faces pinpricked the crowd. The only Raskians present were others who had given themselves to Gemyndian nobles. Perhaps there was sympathy on their faces, but it was difficult to see their expressions in the dark.

The ceremony concluded with Sepult Disren rising, stepping up onto the podium, his blood-red lips stark against his withered grey skin. "As the Astrologer-Elect, I sanction this marriage on behalf of the Stars. I am pleased that my dear friend, Pearth, dutiful head of my guard, can find such beauty in a Raskian. I am honoured to be here, and honoured to acknowledge that, by this marriage, Tollska of Rask becomes Tollska Arden, with all the elevations that marriage to Pearth will grant her."

Sepult Disren kissed both of Tollska's cheeks, tilting her head to either side before stepping away. Pearth then closed the gap between them and placed her lips briefly upon Tollska's before stepping promptly away once more. The courtyard at once became a cacophony of words, applause and laughter as the night's ceremony lapsed into festivities once more despite the winter winds cutting across the gardens.

Warm drinks were served and platters of food carried amongst the guests, but Tollska had no stomach for them. She looked longingly at the gates leading down into the settlement and eventually to Rask and the life she had left behind suddenly seemed so much freer than this one that she had aspired to for all those years.

Chapter Eleven

This new Raskian practice of word-weaving is heresy to the Stars,
but we will allow it as long as Rask still acknowledges the one true
power of the Constellations.
~ The Fourth Astrologer-Elect

The rustle of hessian filled Einya's ears, the fabric scratching at her skin. Strong hands continued dragging her, heels bashing against the cobbles.

Einya tried to shout, but it was drowned by the roar of a jubilant crowd. She was lifted off the street, taken up a few steps. A door slammed. The spiking wicker of a fraying rickety chair prodded into her back as she was lowered into it.

"Found her," a reedy voice said.

"Well, so you have," a thick raspy voice with a Raskian accent drawled nearby.

Einya twisted her head around, straining against the hold on her. A hand lifted her chin up.

"An Astrologer. Listen, star-lover: there is no love for you here."

Someone spat on the floor at her feet, the splatter of it hitting her ankles.

Einya stopped moving, frozen, the sharp tip of a dagger pricked at the edge of her throat.

"Stop that, we need her to be on our side. This isn't just any old Astrologer. This is the cousin of the head of the Constellan Guard... Einya Arden, no less," the raspy voice began again.

Einya breathed out a raggedy barely-contained breath as the dagger tip flicked away from her tender skin. Relief surged through her.

"I know your voice," Einya said after she'd gathered her wits.

"I'd hope so. Remove the bag"

"But..." someone said.

"Do it."

The rough sack was ripped away from Einya's head, and the dim room came into focus. People lined the walls, resting their backs against flaking paint. What was this—who were these people?

Einya's confusion was reserved for the face in front of her, the only familiar one in a sea of strangers. The woman was short, her hair wintery grey with purple smudges throughout. She smelt familiarly of lavender and wild herbs. It couldn't be, could it?

The other people stood around this woman in varying rags and poorly fitting clothing, looking at her uncertainly. The woman's eyes were intense, and a small mischievous smile lifted the edge of her cracked lips.

"Oenska, why... why aren't you at your daughter's wedding?" Her heart felt torn apart, seeing the woman she remembered as soft and warm as melted butter looking so wild.

Oenska stamped her foot, stepping closer. "I wanted her to marry you, that was my plan. Not this. I'm absent because watching my daughter marry that monster would be like watching thorns hammered into her eyes. No, I will go to the feast and say my farewells to Tollska there. "

"She made her choice; she knew what she did."

"Because she had to. They gave her no choice."

"Then what do you want from me? I'm no different from my cousin. Just another Gemyndian oppressor."

The ageing woman gestured, and Einya's hands dropped to her sides as they were released from a tight grip. "You lie, or you are wrong. You're different. If you weren't, I wouldn't have wanted Tollska to marry you, would I? All those years we spent in bright sunlight as you both made your plans. And now they've taken all that you wanted away from you, as much as they have from Tollska."

Einya felt her teeth grinding against each other. "Tollska was every bit a part of that..."

Oenska shook her head, a sombre downturn to her lips apparent when she spoke again. "You don't understand. You've seen what they can do, and I want you to see what it is like for us here. I want to offer you a home away from Gemynd. I've lost a daughter, you've lost your lover and your family. I cannot be all of that to you, but I can give you some family back if you help us."

Einya clasped her hands in her lap, unsure of what to say. "Help you?"

"Yes, win the coming war against Gemynd."

Einya shook her head, a bitter strangled laugh escaping her lips. "Everyone is so sure there will be a war, especially now most of those on the hill think Raskians can curse or poison us. If you want me to help you, why all this charade?"

Oenska's eyes flared, heated to their core. "Of course there'll be a war. Look at our lives here! You can't be blind to the hunger, the illness, surely? Your brother knew."

"My brother's gone, and you have kidnapped me. Why should I help you?" Einya snapped.

The older woman leaned toward her conspiratorially, a playful smirk tugging up at the corners of her lips. "Listen. Would you have come otherwise? You know me, yes, but you don't know *us*. Let me show you what reality is like here."

Her intense eyes stared deep into Einya's. "Down in these piss-stained streets there's a thrumming, a drum beating, an anger rising. Don't be fooled by the laughter you see today. It, too, is a sham."

Einya sighed, slumping against the back of the chair. Fighting this tide seemed pointless; what could she do? "I cannot change that for everyone, and the one person I wanted to change it for has—"

"I know." Oenska hissed a little. "But this isn't just about one person. Or even just those of us here. Look."

The Raskian woman slipped open a small bag thrown over one shoulder, tugging out a battered parchment. "This is a letter from a friend of mine; he writes that his family lacks food. He writes that his wife can no longer feed their babe, because she has not eaten in weeks and her breast milk has dried within her."

Einya pressed her nails into her legs, remembering the many times she'd noticed how thin Tollska was compared to herself. Remembering too vividly the membranous skin stretched sparsely over the bones in her hands. "I wish I could, but I cannot change these things."

"You can ask yourself why, when Rask farms food, do her people go hungry?" Oenska rattled her words out, filling the silence Einya left. "All our rich farmers left for the peak of the hill in Gemynd, taking the little wealth we had. We tried to ask for help, and stop the loss of our wealth, but all they saw were farmers who should serve them. Why buy food from peasants when you can own the production? What land they didn't buy, they took with force."

Einya stood from her chair and glared at Oenska, only a breath away. "What can *I* do about it? Nothing!"

"But we can together, with your help."

Einya snorted, eyes narrowed on the font of strange wisdom that stood before her. "How? I couldn't even save Tollska."

"Because they keep control with the power of those Stars, a promise of divine authority from two lumps of rock, locked within a cave that no one but the Astrologers can enter. And now we have an Astrologer who can tell us all about those very rocks."

Teeth ground against teeth as Einya's jaw tensed. "Why would I do that?"

"Out of your love for my daughter? Gemynd's leaders told tales of celestial beings inside those rocks, and how the

60

magnificent power of them would control the world. And, under the threat of divine retribution from the only country with gods in their midst, Rask opened its gates and gave control to Gemynd."

"It wasn't like that, it was more..."

"What? Even-handed, fair? I'm sure they tell you that."

Oenska crossed the small room, taking a sheaf of parchment from the hands of one of the men. "Take this, read it—it is an account from those days."

Numbly taking the parchment in her hands, Einya felt its surface, cracked and dust-ridden. "Did the child from the letter survive?"

Oenska nodded, a small smile cracked across her dry lips. "She did. Take the paper, read and decide. There are different rebels within Rask, some violent and some not, some plan to stop working the fields and sending Gemynd their corn. But all of us plan to open the eyes of Gemynd and Rask to the truth about the Stars. Be part of the right movement and help us win good lives for ourselves."

Einya turned the scroll in her hands. "I should tell the Astrologer-Elect..."

"I don't think you will."

"Why not?"

"Because my daughter wanted you to be an Astrologer so that you could help us find out the truth about the Star-rocks. I think you know our suffering, just like your brother knows. Tollska loved you for that."

"Then why did she marry my cousin? I gave her another option and would have given her the rank she seems so desperate to have."

Oenska sat down on a creaking stool, sighing, the light slipping away from her eyes. "Did you think it was just about the rank? She doesn't care about that. This was her great sacrifice, to marry a Gemyndian for the cause. She needed to convince you otherwise, else it would never have happened."

"What? I..." Einya stepped back, her eyes wide and breath coming in short, disbelieving gasps.

Oenska shuffled the stool closer to Einya and then stood, her hazel eyes shedding one gentle tear, her voice suddenly softer as she placed one hand on Einya's shoulder. "Peace, she was so in love with you for all you had done for her by the end that she couldn't break your heart. She would have told you everything. But now she is gone, and my hope for her marrying you didn't work. So, I had to tell you instead, in the hope that you will help us because of the love you carry still for Tollska."

Einya trembled and looked around the hut. "I need to think; let me think."

"Think then, Einya, but don't take too long. I will find my daughter to ask her myself, also. I'll be at the wedding feast tonight, hidden in the crowds." Oenska placed a tender kiss on the woman's forehead. "And read. Then, if you decide to help us, cut two wooden notches into your door in the shape of a 'T' and we will talk more."

Einya nodded. Despite being almost thirty years of age, she briefly felt like a child again. "Won't going to Gemynd be risky, if you're heading this rebellion?"

"No one knows who I am, except you and Tollska. I'll be fine."

"Be careful. I can leave then?"

"Yes, go safely," the older woman said, affection softening her voice.

Oenska smiled; it was a long sad smile with a thousand tales carved into it. She gestured, and this time, the bag was placed over Einya's head gently before someone led her out of the small hut. They walked for what felt like an hour, but it could only have been a quarter of that time until they released Einya in some fields at the edge of Rask.

She knew it instantly when she tugged the bag from her head: this was where she and Tollska had first fallen for each other. They had met here by chance when Einya had explored the fields beyond the stone settlement, lamenting the lack of plant-life within its walls.

It was where Einya had enthusiastically told Tollska of her plans, and many years ago, had asked Tollska if she would marry her one day. Of course, they had picked this place to release her, she thought bitterly. It was in this field of many memories that

Einya sagged at last and lay amongst the barley as the sun rose, tears tumbling down her face.

Chapter Twelve

Having Raskians on the Constellan Council only serves to keep
them compliant; they will not understand our ways, so it matters
little.
~ Anonymous Astrologer

Tollska awoke to the unfamiliar sensation of lips brushing her neck, and one hand resting on the small of her back. It took a moment to gather her thoughts. "Good Morning, Pearth."

Pearth's eyes stared intently at her as sleep fell away, and the strange new world greeted her like a stone plummeting into a pool. "And to you, sweet love."

The second kiss pressed deep into the line of her jaw, and Tollska swallowed at the sensation. She said nothing, but tentatively found Pearth's lips with her own. She gasped a little and broke from the kiss when a maid entered the room. Pearth shrugged, even as Tollska drew the covers up around her shoulders, seeming unfazed as the woman hurried around the room.

Tollska tentatively shuffled her way upright with the covers still clung closely to her chest as the drapes around the four posts of the bed were pulled back and hot drinks were placed on trays beside them both.

Pearth began leafing through a stack of papers that had been placed next to her. "Now, Tollska, a lot has been prepared for you today. Well, this evening really."

"Such as? Will you be here, too?"

"So impatient!" Pearth smirked and pecked her cheek. "First, get yourself dressed, then we will breakfast. I then have some business, but you will be looked after. This evening, you will address the Council as its newest member. Then there will be a dinner."

Tollska laced her fingers into a complicated mess, nerves thrumming through her. "I see. I haven't met the Council yet. I haven't been told what to do or heard anything since they wrote to accept me. What will be required of me?"

"You'll be asked to make a speech."

Tollska felt her heart pound against her chest in one nervous strike. "I haven't written one…"

Pearth's hand brushed across Tollska's lips. "Calm yourself. It will be written for you. It's for you as part of the Council to establish a testament of the way peace is threatened in Gemynd and a doctrine for how we will combat the breaking of our peace. Just read the speech, simple, and the Astrologer-Elect will be pleased for it."

Tollska ran one hand over her face, brushing straggles of hair from her eyes and biting her lip in confusion. "A testament? I'd feel much better if I wrote my own…"

"Tollska, I know, I understand. Believe me, I do. But this goes so much wider, and there's a need to maintain peace and keep Rask and Gemynd close together or we'll be vulnerable to external threats."

"External threats? To what?"

"Sovereignty of the Stars. It doesn't hold the strength it once did, sweet love. Come, let's go to breakfast." Pearth got up from the bed, naked and unbothered as the maid approached her with a robe.

The maid closest to Tollska gestured for her to stand. She tentatively slipped one foot out from the silken duvet onto the cold timber slabs of the floor.

A large wardrobe had been opened, full with opulent gowns Tollska had never seen before. The maid rifled through the garments and then stepped out, holding out a fine black gown embroidered with gold flowers. Tollska just nodded as the maid unbuttoned her silk nightdress, thoughts burning through her mind. As the maid slipped the nightdress over Tollska's exposed skin, she politely looked away.

Don't blush; show them you can be part of this world.

It was strange, being undressed like a child.

"What's your name?" Tollska said, just to fill the awkward silence as she stood naked and shivering.

"Irinsk, ma'am."

"Please call me Tollska."

"I couldn't, ma'am, sorry."

The heavy dress was then dropped over her head, slapping heavily onto her shoulders before being tightly buttoned up at the back. Tollska silently allowed herself to be wrapped and prepared, like the speech she had not seen.

A while later, she sat in the breakfast room and felt, not for the first time, a longing for familiar simplicity. There were luxuries here that she didn't know what to do with, even though she'd aimed for them for all these years.

Pearth had made a great show of affection towards her, and she sat at a table painted with gold leaf, surrounded by lavish gifts and gilded trinkets. Three small hounds with feathery plumes for tails scrambled around her ankles. A maid stood to one side and occasionally passed her a bowl of berries and chocolates. She hadn't asked for the dogs, or the berries, but this was clearly how she was expected to spend her days.

Tollska made sure she ate heartily, though she didn't feel like it. The exuberance of the dogs at least feeling like a reason to smile, that part wasn't so hard as they scrapped and tumbled across the slick stone floors. When Pearth left after breakfast, it was with every warmth that a spouse could hope for; a gentle squeeze of her hand, a pleasant wish for a lovely day, tender nuzzles against her cheek. She had to remind herself that all of this was a kindness shown to a creature in a gilded cage.

As soon as the heavy wooden door clicked shut behind her new spouse, Tollska ambled to the window, taking a morsel of food with her. Looks of confusion spread across the faces of the Raskian servants as she smiled at them awkwardly. She felt like a pigeon wearing a fancy coat in a world of peacocks, dressed up properly but still shabby underneath.

All of that was forgotten when she looked out of the tall window that revealed the expanse of the settlement. From their rooms overlooking Gemynd, and even Rask beyond, the rising of the sun mirrored radiantly off the polished stones and dappled the farmland in the distance. The wide streets of Gemynd had begun to bustle; in a square just a few streets away, a colourful market was opening with finely dressed patrons wearing vibrant outfits.

Eventually, Tollska allowed herself to be ushered away to take tea in the library, hearing the clatter of dishes taken from the table behind her. Settling herself in the adjacent room, which was floor to ceiling in leather-bound books, a surreal sense of peace finally descended. Tollska remembered the times Einya had snuck her books to read; the fine texts had seemed out of place in her rickety shack, but nonetheless, she had always asked for more.

The three dogs slumped on the overstuffed cushions on the chairs, leaving little room for her. Instead, Tollska sat at an opulent writing desk in one corner, took a quill from the holder and dipped it into the inkwell.

> *Einya,*
> *Whilst I think I can live with this, it will*
> *never be what I wanted.*
> *Please let me see you, let me explain.*
> *T*

She sealed the parchment and tucked it into the lining of her gown, knowing it would never be delivered.

Tollska spent the bulk of the day idling in this room, reading snatches of different books and leaving them stacked on the writing desk. At some point, she had been brought a selection of pies and fruits, which she picked at intermittently.

Tollska thumbed through an old text on the history of Gemynd, an account from before the Stars had come to the settlement. Her eyes were still flicking through significant passages when she felt a gentle stroke down her spine as Pearth came to stand behind her, grinning. It must have been late in the afternoon, and Tollska yawned and slid the book gently down onto the pile so as to avoid Pearth noticing the title.

"Tollska, you're reading?"

"I like to read," Tollska said, looking up at the note of surprise in Pearth's words.

"At least one of us does; I'm not so patient to be able to sit and read."

"Really?"

"Yes, it's true, I'm afraid. Just so much activity in my life, sitting for longer than an hour makes my legs twitch." Pearth grinned again.

Tollska just nodded, her words snagging in her throat slightly, pushing up some bravery within herself. "My speech, I need to ask you about it."

"Yes, here." Pulling a folded parchment from the pockets of her embroidered doublet, Pearth passed it to Tollska. "Short, and effective. That's all it needs to be."

"Is that all? I still think I should have written it."

"They won't know, I promise."

"*I'll* know. I worked for this…"

"Tollska, it really doesn't matter. This is just the frills; you'll still have the position."

Pearth knelt at her feet, gently running her hands down Tollska's forearms, causing Tollska to smile faintly back.

"You'll write them in future, I promise. The Astrologer-Elect gave me it, he insisted. He wants this testament mentioned; we need to ensure peace, unity and strength with neighbouring settlements. So, please read it? For me?"

The sealed parchment, heavy in her hands, felt lead-like in its weight. "I will, then."

"Thank you. Are you ready then, sweet love?" Pearth's soft smile, her kiss and soft-misting breath warmed Tollska's cheek.

"Of course," Tollska whispered, struggling to not feel a little tenderness toward Pearth. Standing, she noticed the crumple of the parchment for Einya against her skin and—not for the first time—felt a guilty stab through her heart.

Their arrival at the Council was heralded by a trumpeter in the entrance to the Council Halls, a lavish building where decisions made by the Astrologers were ratified. Carved into the stone archway above the entrance were the words: *Sanction the will of the Stars, sanction the will of Astrologers, uphold the glory of our settlement.*

The great wooden doors beneath the words had been left open, and another herald called their names as they entered the candle-lit hall that was decorated with banners of the Constellan Council.

Around the room, there also hung artworks depicting famous events where the Council had either challenged or upheld a crucial law proposed by the Astrologers. At the end of the great hall, a mural painted on the wall showed the falling of the Stars and the divine starlight shining on the founders of the Council, the Astrologers, and their protectors, the Constellan Guard.

Tollska had been here once before when she had offered herself as a member of the Council. It was a long day, establishing if she was worthy enough despite her Raskian blood. She had been examined, questioned and asked to display her loyalty to the Constellations. Now she was paraded about, smirks and smiles on every face admitting her as one of them, and Pearth introduced her with the flourish of someone clearly showing off a grand achievement.

The dinner passed in brief spurts of conversation with an assortment of strangers. Someone asked her how she felt about recent Gemyndian art as opposed to pre-Constellan art before the Stars had fallen. Tollska fumbled for an answer, and then the noble who had asked her lost interest and instead addressed a question to

Pearth about the Constellan Guard or some political happening that Tollska knew nothing about.

The dishes of food before her were unusual, with strange smells and textures. There was never anything this lavish in Rask. A whole deer, roasted in capons and butter, had been placed on the table in front of them. Tollska had never seen one cooked before. No one dared to hunt deer in the forests for fear of death around Rask; game meat belonged to the nobles.

She cast her eyes down the hall; few Raskian faces were amongst their number and she was the finest dressed of them all. Raskians were often brought up from the settlement to wait on tables when the Council had grand events, and she looked around for a familiar face. Not one there.

A trembling note from a gong signified the speeches, and when Pearth nudged her, she stood, feeling the eyes across the room burning into her like flames melting wax.

"I am pleased to take this position and I'm exceedingly grateful to Pearth Arden for the opportunity, and the love, she gives me."

Polite taps on tables echoed through the hall. She looked sideways at Pearth, a perfect grin on the woman's face, before turning back to the crowd.

"I hope you will find me as I am, an educated Raskian with ambition to match. I will give all I am to uphold the Council's understanding of Rask. I will serve the Stars and be thankful for their guidance. I will make decisions with the Stars in my heart and in my mind."

Taps pattered on the tables again, and she continued: "My place here is one of unity, one of peace. We must be strong inwardly to safeguard against outward forces that might seek to gain strength over us; neighbouring settlements such as Parlenta and Aisren look to our Stars with greedy eyes in these changing days."

The last paragraph, in its slanted crimson scrolling, seemed unnaturally bright. She felt her knees clack together under her long skirt before forcing her lips to speak once again.

"Unity in Gemynd and Rask, our fair settlement, will be our strength. My union with Pearth Arden is the epitome of this strength. Which leads me to say, in response to the rising spikes of rebellion in Rask, most recently characterised by the sad attack on the Thennet child and poisonous pamphlets against the protective rule of Gemynd. Measures will be taken to cease this behaviour. Like of old, a testament will be published and all who push against the unity that keeps us strong will be listed. The first names upon this list are…"

Tollska paused, feeling blood run through her mouth as she dug a sharp tooth into her tongue. Struggling to get her voice to start again, stern gazes crept across her skin in expectation of her next words. "These names are… Oenska of Rask and Briarth Arden, as well as anyone who hides them. The last has fled the settlement but will be found. Let us align in unity under the sovereignty of our twin fallen Stars. Thank you once again for my place here."

Applause clattered, loud enough to drown her thoughts. She tore her head around to Pearth, forced herself to steady her limping breath. "Will you take those on the list to the tower dungeons?"

"Only if peace is not achieved; it's a deterrent for now. Nothing more."

The feast recommenced, so she tried to smile, eat and drink. Conversation, music and laughter rose loudly around her, but her voice saying the two names still echoed in her thoughts.

In the crowds, she saw the face she both dreaded and desired to see. Her mother, weaving between the tables, collecting dishes, filling glasses. A tight headscarf barely concealed the purple streaks in her hair, but Tollska saw them clearly.

Her nails dug deep into her hand, leaving trenches in her skin. She slid one hand across the table and tipped over a glass so red wine cascaded over the sleeve of her white-gold dress.

"I… oh no, I'm sorry," Tollska said, frantically trying to pad the wine out with a napkin.

"Are you still nervous from the speech?" Pearth said, taking the napkin from her and brushing the worst of the wine away.

"A little, I'm sorry."

"Don't be, sweet love." Pearth squeezed her hand, which still dripped with wine.

"I must get this cleaned." She squeezed Pearth's shoulder and stood, the bright crimson stain picking out the brocading detail on her gown.

Tollska followed her mother's path away toward the door to the kitchens, cornering a maid on the way and gesturing obviously to the stain on her gown.

"I'll need some salted water, please."

"I'll get you the water, but let one of us clean it, ma'am." The maid hurried off, giving her a strange sideways look. "If you'll wait over there."

Tollska nodded and stepped into a small seating area to the side of the grand hall for entertaining smaller groups. It was quiet, with lavish seating and only a small hatch into the kitchen. Waiting until no one was looking, Tollska opened the little hatch door and knocked on the side of it when her mother bustled past.

Oenska looked around, dumping the wooden dishes she held on the large stone table before hurrying out into the seating area. Tollska felt the strong arms reach around her, and the scent of roses and lavender engulfed her.

Her mother kissed her hair repeatedly. "Little one, sweet girl."

"Everything is hollow without you, Mama."

"I'm here to make it better."

"I know. I know, but you need to go. Didn't you hear your name?" Tollska whispered, gripping tighter, knowing this moment would only be as brief as the sun fleeting between stormy clouds.

Oenska smoothed Tollska's hair from her eyes. "Listen, sweet child. It won't always be like this."

"You need to go, please."

"They don't know my name, I gave a different one."

"What if someone recognises you?"

"Only Einya knows me, and do you think she would say anything if she saw me in the settlement?"

Tollska clutched her tighter, pressing her nose into her mother's hair. "Ma, I want to come home. I thought I could play this game, but I don't think I can…"

"You can, and you know it. One day we'll be together, once we have made a better world for us here, but for now, pretend to disown me. We must focus on survival, sweetest Tollska."

They held onto each other for a final bittersweet second before Oenska pulled away, smiling through the grimace. "We need to go on. We are fighters."

"I know, and I will."

"I'll see you again soon."

Tollska choked back a sob, resting her forehead against her mother's for a fleeting moment before Oenska slipped away into the kitchen.

The maid found her quickly after that, sponging away the wine whilst Tollska sat there biting her lip. The stain faded a little and Tollska stood, stepping back into the hall and her hollow life. With every step back towards Pearth, she reminded herself of the purpose of all of this, knowing that—despite the treachery that seemed seared into the fabric of her life now—she must smile and pretend.

Tollska dipped into a low curtsey as she approached Pearth once again and, sitting, leant in to gently kiss the other woman's cheek. "Mostly removed, love."

"Good, you can barely tell," Pearth said, gently brushing the hair away from Tollska's neck.

The morning after began in the same way as the one before, with the ritual of being dressed and ushered to breakfast. After they had eaten, Pearth stood.

"I've something for you," she half-whispered.

"I don't need…"

"Hush. Come with me."

Still bare-footed as they pattered out of the room, Tollska stepped tentatively down the spiral steps to the courtyard with Pearth's warm hand pressed against her back.

A brief spike of a gasp hitched in Tollska's throat.

In the yard stood a magnificent grey mare, speckled with white spots that looked like Stars dotted on a stormy sky.

"For you." Pearth smiled broadly, the glow of the grin reaching her crystal-blue eyes.

Her own heart fluttered a little, but she caught herself and shook her head slightly. Swallowing, feeling like the gifts could be the honey to trap a fly, Tollska stepped toward the horse and reached out to stroke its silken neck.

Pearth placed one hand on her chin, tilting Tollska's head up toward her own. "Which reminds me, I've something to ask you."

"Oh?"

"I've heard that some Raskians might be planning more pamphlets..."

Tollska brushed the feather-light horse's mane, feigning deep interest in the tiny follicles of hair as she listened. "About what?"

"Rebellion, rejection of the Stars. I need to know what they're saying, what they're planning."

"I don't know anything about this..."

"They are saying Gemynd has no right to rule Rask, apparently. One of my guards found some. This is not a time for us to be divided."

Tollska bit her lip, turning to face Pearth. "Nothing I've ever seen."

"Even though you are from Rask..."

"How would I? I'm here. Have been for a month or so."

"Ask your friends, for me, please? I want to keep the peace, not just take the Guard in there. That won't help anything."

Tollska knew the meaning behind the words. Spying. She knew her answer but fumbled with her fingers as if uncertain. "I will ask, then, my love. If it will help you."

"Thank you."

"What should I look for?"

"Sedition, lies, propaganda. You'll know it when you see it. Let's work to make the peace last here. Let's find names for this testament and use them as a deterrent. It'll be for the best, trust me."

Tollska wrangled her lips into a smile. "I'll try my best."

75

Pearth dragged her into a tight embrace and Tollska gripped tightly in return. She gazed out over her spouse's shoulder to look back down over the settlement, grinning for the first time since she had been married. This was her excuse to go home.

Chapter Thirteen

Your trade policies will be the death of us, I beg you to reconsider.
~ Letter from the Rask Word-Weaver to the Astrologer-Elect

In the months that followed, Einya dug herself into her new life. Winter had thrown its cloak over the skies of Gemynd and Rask, and the trees of Rask were now barely visible, skeletal branches at the edge of the horizon.

Einya spent her days in the regular duties required of the Astrologers, praying for the dead, assigning birth-Stars to newborns and presiding over weddings. As well as this, she visited the cavern every day and tried different methods for speaking to the Stars, and Sepult Disren asked after her progress regularly.

There were so many ceremonies and protocols for different occasions and detailed guides about how to find out the truth from the Stars, that she felt lost in the seemingly limitless maze of options. In every instance, there was reference to running one's tongue over the stones, and Einya had lost track of the times she'd felt the rough jagged rock grate against her tongue now.

Einya dropped the heavy book to the floor of the cavern again, the thump echoing around the chamber. She'd come here as darkness had fallen, and she was sure it must be close to midnight by now. It felt like she had tried over a hundred times, so much so that she knew the book's words thoroughly. She ran one hand through her hair. As the book instructed, she'd lit the circle of candles, licked the Star-rocks and asked her questions to the Stars.

But the twin Star-rocks still remained silent, and Einya began to wonder if the book was even right. It seemed like a joke; one of the suggested practices of licking the Stars seemed such an odd thing to do. The tome had so many different methods for speaking to the Stars, it was hard to know which to pick. It was a catalogue of all the attempts of the Astrologers from when the Stars had fallen. It seemed only a few had succeeded.

She flicked through the pages again, wondering which method she should try next. There was a whole passage about 'asking with need in your heart' that Einya had read over and over, but with no revelation about how to achieve that.

It was the Astamitra, or Star-blood, that seemed to be the key to hearing the star's voices. It was mentioned in almost every chapter. Sighing after reading the passage again, she stood and wove her way up the stairs into the Astrologer-Elect's manor. The wait wasn't long before the older man stepped into the entrance hall, told of her arrival by a maid.

"How can I help you, Einya?"

She swallowed. "Elect, the book mentions Astamitra being needed to speak to the Stars. How might I find some?"

"Why, that is what's in the font. In a weakened form. It forges a connection to the Stars."

"I know, Sepult. That is, I need the strongest form. Undiluted, apparently."

The Astrologer-Elect furrowed his brow. "I will seek some for you, but use it carefully. There is reason we dilute it, Einya."

"Where does it come from?"

The wrinkled man paused, frowning still. "I will tell you, but you must not tell a soul. Only me and a few other ranked

Gemyndians know. Parlenta mine their Stars, closely guarding the secret how. I do not believe this practice of taking energy from our beloved Stars is right. I have long appealed to them to stop, to little effect. But this seems cause enough for us to need it."

"They mine the Stars?"

"Yes. But tell no one. We must not admit they have knowledge of the Stars greater than our own; we are still astrologically superior."

She paused, uncertain, but forced a smile. "Understood, Elect."

Rising to leave, her thoughts raced. What strange conflict was this? Was there some tension with Parlenta she'd not seen before? How could they mine the Stars?

Following the stairs back into the cavern, thoughts still racing, she strode to the carved font at the centre of the cave. The Star-blood still swilled around inside. Einya had dipped her hand in a few times but found a pit of reluctance bubble up within her every time she considered drinking some again. The memory of the undulating floor from her initiation still made her feel a little nauseous, and it still hadn't begun to feel normal. What would it be like with undiluted Astamitra?

Packing her belongings, she returned to her rooms. The sun was rising, and the markets had begun to fill with stalls. People would nod in deference now they knew she was an Astrologer, and Einya would smile awkwardly back, unsure how to respond now people saw her as powerful. In her rooms, she placed the star book on a high shelf, before meandering aimlessly around the large room for a few moments until she found a loose board in the wooden floor. Stepping on one end tipped up the plank, revealing the wooden box she'd tucked away beneath it.

She glanced at the door, making sure no one was coming. Then she opened the box. Inside, the historic scroll rested on velvet lining. The sealed note with Bri's location still sat there, as it did every day when she checked. Butterflies of relief fluttered in her throat.

Very gently, she eased out the scroll and rolled it open on the floor. She'd barely dared to look at it, leaving it hidden away in the hope she wouldn't think about it. The rasping of the rough edges of the scroll against itself caused her to jump. Einya tutted at the nervous jitterings of her fingers. The scroll was ornately written:

An account of the Stars falling.

They broke through the roofing of the Astrologer-Elect's manor and cratered the hill beneath it. She instantly proclaimed it a miracle, of Gemynd's divine right over the farming lands in the Raskian part of the settlement. She told all who would listen.

Travellers even came from the neighbouring settlements once word spread. Astrologers from Aisren and Parlenta, who had seen the Stars fall, flocked into Gemynd. The celebrations lasted for a month, and all were permitted to visit the Stars. People brought their sick and dying family, held them to the heat of the Stars and saw them instantly healed with a strange energy that burst from the twin-rocks.

It was in the days of these festivals that the Gemyndian Astrologer-Elect suddenly disappeared, and the freedom to see the Stars that she had granted to everyone ceased abruptly. Soon after, a cavern was constructed from Parlentan stone around the Stars, and it was almost as if people forgot they were ever openly accessible.

The new Astrologer-Elect, Kareth, proclaimed that the Stars had spoken to him and that they wished for unity of the settlements under one leader. The festivities ended abruptly, and the Astrologer-Elects of the three settlements spoke behind closed doors. There is no record of what was said, but the outcome was clear to all.

Aisrenese Astrologers left Gemynd in disgust. Rask's Astrologer-Elect renounced his title and offered tithes of taxes and control over Rask's

agriculture to Gemynd, in turn moving up from the
slums onto the Gemyndian hill.

Kareth became the first Astrologer-Elect of
both Gemynd and Rask, and soon Gemynd's wealth
built up on the benefits of trading Raskian goods.
Kareth slowly built up laws securing Gemynd's
financial and political power over Rask...

Einya exhaled as she finished reading, dislodging a deep breath that had snagged in her throat. The words faded after this and became illegible, but she had seen enough. How could they have done this, devalue life like that? This history was never taught, and the schools and scholars only referred to Rask as always having been part of Gemynd. Still sat on the floor, Einya traced one finger over the grains in the wooden boards before abruptly standing, slinging on her coat and tugging on her boots. She stashed the scroll before leaving.

Hurrying through the settlement, the marble streets seemed more glaringly bright than ever and the ice-cold of winter setting crisped her breath in front of her lips. She knew the route she would take, one she remembered from one free and wild night where she and Bri had fled into Rask to escape the Gemyndian monotony years ago. Stepping into the shadowy streets and uncaring of who would see her, she emerged from the steps down from Gemynd into Rask. The gate guard stood on the street side, frowning and clutching a pike with white-knuckled fingers. He seemed nervous, but Einya didn't pause to pay him much attention.

The streets were as rough as she remembered, but they seemed more vivid now as if there were some elements picked out in bright oil paints for her to see more clearly. Small groups stood in shadowy corners, some looking over parchments stretched on splintered tables.

A man with ragged hair and yellow eyes sagged against the steps to a small building nearby, where people hustled along the street without looking down. Einya's suede shoes splattered in a muddy puddle when she stepped up to him, his eyes watching her nervously. She placed a large coin in his hand, smiling a little.

"A Myndat won't go far down here," he said, voice quiet.

"Really?" Einya knew she could buy two lavish meals in a tavern for that cost in Gemynd.

"There's less food, Lady, so it costs more."

Shock coursed through her. "How long has that been the case?"

"Since a year ago, Lady, when the amount of food Rask was told to trade went up. Lack of supply increases demand, increases cost. In short, your laws starve us."

Einya felt her heart squirming in her chest. What could she say to a man starving, when she had all the food she could want? Giving him two more Myndats, she smiled in an attempt at sympathy, before hurrying on, aware that whatever she did would be imperfect.

Her burning list of questions was growing more detailed. By the time she had reached *The Dead Mule*, she had seen many more examples that made a reality of the stories Tollska and Briarth had always told her. How had she missed this all these years?

The rickety door swung open easily, a broad-shouldered woman bustling behind the bar.

"Luskena..." Einya called out, criss-crossing between the tightly packed tables.

"Bri's sister, well as I live and breathe. Didn't think you'd care to dirty your skirts down here."

"I am trying to find Tollska's mother."

"Have you heard from Bri?"

"No..." Einya thought Luskena's shoulders sagged at that.

Luskena paused, painstakingly rubbing a stain from the counter. "No surprise, I guess."

"Have you?"

"No, and you shouldn't be here."

"I need to..."

"It's too obvious; *you're* too obvious. Look at you, dressed in all your finery."

Einya tried to look a little less out of place as she leant forward. "Please, Luskena, I know you were friends with Bri. Please, help me."

"Friends? That's what he told you?"

Einya toyed with the glass, rolling the base in circles on the splintering bar. "He told me nothing."

"I suppose love only happens in Gemynd."

"I never said…"

"I'll take a message to her. That's all."

"Thank you. Can you tell her I need to know where she got the scroll from?"

Luskena laughed, loudly moving glasses across the bar-top to mask the sound of their whispered conversation. She poured a shot of a strong whisky and slid it to Einya, swigging from the bottle before returning it to its shelf. "We all know that, Astrologer."

"Really? Where was it found?"

Luskena tilted her head, lips pinched tight together as Einya waited for the answer. "Tollska stole it from the Astrologer-Elect, I bet they know she did it, too. I bet they used it against her to get her to agree to marry that beast."

Einya shook her head, feeling panic well up in her throat. "That cannot be true, that has to be rumour."

"Maybe, but do you know everything she did? How much did you really know her at all?"

"I need to go." Einya hadn't intended to drink the whisky, but now she gulped it down without a second thought. Anything to cope with the madness that engulfed her. She quickly crossed the room and hurried out onto the street. Einya steadied herself against the wall, head spinning. A crowd bustled past.

"Drank too much, eh, Gemyndian? Can't take Raskian liquor." The crowd laughed at the remark, but Einya didn't look to see who had made it.

She hadn't even noticed that Luskena had followed her outside until the mouse-haired woman yelled at them to hop it away from her inn, before turning back again. "Einya, listen, you should get back to Gemynd. Ain't safe for you here at the moment."

"I never knew Tollska was so… so involved." Einya fumbled for the words, haltingly.

"She's not just involved, she's a Knight in this game of Chess."

"I knew she was intelligent, but I never knew she was cunning."

"Then you didn't pay enough attention," Luskena spat.

The two women shifted slightly, resting with their backs against the flaking walls of the inn. Einya looked around her, seeing more and more of the deprivation there.

"Luskena, can I ask, how do you get by if Myndats are worth so little in Rask?"

"We get by how we can, there's not much more I can say. At least they're not as worthless as Raski-rust coins have become. "

"How do you buy enough food?"

"In truth, everyone does it differently. For me, your brother helped."

"He did? I never knew—"

"Seems that's true of a lot, Astrologer." Luskena smiled a little, despite her words.

"I knew he came here sometimes," Einya said, remembering the days when Bri would return wearing threadbare clothes.

Luskena stood and headed back to open the door into the bar. "He made my life warmer, for the years that I knew him. For that, I at least have some joy in me. You said you were leaving?"

"I must…"

"Then go, and do me a favour: don't go find Tollska. You'll make her life hard if you turn up asking all these questions. Forget her and go about your life. If you want to speak to her Ma, you know what you have to do."

Einya nodded, feeling stretched between so many different thoughts. She pushed herself off the sludge-covered wall and left, trudging back through the streets of Rask and up the steps towards Gemynd, with even more questions burning on her tongue. Creeping into her home under the night's canopy, her head pulsing, she felt like an intruder in her own home. Sagging into a chair, she reached for a bottle of wine and tugged the cork out with her teeth. What was she going to do now?

Chapter Fourteen

Star-blood is a little-known science, but we will learn for the good of all and so our trade may continue.
~ Parlentan letter to Gemynd

The frost-laden winds stung harshly. Bri rubbed his hands together again to force some heat into them. He'd squeezed Prethi's coat over his broad shoulders and huddled them over, trying to get warm before his turn with the coat ended. The mud path through the woods was shielded by an arch of stretched out willow bowers that formed a neat V-shape above their heads. Prethi blew a tune through a simple wooden flute as they walked, the man's breath misting into a silver cloud with every trembling note.

Beyond the woodland that bordered Rask, Bri had spread the map out on the ground, running his thumb over the various faded ink lines. "I think it's that way," he mumbled, pointing at one of three straight roads available to them. Prethi only nodded, and they wove onwards, occasionally singing together in close harmony to distract themselves from the cold.

A little way onwards, they stopped in an abandoned farmhouse and slept with their backs to each other, sharing in each other's warmth. The next day, they managed to swap a few coins at a farmhouse for a hot broth, which was a welcome change from the frozen berries they'd been snaffling from the forest paths until then. Prethi had often prodded Bri in the ribs, saying: "Next time you run away, plan it better."

Two days later, luck finally joined them on their journey, and Prethi managed to buy two pack horses from a stable hand for a ridiculous stack of Myndats. With the warmth of the beasts beneath them, they set off at a faster pace, with a few saddlebags filled with some bread and dried meats.

Bri looked again at the map and compared the mountainous features penned on it to the route they were following, where the fields were now strewn with rock fragments and in the distance tall pinnacles of mountains could be seen.

"I'm no longer sure what day it is," Prethi said after they'd rode a little way further into a small rocky ravine.

Bri's laughter echoed a little around the steep stones on either side of the road. "I've not known for some time, but at least we're going the right way."

"And when we get there, what then?"

"See if they'll help Rask. I have a fairly unformed idea, but it might work."

"Oh good, another unformed idea. What a relief," Prethi muttered, smirking.

As they rounded the edge of the ravine and their horses plodded out onto the open road, the pair of Gemyndians could see two towering rock gates looming in the middle-distance. It looked as if the gates were cut from the mountain itself and, as they got closer, they could see through the open gateway that there was a hollowed-out crater beyond where the settlement of Parlenta was built.

The empty plain before the gates was jagged with rocks, all capped with web-like patterns of frost across their black surfaces. Only the dirt path down the middle of the stone meadow was traversable, and Bri twisted his horse this way and that to avoid the sharper rocks on the road. It was wide enough, though, proven when Bri turned at a scraping noise to see a carriage clattering up the road behind them.

They shifted their horses off to the side before dismounting briefly, and Bri was rooting through the saddlebag for some food when he felt a rough shove. Slipping on the icy rocks, he tumbled down and, looking up, saw Prethi pointing behind the large rock nearby. Bri crawled behind it, his arms scraping on the jagged stones, and huddled himself just in time to see a big black carriage roll by with the large, emblazoned gold star of the Constellan Guard painted on the side.

Bri brushed the fragments of stone off his now battered clothes as he stood up when the carriage had clattered away.

"That's not good, they'll wonder at two horses and one rider," he spoke.

"Maybe, and hopefully they didn't see your doublet."

"It's now in tatters, I doubt the gold is radiant anymore."

Prethi plucked at the fraying gold threads of Bri's doublet and tutted a little, smirking. "Hopefully they didn't see or recognise you then. So, what now?"

"We go on and hope they don't say anything about me. If they do, then you get out."

The last stretch of the jagged road that led into the settlement was strewn with a carpet of spiked stones. The horses skittered around them. Jutting out into the sky above them were two stone walls on either side of the road leading to the black rock gate, carved to look like the mountain that the settlement of Parlenta cowered beneath.

Trade caravans slowly dragged their wheels in and out of the gates. Bri let one hand rest against his leg as he slumped low in the saddle, navigating the horse with only one hand on the reins. He flexed his hand out slightly, stretching to brush his fingers over the dagger hilt tucked into his boot. It'd be better to throw that at range if needed than risk close combat with his rapier.

As they trotted through the gates, the faint rasping of Bri's breath was loud to his own ears. He forced a smile at the sentries standing as still as if they were made from the same stone as the gate pillars, riding on to search for the renowned Parlentan mountain palace.

Chapter Fifteen

Stars are lies, words are all. Have the Stars even spoken?
~ Pamphlet found in Rask

"I'm going to Rask today." Tollska stood in the shade of the courtyard, hands on her hips and her hair tightly coiled into an elaborate design.

Pearth crossed the cobblestones and rested the tip of her sword against the ground. She leant in close to Tollska, taking the first break in her sparring for the whole morning. "On the business we discussed?"

"Yes."

"Be careful, then." Pearth rose and gently kissed Tollska.

"You can be sure of it. Until later, then." Tollska smiled; though forcing her muscles to do so felt like trying to gently crack porcelain open. Each crack made it easier to do again.

The days that had passed since Tollska had agreed to spy for Pearth had been good between them, and Tollska felt that a worry of Pearth's had slipped away. There had been laughter and pleasant evenings dining under the canopy of Stars.

Tollska pecked Pearth on the cheek, turning and taking the steps up out of the courtyard in three quick leaps. Every day she spent with Pearth, the harder she had to try to remember why she was doing all of this. Going to Rask would help her remember. She stopped by the kitchens and requested a small parcel of food to take with her. She stashed it in a bag she slung over one shoulder and strode through the wide avenues of Gemynd towards the crumbling spiral stairs down to Rask.

Strange looks and tentative mutters stalked after her. Her embroidered black coat with fur trim seemed out of place in the austere surroundings. An icy wind battered through the rickety street, a harsh reminder of the reality of Rask.

People looked the other way as she passed, nervous and distrusting. Did they still recognise her? Did they know about the spying on Gemynd?

Despite all this, Tollska bounded up to the door when she reached the little cottage. It was nestled next to the fields and was distinguished from the others by a painted blue door. Beyond the fields, she could see the towering mountain of Parlenta, the spiralling smoke jetting from within dark in colour against the pale sky.

Looking away, she slipped in through the door. The familiar acrid scent of ink filled the empty room, and at the centre stood a large wood and metal contraption. Voluminous stacks of papers stood by it, and scattered on the old cottage table were the small stamps that made up the letters of the printing press. A familiar echo of voices was audible from behind the door into the cottage kitchen. Tollska quickly crossed to it and turned the rotting wooden door handle. Inside, five people clustered, close enough to rub elbows in the small room.

"What, you're here in Rask, girl?" a man she knew, Gunsk, greeted her.

"I am, with important things to tell you."

"Best not be calling her *girl*, Gunsk, she's more than all of us now," another man, Terskan, spoke.

Tollska raised one hand to wave away the man's words. "I'm here to see my mother, and whoever is doing the printing these days."

"That'd be Luskena."

"Explains a lot. The Guard knows about the pamphlets. They think you're planning a rebellion. They've begun a list of names. They asked me to come here and find out who is behind the pamphlets…"

Panicked eyes tripped from one member of the small group to another.

"Gunsk, we gotta get out of this if they know," one man said, his voice squeaking on the last syllable.

"No, we ain't. There's too much at play here for that. Got no faith in Oenska, do you?"

Tollska tutted, put one hand to her lips and felt the silence of the room rise around her. "You should have faith in my mother."

Gunsk glared. "I always will, Tollska. Heck, you even sound like them, you know? Imperious."

"I have to."

"Suppose that's a fair point, but don't mean I like it."

Silence accompanied the uneasy glances that passed between the room's occupants.

"Look," Tollska said. "I know it's hard, it's hard for me too. I did this because of everything we've suffered—the hunger, the hardship. Let's talk about plans."

The door creaked open, and Tollska exhaled a repressed breath she'd held tightly onto. Oenska entered, surprise on her face, and behind her, Luskena and a handful of Raskians followed. The door was shut quickly, and Tollska restrained herself from rushing to embrace her mother.

"Tollska? What are you doing here?"

"I have something to tell you. To tell you all."

"Go on then." Oenska moved to rest against the printing press at the centre of the room.

"Pearth—I mean, the Guards know about the pamphlets. They've asked me to find out more."

"How?" Luskena said, a snarl forming on her lips.

"They found some."

The hulking form of Gunsk dominated the small room as he stood. "Tell them about the list."

All eyes in the room pulsed from Gunsk back to Tollska. "They've got a list. You heard of it at the banquet, Ma. They're saying it'll be ratified by the Stars, this list, and that it'll bring peace everlasting between Gemynd and Rask."

"How, sweet one?" Oenska reached out, and Tollska felt the firm reassuring grip upon her skin as well as all eyes searing into her with interest.

"The list will be of all those seeking to make war with Gemynd, anyone who doesn't respect the Stars. I have been sent here to find names for it."

"So now you're their spy?" Luskena spat on the floor and stepped up close to Tollska, their eyes digging at each other. A few people murmured in agreement.

Tollska didn't step away or blink. How could they think this, after all she'd done for them? "Only so much as it helps us find out more, so don't bring your rage to me because you want to be up in Gemynd."

"How dare you."

"Everyone knows it." Neither woman looked away from the other and Tollska used her height to tower over Luskena. A susurration of clipped murmurs tiptoed round the room between the Raskians present.

"Stop this." Oenska pushed Tollska's cheek away so the tense stare broke. "We are all on the same side. Tollska, continue."

"I am going to use the excuse of finding out more about the pamphlets to bring you information."

"And when they ask you for what you know?" Gunsk asked, causing Tollska to smile mischievously.

"Then I will tell them what *we* want them to know. It has to be this way if we're ever going to prove that the Stars are being used in lies against us."

Oenska brushed her daughter's cheek with a kiss, before turning to the group. "This, friends, is what we need. Now we might have two ways to learn more."

"Two, Ma?"

"I'll tell you later."

"So, what now?" Luskena spoke again, with only a little less venom in her words.

"You will give Tollska some old pamphlets to return with. Tollska, you then make out you found these pinned to gaslights in the streets. Then, find out what the Guard will do and tell us when you come here next."

"And then what?" Tollska whispered, feeling daft for hushing her voice.

"It's best we keep our plans quiet, for your own safety."

"They expect me to ask people I know, what shall I tell them if asked who I saw?"

No one spoke immediately. Birds chirped outside the hut, filling the silence. The small hut pressed tight with bodies had become humid, and the toxicity of the ink had crept an acidic taste into the mouths of all those in the room.

"Tell them my name," Gunsk answered finally, his amber eyes set like stone in his wrinkled face.

"No—" The reed-voiced man, Terskan, gripped Gunsk's arm.

"I got no one since my daughter died. I make the most sense, and I can leave easy enough, what with living close to the woods between Rask and Parlenta."

"You sure?"

"Yes, Tollska, this has gotta seem convincing if your plan is gonna work."

Tollska nodded numbly, feeling stupid. It hadn't occurred to her what would happen to the people she knew when Pearth asked who she'd seen.

Oenska stood, and all words ceased. Her mother's rasping voice filled the room. "Friends, this was always going to be hard. To get where we want to go, we need to be strong, we need to know what they know and find a way to have negotiating power over them once again. Let's use this opportunity to get our rights back."

A mumble of ascent, and people began to file out.

"See you around, girl," Gunsk said, smiling broadly before shuffling through the door.

Tollska smiled feebly back. Then it was just her, her mother and Luskena in the room.

"Luskena, we will talk later about what to print next. Let's start getting ready, as we discussed."

"The sooner the better, let's tear them down now."

"No, when we are ready. When I say. Now, will you dig out those old pamphlets?"

Luskena shrugged, huffing slightly, and headed over to a splintering crate by the window. Oenska sighed, pulled the scruffy hat from her head and let the grey and purple hair tip out over her shoulders. She looked sideways at her daughter.

"Tollska, here's the thing. It's excellent you can bring us information and knowing what the Guard knows is going to be valuable. But we need this to be political, too, as you know, and you need to keep your position of power, so openly campaigning for Rask on the Council will not win you friends. You will be seen as just a low-caste Raskian and excluded."

Tollska nodded; she knew very much now that her position on the Council seemed to mostly be honorary. She'd only been called to the Chamber twice since taking her position, to vote on a very minor law change. She'd been other times too, of course, but until the Astrologers called on her, there was little power to do anything at all. It made her angry. Why bother with the formality of having the Council, if their purpose was just to agree laws they had already decided on?

"So, what next?" she asked.

"Well, here it is. I need someone who can tell us the will of the Stars and be listened to. So, we know whether this list is just set by Gemynd to keep us down-trodden, or if the Stars are really agreeing this. I've asked Einya if she will help us. I'm waiting for her answer, but if she says yes then she may be able to find this."

"What?" Tollska took her mother's hand, gripping tightly. "Please, no, I want her free of all this."

"I know, but we need her. Do you think any other Astrologer will help us? We need someone who will make our case to the Astrologer-Elect, we need someone who can tell us whether the Stars really care about the Gemyndian control of Rask."

Tollska's jaw clenched, her teeth grinding against each other. "Don't let her get hurt. They will kill her if they find out she has helped you. They put her brother on the list…"

"I will hold her gently away from everything we do, I promise. Don't tell her you know."

"I don't see her anyway." Tollska bit her lip and sighed.

"Tollska, I am very glad you're able to see us. Be careful, don't come too often."

"Of course."

"And how is your marriage?"

"Good as can be expected, she dotes on me and it surprises me."

"Then keep in her good book."

Tollska smiled, a little of the merriment creeping back into her eyes. She took from her bag the food she'd brought from the kitchen and placed it in Oenska's hands. "For you."

Before leaving, she wordlessly accepted the handful of pamphlets from Luskena, who also said nothing. Tollska headed from the hut and slowly walked up the straw-lined street. Raised voices snaked through the breeze behind her, but the words drifted away, unheard on the wind.

Each of her steps echoed in the narrow streets. Another thought rushed through her mind: how would she explain this to Pearth? In the distance, the beginnings of the winter clouds were clustering above the broad hill that she now called home.

Chapter Sixteen

Birth-Stars set a dangerous precedent; people believe they are set in a certain way and always must be so. It gives no room for change.
~ The Word Weaver of Rask

Einya broke her habits after a while, tired of her usual regimented day. A package from the Astrologer-Elect that had been brought to her rooms contained a few small vials of blue powder with a note saying: *use it carefully, more to follow.* An uneasy impatience bubbled up in her.

Even so, Einya stashed the vials in her bag and started the day as normal, performing the duties required of an Astrologer. In her ward, there had been a birth, and she'd reluctantly visited the grand manor of the Tarenen family to assign a birth-Constellation to the newborn. The process had thankfully been quick; she'd taken the little Star-gems out of their velvet pouch and scattered them across the rug in the room where the child was born.

She knew the gems didn't always settle into a recognisable pattern quickly, but today they fell correctly after only two tries. They'd formed a twisted, snake-like form.

"It's the adder, Lady Tarenen," Einya declared.

"Really? No, please, look again."

"It is the same, but the adder is a good sign—wisdom and knowledge."

"And a poisonous lust for secrets…"

"I assure you, not always. It's just the time of year for hidden knowledge, sometimes there's wisdom in that."

"Thank you then, Astrologer Arden."

Ejected onto the street like a bad omen, Einya headed to the Star cavern in the day instead of her usual nighttime visits.

The little door gave easily, and Einya saw that the torches leading into the cavern had already been lit. It was not uncommon for other Astrologers to come here to pray, and Einya continued. She unpacked her satchel, which she always kept with her now.

The contents of candles, salts, pumice stone, fragments of granite and ground-up marble all formed part of the menagerie. The last item she removed were the vials, carefully wrapped in a silk cloth inside a small box. The Astamitra in its purest form shone in the vial of translucent crushed crystals, unlike the liquid in the font.

Einya's hands trembled as she placed one of the thin vials from the silk cloth on the stone floor, and carefully tucked the others away again. She thought, not for the first time, about how far she would go to hear the Star's words. Would it be worth it? Her determination already struck inside her like a spark, lighting a dangerous fire within her.

She held that thought in her mind, tipping a tiny amount of the azure phosphorescent powder onto the tip of one finger. Pausing for a brief moment to admire the shifting colours of the stones, Einya took a deep breath and licked it up before kneeling at the foot of the largest star.

The taste instantly sizzled on her tongue in its same smoky, strangely floral, taste. But it was stronger this time. The aroma stabbed again at her lungs with an intensity that made her eyes water, hauling throat-grating coughs through her windpipe.

She remembered the light-headed sensation from her initiation, but it didn't prepare her for the feeling that overtook her now. Stronger, nauseating: like being lifted up high and then dropped out of the star-studded sky to plummet to earth. Were her knees still on the dusty floor?

Three sharp steps sounded from the shadows. Long loose hair framed the shoulders in the dark, and blue eyes shone in the lantern light as the intruder knelt next to her.

"Pearth, how are you here?"

"I need to talk to you, cousin."

"I'm trying to speak to the Stars."

"I know. Sepult and I talk, we need you to seek answers from them to keep us all safe. Protect us from Raskian attacks and lies with the truth."

"Why now? Why get me to ask the Stars now?"

"Because of the Thennet boy. You couldn't save him, so make sure it doesn't happen again."

Einya spluttered, stomach churning and head spinning wildly. "I'll need silence."

"Then I shall be brief."

Einya tried to focus her eyes on Pearth but felt like she'd suddenly been wrenched from her feet again. A hazy blue sheen burst from the Stars, obscuring all else in the cavern.

Pearth's voice continued its monotone drawl, pulsing through Einya's already throbbing mind. "I know, of course, that you once cared for my Tollska."

"What? That doesn't matter to me now." Einya clenched her teeth on her tongue as punishment for the lie.

"Then be aware, she's spying on dissidents in Rask for me. I need your help, too. Help me keep her safe."

The cavern seemed to lurch sideways. Einya spluttered and gripped one hand into Pearth's tunic to steady herself. "Why are you telling me this?"

"I care for her, in my own way, and so do you. But, what's more, I need her information. If she needs help, I want you to help her. I know you have friends in Rask from when your brother wasted his life there. So, help her. Please."

Einya heard her stabbing words string together in shouts she couldn't control. "How can you ask Tollska to do this? They won't let her go if they find out. If they'd kill a child then what'd they do to an adult? There's got to be a better way to find peace."

Einya's heart drummed against her chest, her fingers weakly grasping the collar of Pearth's tunic.

"She's the only one who can get this information. It'll save lives, Einya. I hope you find the answers we need, to help us keep peace." Pearth wrapped one hand gently around Einya's trembling one.

"Then leave me to find them…"

"I have more to tell you, more I need your help with. I want you to find Tollska's Constellation. Come to the manor, then we'll talk."

Einya's jaw clicked open and shut, lips limply failing to find any words. Her muscles flailed feebly, feverish. The radiant glow of the Stars pulsed through the cavern in fresh waves of heat, but she couldn't see Pearth wincing or acknowledging the strange light at all. Was it invisible to everyone else?

Pearth stood and strode out of the cavern. Einya crumpled like a paper doll against the rock as the gentle lullaby of the Stars saturated her thoughts. The glow still pulsed; the sound of a thousand whispered memories undulating through the cavern.

Einya struggled to refocus and find the question burning in her mind. All she could think of was Tollska's face and her own outrage at the danger she would be in. A strange high-pitched noise echoed around the cave, stabs of images appeared in the light, and Einya realised the noise was her own terrified howl circling around the room.

The strange vision from before came again. In the swirling blue light, whichever way she looked, rows of bodies with serrated teeth loomed. One stone-grey face, tantalisingly masked in the shadows, had a single crimson tear dribbling out of its eye, leaving a deep gouge in its skin.

A tall figure loomed over them all, and Einya felt herself amongst the press of bodies as a soft finger ran over her lips. Tendril-like stabs pressed into her mind, connecting, prying into every thought and emotion.

She managed to babble a question, focusing on them in her mind. *Do you care about Rask being in thrall to Gemynd?*

She clenched her fists, the answer surging against her like a wave hitting a cliff. It felt like water was ripping through her veins, bursting them, surging through her ears to shatter them apart like glass. The Stars thrummed, drum-like, with a tremulous undercurrent of howling air.

The answer was clear in her mind, pulsing rumblings bursting from within the Star-rocks. *"We only care about memory and truth, all else is nothing. We are only historians to you, here to speak to you of what we know."*

Her jaw ached like her lips had been stretched too wide, the words belonging to the Stars tumbling from her lips. The feverish thrill of the Star-blood thrummed through her. She realised with a brutal stabbing horror that they were using her mouth to speak. Unable to control her body, spasms still rippling through it, Einya trembled on the cavern floor. She held no doubts now why the Astrologer-Elect didn't just speak to the Stars himself: this was the path to madness. How many more had gone before, now just jabbering wrecks in the prison cells of the Tower?

The star's light faded into dull rock again, but the voice stayed echoing, churning words around her mind like a tumultuous sea.

Einya took several deep breaths as her eyes focused, slowly feeling strength return. The question from earlier returned to her thoughts, unbidden: was this all really worth it? Stumbling to her feet, she staggered to the door and into the fresh air before coughing up blue bile onto the cobblestones.

It was impossible to believe that all the doctrines suggesting the Stars wanting Rask under Gemynd rule had just been smoke and mirrors. Had this just been the drug-like effects of Astamitra, churning strange thoughts through her mind? No one else had heard the Stars; so why her?

The grey clouds above began scattering heavy snow between the cobbles, their flakes dripping refreshingly over Einya's burning face. She inhaled the blizzard, snow filling her lungs and mind with icy clarity. Striding back through the door toward the Stars, she looked around the now dim room before tossing everything into her pack—except for the glass vials, which she gently tucked into her pocket.

Outside again, the snow lashed against her as she set a steady fast pace back to her home, shoulders hunched over and hood pulled low. Reaching her door, she tugged the stone handle of her blade out of its sheath and raised it without hesitation.

As the snow drift swirled around her, she cut a simple 'T' deep into the door's wood and turned to look out across the sprawling mess of Raskian streets below her. She stamped her frosted feet against the flagstones leading to the door, noticing for the first time that they alternated in shades of ivory and ebony. Einya felt as if she was snared on a chess board as she stared into the distance, feeling a tug in her chest and a desire to see Tollska kindling itself from the burnt-out ashes of her heart.

Chapter Seventeen

Without their birth-Star, a person can amount to nothing.
~ The Testament of the Stars

Tollska found Pearth in the guard outpost near the Astrologer-Elect's manor, as she'd been told she would by the servants. She dragged in a nervous, shuddering breath. It was a relief, in some ways, to not have this conversation in their home.

Pearth sat with her legs straddled over a bench in the small room the guards had pointed to. The head of the Guard still held a sword in her hand and looked more militant than Einya had ever seen her before. Something powerful, and almost regal, in the strength of this woman struck Tollska. Smatterings of blood scattered the sand-strewn floor and a few fresh scratches criss-crossed on Pearth's bare arms.

"Training?" Tollska mumbled, hoping she wasn't blushing. It was tricky to keep her voice from wavering, especially when Pearth's head turned to her. The Guardswoman's gaze was bright and intense, causing Tollska to squirm a little. She shook her head, forcing a thought away to avoid getting distracted. "Pearth—"

"Shh. Don't speak."

Pearth stood, a slight swagger in her step as she crossed the distance between them and pressed a deep kiss into Tollska's lips. Pearth's strong arms pushed her back against the wall of the small training room, and Tollska felt the stone cold against her shoulders as she returned the kiss as best as she could at the awkward angle. Pearth's movements were focused, but tender. *Unexpected, but not unwelcome though.* The thought surprised her, had she been so lonely that this felt that *good?* A light-headed mist permeated her thoughts, stealing away her focus, as their bodies pressed closer together.

They lay, sometime later, with sand clinging to their clothes and skin.

Tollska bit her lip and exhaled as her stomach fluttered. She grabbed her coat and pulled it over herself. "Pearth, I need to tell you about what happened."

"Later. I want to teach you to defend yourself, sweet love."

"I… thank you."

"I won't let you be easy to push around." Pearth sat up, brushing Tollska's hair from her eyes.

"I'm not, in the ways that count."

"All ways count, so I need you to learn."

Pearth stood up, helped Tollska to her feet and started to button up her own tunic. Tollska moved to reclaim her dress, unsure how to answer such direct truths. She swallowed.

"Then I would like to learn."

"Good. That is for you."

Tollska looked up to see Pearth gesturing to a box on the table to the side of the room. She forced a smile, fiddling with the metal clasp until it clicked open. The velvet-lined case held an ornate rapier within it, with her married name initials engraved into the blade.

She flinched as Pearth's arms wove around her waist, feeling the humid brush of breath as the guard whispered in her ear.

"I want to find your birth-Constellation, and have it added here in the gap between the filigree."

"How? Is it possible? The Constellation, I mean. I thought—"

"I know someone who will find a way. Even though you're from Rask, I want you to know yours."

"Do you mean…"

"Yes, but do not worry. Einya has told me she's not concerned about us."

Tollska blinked twice. "She said that?"

"Yes, of course. She relinquished all claims; did you think I didn't know?"

"No, of course not. I'm glad, then you and I can be together and not worry."

"Exactly, and I will not have my wife live without her Constellation. Einya will find your birth-Star."

Tollska twisted round to face Pearth, tricking her lips into smiling, desperate to change the conversation. How could she face Einya? "Thank you, the sword is beautiful."

"And practical, we will see you be a blade-mistress yet."

"We'll see."

"I will teach you myself, my love. Every morning, bright and early. If this disillusion with us rises, I want you to be able to protect yourself."

They finished dressing and took a carriage back to the manor where an elaborate dinner waited for them. It was smaller than the feast laid on when she had made her speech, but there were still rich dishes of cured hams and roasted veal. After they had eaten, they both went through to the library where they were brought large goblets of fine brandy. Tollska tentatively sipped without drinking much at all, unsure how to proceed. But she was spared the concern, as Pearth didn't wait.

As soon as they were seated, Pearth's eyes shone eagerly as she leant forward. "So, tell me about Rask."

The speed of the change took her by surprise, and Tollska took a sip of brandy to give her time to think about what to say. "I found the things they're printing, a few actually."

"Show me."

Tollska folded them out from her pockets with trembling fingers and felt the papers tear slightly as they were ripped from her hands before Pearth read through them. The largest letters stood out boldly: *Gemynd lied about the Stars, no one can prove the Stars want us to give away our freedom. Gemynd trades all our goods and leaves us in poverty.*

"Where were they?" Pearth leant forward again, speaking quickly.

"On a street, tied to street lanterns."

"No indication of who put them there?"

"Not really."

Pearth looked at her closely, appraisingly, the softness of her words gone and in their place, granite-like syllables. "Tell me, please, anything at all."

"Well…"

"I need to know. I understand this is hard for you, but I won't have more children dying."

Tollska fumbled with the edge of her sleeve, trying to seem uncertain and reluctant. "There's a name, someone I know—he's a good man."

"Tell me." Pearth sat on the edge of her chair, looking as if she was about to spring up and rip the words from Tollska's lips.

"A man called Gunsk, I think he puts them up. That's all I know."

"Can you speak more to this man, find out more? Get other names?"

"Yes. His daughter and I played together when we were little, I know him well…"

"Good. That's how we will proceed. I need to know what they intend to do with these beliefs."

"You want me to go back?"

"Naturally. I need details, Tollska, on who he is. Who he knows."

Tollska looked around the plush room; the odd position of power tasted like molten metal in her mouth. "Well, I can try. What will you do with the testament?"

"Wait. See if they move against us again."

Tollska bit her lip. "And then?"

"We shall see. It depends how far this little game goes."

"Little game?"

"I'm sorry, love, I know this must be strange for you. I can trust you to want the best for them."

Tollska forced a smile as Pearth took her hand and gently kissed it. She didn't trust herself to speak. As they stood amongst the dust and books, she thought about the blurry and unmapped path ahead, reminding herself that she was the Queen in this waiting game. Even if it didn't feel that way.

Chapter Eighteen

We don't want much, just freedom to trade our own food. Freedom
to not starve.
~ Pamphlet found in Rask

Einya stayed hidden at home for days after she'd staggered
back from the Star caverns, half-blind in the blizzard. Glittering
lights left a piercing aura in her vision, and it tricked and dogged
her senses for many days after she had left the cavern. She had
curled into a ball by the lit fire, feeling its heat drying her skin as
though she was soaked with icy water still. Lying by the flames
while still trembling, nauseous, she'd forced herself to swallow
some dry bread. It just tasted of the tangy salt-like taint on her
tongue from the Astamitra, and it was hard to swallow down her
swollen throat.

The Star's words still clung to her like cobwebs, and when
she strayed from the fireside, she trembled. Sprawled on the
wooden planks and reaching for the loose floorboard, she clawed

out the small chest hidden within. She lay there, clutching the parchment written by Bri close to her chest. Torn wisps of conversations with herself tumbled in and out of her awareness. *Is now the time to go find him? No, there's more to do.*

Day blended into night twice that she counted as she lay on her floor, only half awake. Her eyelids felt weighted as if held down by chains, and half-burbled voices snaked through every thought and stayed as her constant companions while she slept.

A clear voice cut through the fog at some point. Someone was lifting her from the cold floor. Feeling the heavy weight of her quilt being draped around her shoulders and the soft sinking comfort of her bed, she tried to open her eyes. The curtains had been opened and the intricate herbal smell of Raskian cooking permeated the rooms as she felt herself waking up.

"Wake up, Einya." The familiar face of Oenska greeted her, the woman sat on the side of the bed, her soft scent of lavender woven into the smell of cooking. Einya stumbled over her words, head spinning.

"How…? When did you get here?"

"Yesterday some time, you were lying on the frozen floor."

Einya tried to sit up but found her arms limp at her side. She felt warm, at least, and it seemed a long time since she remembered feeling anything other than frostbitten.

Oenska gently placed her hand on Einya's forehead, a soft smile tugging at her lips. The elder woman carefully lifted her upright on the bed.

Before long, Einya was sitting up properly with Oenska resting next to her to stop her slumping sideways. She sipped tentatively from a bowl of heated broth, relieved to taste the herbs and not the strange stinging of the Astamitra.

"Oenska, the Stars—I spoke to them. At least, maybe, I'm not really sure." Einya spluttered as she choked out the words in a rush.

Oenska plucked the bowl from between Einya's hands, swapping it with a glass of water. "I'd assumed that was why you marked your door," she replied, as Einya sipped tentatively.

"Not only that, but yes. Listen, there was a boy who died. I need to know if…"

"Finish eating, then we'll talk."

"Did Raskians kill the Thennet boy?"

Oenska sighed. "If they did, it wasn't at my order. I promise you that. I can't control all the angry Raskians, much as I wish I could stop atrocities like that."

Einya nodded, hoping it was true. They sat close in occasional conversation whilst Einya slowly chewed through the meat chunks in the broth. She found herself shifting closer to Oenska slightly, realising how much she'd missed warmth and company.

Eventually, she set down her bowl and began to think through all she wanted to say. "The Stars don't care—they're just interested in memory and truth."

Oenska turned to face her, and Einya felt the intensity of her stare crawling over her skin. Warm, but firm and fierce.

Einya forced herself to continue speaking, feeling out of practice like she hadn't properly spoken to anyone in months. "They watch and want us to know of the past, and how we'll act based on our past. They don't care who rules where, they don't care about the list. They called themselves *historians*."

"As suspected, and now confirmed. Thank you." Oenska ran her fingers over Einya's cheek, causing her to blush. Oenska used to brush Tollska's cheek that way.

"How did you know?"

"I didn't, but when you've never heard them speak, it's hard not to wonder."

"No one does up here."

Oenska just shrugged. "They are not starving, Einya. They don't have to sneak food out of the deliveries to Gemynd, treading the line between famine and arrest. They don't live in fear of what will happen to those on this testament that your cousin is talking about now."

Einya swallowed. "I never knew how bad it was down there."

"Did Tollska never tell you? Did she never say that as a child, she'd wait underneath the promontories when the carts are sent over, just in case some food might fall over the edge? Lots of children do that, we call them bread-catchers. Sunrise every day, you'll see them there."

Einya looked away, feeling guilty that Oenska had just cooked for her. "You shouldn't have…"

Oenska's fingers tipped her jaw gently back towards her, her fingers rough like sandpaper on Einya's soft skin. "None of that, Einya, Tollska sends me food from your family's kitchen these days. I eat like a queen!"

The elderly woman shuffled off the side of the bed and moved around the room with a bright energy, whistling a little as she looked out of the windows. "I like these rooms, lovely! Better than a drafty manor." Oenska bounced around the room with the energy of someone half her age.

Einya smiled slightly and tentatively rolled out of the thick covers and, reaching for a gown to wrap herself in, stepped onto the wooden floorboards. Oenska's infectious energy, much like her daughter's, jolted her with an old spark of joy at running through the maize fields and getting lost in the forests of Rask.

Then she sighed, her energy seeping away again. "I'm out of my depth in all this. All I wanted was to be with Tols, to take her away from all of this, and now she has forgotten me."

"You're not, and she hasn't." Oenska plucked at some flowers resting in a vase, rearranging them slightly. "One day, when we have our freedom, things will be different."

How could Raskians endure so much, and still have optimism? Einya emptied her lungs with a heavy sigh. "She will still be married. Where does this end, Oenska?"

"I don't know. It can't continue as it is." She grinned. "Half the battle is finding our new path."

"What about Tollska? What is her role in this?"

"She'll tell us if the Guards are coming to Rask, and she controls the names we tell Gemynd."

"Well, then I will try to control the response from the Stars."

Oenska ceased in her travels around the room, her sharp eyes focusing on Einya. "Yes, but also take the evidence to the Astrologers. Be our voice."

"And tell them what?" Einya spat, trying desperately to keep the edge from her voice.

"Less mandatory trade for Rask, equal rights, let us own our goods and trade as we see fit."

"I am worried, I won't pretend I'm not. It's dangerous. But I will, for her, and for you."

Oenska smiled. "Thank you."

They said nothing for a short while, Einya slowly pacing around the room and gathering her thoughts. "How long will you stay?" she asked. "Stay as long as you're safe to, and happy."

Oenska smiled from where she was now sitting by the fire, watching the brass kettle humming on the range. "I need to go back I'm afraid; things are starting to move. I wanted to see you, see that you're managing and make sure you know what to do. You're a good woman, Einya."

They sat together for another hour, sipped tea and nibbled on cakes, talking about memories and brighter times. For that short time, both forgot the rising tide of tension and the shattering differences between their lives. When Oenska finally stood to leave, the room seemed to dim slightly to Einya. She looked out of the now open door to see if clouds had canvassed across the sky.

Grabbing the Raskian woman's sleeve, a frantic thought stabbed through her brain. "Keep her safe."

"She's my daughter; I always will."

Einya nodded numbly as the splattering of rain began to patter on the paving stones.

"We will come find you if it all starts. Stay safe, my Einya."

Einya watched her stride away with an ache in her heart, Oenska's plum-coloured hair and olive-green coat vibrantly conflicting with the drab grey rain-beaten rock facades of Gemynd.

Chapter Nineteen

Parlenta offers us hidden knowledge of the Stars through
Astamitra, which is worth the spending of Myndats.
~ Astrologer-Elect Sepult Disren

The steep switch-back stair that led away from the small canvas hovels by the gate of Parlenta was wide, despite being hacked into the side of the mountain. Bri felt his legs straining as he slowly trudged higher up the mountain, grudgingly thinking back to the guard who'd pointed them up this way.

Above the pathway, the looming turrets and buttresses of the Parlentan Palace hung over them. Prethi had remarked several times that he hoped it was only an illusion, and that the hulking fortress wasn't in fact directly above them waiting to plummet down on their heads.

They had left the horses tethered at an inn at the bottom. The wind snagged at the travellers as they wove up the precarious path on foot, and Bri tugged his doublet collar up higher in a vain hope of keeping the gale from blowing cold winds down this neck. The guards had pointed them to this stair, it being the one that uninvited guests to the palace took.

Bri's thin-soled shoes had started to wear through, and stabbing lances of pain were digging into his feet where stones pushed through the leather. "Not much further, Prethi, let's hope our fellow Gemyndians didn't go up by the honoured visitors' route, which I am sure must be quicker than this! This better be worth it!"

The route turned out to be even slower than they had imagined, and after another hour of walking, the pair finally reached the sprawling plateau that led up to the palace. The plateau appeared to be in a crater with curved walls scraping the sky as if something had been hurled into the mountain to create the strange bowl-shape they now stood in.

The palace had broad turrets that reached upward like stalagmites, similar in colour to the yellowing sludge that slumped over the sides of the mountain stone they were carved from.

A soldier, wearing black mottled armour and a helmet concealing his entire face, stepped to block their way as they headed towards the palace. "What brings you here? Who are you here to see?"

Bri tried to see the man's eyes through the visor but his gaze was shadowed by the lack of sunlight reaching the crater. "The ruler here, I've important words from Gemynd."

"From the Gemyndian delegation that arrived earlier? Why are you not with them?"

Bri smiled, ignoring Prethi fidgeting next to him. "I wished to see the settlement before I came to the palace. My servant here will go and make some quarters ready for me this evening, now he has seen me here. You can go." He waved his hand.

Prethi stammered a little. "Go? But…"

"Like we discussed, remember? Go, do what I told you to before. Don't make me repeat it."

The soldier reached out as Prethi turned away, and Bri felt tension twinge through his shoulders as the soldier barred Prethi's way. "He comes with you, Gemyndian."

"Would you deny me my servant preparing a suitable quartering for me? I am a noble, after all, though the travels took a little toll on my clothing."

"What is your name, Gemyndian? I have orders…"

"Oh, my name? Lord Prethi, thank you very much," Bri said.

Another soldier came striding over. "Is it the Arden man? They said he'd be better dressed than this."

"Apparently not," the first guard muttered back.

"Let him pass then, honestly."

Bri grinned and bowed low with a flourish of his arm, grateful he had thought to not use his name. "Stars bless you, gentlemen." He straightened and waved one hand dismissively at Prethi, whilst sneaking a wink with one eye. "Go on then, servant, do as I instruct."

As his raggedy-haired friend turned and trundled back toward the edge of the plateau, Bri felt gratitude, guilt and regret churn through him. He swallowed, packed it away with all his concerns for Einya, and bowed again to the soldiers before striding toward the doors of the palace.

These were heaved open for him by four guards, leaving Bri to admire the glittered gems set into the heavy rock of the doors as he stepped over the threshold. The cavernous hall was gilded with gems too; large emeralds, sapphires and garnets dressed each pillar. He'd expected it to be dim, but the hall dazzled with torches and lanterns hanging low, flames ricocheting light off the angles of the precious stones.

At the grand doors, a small group of guards stopped him and took the rapier and dagger from Bri's belt without so much as a word. It was lazily done; luckily, they missed the short blade in his boot. Bri sighed, relieved, and smiled as if this was all expected to him. Each guard had a blue crystal set into their breastplates, and all seemed to have eyes stripped of their natural colour.

Strange, he thought.

Only two people occupied the grand platform at the end of the room, one on a lofty dais made of plush scarlet velvet, mounted atop four pillars with an intricately carved stone staircase rising up to it. A grey-skinned woman lay delicately sprawled on a chaise, her chin resting on her hand. She wore an elaborate dress with diamonds encrusted into the puffed sleeves.

Below stood a man who was more simply attired, except for the garnet-laden chain of office slumped over his shoulders.

The woman stretched out like a cat, her arms long and fingernails lengthy enough to be claws. She gracefully sat up, tilting her head to either side as if assessing Bri as he approached.

"Well, man from Gemynd. Lord, is it? Welcome. I have expected you."

"Me, my lady?" Bri bowed low. "I'd not expected you, in such finery."

"Then you are ill-informed. I am the Queen of Parlenta."

"Then forgive me, your glittering Majesty."

The woman laughed, her parted lips starkly red against her stone-grey skin. "Better, Lordling." She stood, and even her eyes seemed bright like gems as she sauntered down the steps with the gems sewn into the tail of her dress twinkling against the stone staircase. "What is it you travel all this way to assail me with, pleasant and diverting nothings, I hope?"

The Queen brushed the thumb of her right hand over Bri's brow. "The frown on your face says otherwise. Sit with me, unburden your troubles."

She turned before Bri could speak and sat upon one of the steps, her legs neatly coiled beneath her. She clapped her hands, her claw-like nails clicking against each other. Moments later, a servant brought out steaming cups on a marble platter, which he offered to the Queen first and then to Bri. The pungent sweet liquid was almost too hot, but Bri glugged it down anyway, grateful for the warmth.

"So, you're here. What for, Lordling?" the grey woman asked.

Bri knelt, it somehow seemed like the thing to do, even with his cup in one hand. "To ask you about Gemynd, glittering lady."

"What a flatterer you are. Speak plainly as I imagine you know more of Gemynd than I ever will."

Bri shook his head a little, chuckling. Why did he always try his hand at politics? It still was not his strength. "My sister would tell me not to say this, would say it's impolitic, but I will tell you anyway. Gemynd wants to expand, always has, and everything they do entwines the Stars they have... they are a claim to righteous power."

The Queen shrugged. "We have our own Star."

"I have heard, but they have two. Twice times the claim to astrological power."

"So?"

"Like Rask beneath them, would you just become another vein of Gemynd?"

The Queen stood. The delicacy of her gentle saunter gone, now she strode back up the stairs to her throne. "You mistake yourself. I have a palace, a mountain and soldiers. I am safe, and what is more: I have knowledge of the Stars your settlement does not possess. Your Astrologer-Elect needs me more than I do him."

"Are you so sure, what about when they want what you have?"

"He will never grasp the knowledge to do what we do."

The man stood beside the throne chuckled, and the Queen pointed at him with an unbent arm. "This is my Mineral Master, he knows more than Gemynd ever will about the use of the Stars. You see, the power of the one we have far outstrips the two your people fail to use properly."

Bri stood. "Look, what if I told you my name was Briarth of the Arden family. My cousin is the head of our military, and I know what she is capable of..."

"I know who you are. The traders who regularly come here brought me warnings of you from your dear cousin to not listen to anything you say. I know your reputation. So, no lies, what is your interest in my settlement?"

"My reputation, Lady?"

"She said you've fabricated a war to undermine her."

"I came to help you stay free, Queen, that's all. Gemynd oppresses her own people, even though they are one settlement. My cousin seeks absolute power over them. The sovereignty of the Stars is everything to her. How long until you're next? End the chaos in Rask, save the people and save yourselves."

"Chaos?"

"A civil war was brewing as I left; I don't know if it has started. I hope it has."

The Queen stood, the gem-encrusted train of her dress clattering around the stone stairs. "You came for an army, then? Foolish words. The winter will be harsh to you, Arden, and the money of Gemynd will still flow in trade. We have what they cannot get. No. I'll not march to save Rask."

Bri's voice echoed around the stone hall, a crescendo trembling through his speech. "What happens when they come for your people, come to take your star, expanding their little hill into a sprawling settlement-state?"

The elaborately dressed woman sighed and threw her arms in the air. "There is no worry for us there. Mineral Master, show him why our star is superior and get him away from me. I will not throw my soldiers against the allies that I trade with."

Bri panicked a little then, a thought cutting through it: *Have I said too much? Probably.* He bowed again, out of habit more than politeness, and kept his eyes fixed on the Queen's, noticing how her smooth grey-hued skin blurred seamlessly into the stone throne. She sat again and stretched out, apparently uncaring, with one leg dropped extravagantly over the gem-encrusted arm.

As they left the grand palace, the Mineral Master took Bri through a grand arch that led toward a slope, which towered even higher up the mountain. The frail man gripped the guide rope tightly as he ascended the mountain, competently scaling the loose shingle surface with surprising dexterity.

When the Mineral Master stopped, Bri looked around, the view over Parlenta far-reaching. On the mountain, towering over the two men, loomed an iron door. What was he getting himself into?

"The Star is in here."

"Appreciated. Will you enter with me?"

"The custodian of the Star will see to your needs. She will help you in every way."

Bri gulped a little, but as directed turned the heavy iron handle and stepped into the musty darkness. Was this a good idea? Little choice now, anyway. He felt the bumps and crevasses in the wall as he ran his fingers along it, stepping further in. A very faint trembling of amber torchlight flickered deep in the cave and Bri stumbled toward it, bashing and scraping his knees on stalactites.

As the cavern finally widened and brightened, Bri gasped, the glittering spire of hewn rock spiking up high above him with gems glowing in the dim distance. In the centre of the mine's cavern, the Star-rock loomed, a pitifully misshapen form with deep drill holes struck down into its very core. Bri coughed a little, acidic bile rising in his throat at the mining of the star. Who would have thought he could feel sorry for a Star-rock?

"Is anyone here?"

"Yes. Admiring our work?" a voice sounded, and a haggard woman stepped from the shadows.

"A little. Are you the custodian? I wish to see the Star up close."

"I know, the Mineral Master wouldn't be here otherwise. Let me show you her beauty. Look here."

The withered woman pointed at a deep bore hole, and at the centre, a blue glow quivered as if a wind rippled its surface. "That's the Astamitra that Gemynd purchases from us."

"They buy it from you? Why, when they have their own Stars?"

"They don't know how to mine it. Everything your people do with the Stars is clumsy. They don't know anything about them because they pride themselves over everything."

"Can you show me more?"

"Boy, we are rich because of Gemynd's ignorance. Gemynd's beliefs are possible because of their ignorance. You see, we're all too happy with the way things are between us."

It was then Bri saw two shadows shifting at the edge of the glittering cavern. He turned, tugging the short blade from his boot and tightly gripping its archaic carved wood handle.

The first shadow rushed him, and as it emerged, Bri saw that it was a huge woman armed with a mining pick. Bri ducked as the pick swung into the rock of the Star. He thrust his dagger into the woman's ribs and, even as she howled, he turned to find the other shadow.

The second shadow emerged into a rag-dressed man with two daggers and a gaunt expression. Bri struggled to dart out the way of the whirling slashing blades, parrying the heavy blows as best he could. The man was too fast for him. He wasn't surprised when he looked down and saw a deep gash in his side, the blood cascading like a waterfall to the floor.

"Fool, she wanted him to experiment on. Not to die." The withered woman beat the dagger man round the head with her hands until he stepped away from where he towered over Bri, who had sagged to the floor. He pressed his fingers against the wound, but still the river of blood ran free.

"I'll die if you don't help me," he said, taking his chance to speak between pained gasps.

The withered woman tutted and sighed. She ground one foot after the other into the stone floor as she shuffled towards him. Snatches of light drifted in and out of his vision. *You've gone and done it now*, he thought as he began panting heavily with the pain.

Injured on the cave floor, he couldn't object as the large woman held him down and stitched together his wound. The first few punctures of the needle stabbing through his flesh hurt immensely until he felt his awareness fade into nothingness.

Sometime later, his eyes flickered open, wet and sticky with tears. His tongue scraped against the roof of his parched mouth like sandpaper. Twisting his wrists together, finding them coiled up in a rough rope, he realised he lay in his drying blood on the mine floor.

"I thought he'd be uglier than this," the large woman was saying, the three mine dwellers clustered around him and staring intently. "He's fineness itself."

"Isn't he? Shame about all this, then."

Bri chuckled a little, but the laugh mutated into a little cough of pain. "When you're done admiring me, mind telling me what's happening here?"

The three exchanged uncertain glances, which Bri frowned a little at. "Gemynd don't want you digging around here. So, we're here to make you feel right at home."

"Stop talking. Let's get this done." The small man with the daggers was watching intently, and Bri noticed in that moment the small gold-star pin of the Gemynd guard on the collar of his coat. So, there was more to this.

"What did I do that led to this?" Bri whispered, turning to look directly at the man.

The man, with a face like the stones around them, sneered. "This is because the lives of Raskians and Gemyndians alike are just pieces in your little game. Your people must be tired of your schemes. Your cousin certainly is."

The small man slammed a fist into his stomach. Bri wheezed, crumpling like a snapped twig.

The custodian's words ground roughly in his ears. "Now you are a pawn in our Queen's game."

The three mine dwellers pinned him against the Star, clammy hands pincered around his neck. Bri exhaled with a grating discomfort as the elderly custodian hobbled over to him. "Listen, lady, I have money I can pay you. This has gone a little far. Please, let's not do this."

"Quiet." She pulled a pouch from her pocket, her withered fingers easing the strings apart with difficulty. He tried, but failed, to see what was inside until it was too late. The blue smudge of powder was rubbed into his eyes before he even got a moment to look at it. It stung, and he writhed as more was rubbed in, even as he began to groan with the pain. The wrinkles of her hands pressed into his eyeballs until bright lights sparked within his vision.

"My problem is I never learnt how to lie, a bad thing for anyone who dabbles in politics," Bri mumbled, and the last thing he saw before his sight and mind slipped away into a light and tingly nothingness was the crumpled face of the old woman peering curiously at him.

Chapter Twenty

Star-blood clouds their minds, blinds them to our strife.
~ The Word-Weaver of Rask

In the days after Oenska left, Einya hid the book about the Stars away and allowed herself freedom from them for a short respite. She spent the days with parchment strewn across the floor, sketching and painting bright scenes across the textured papers. Mostly, these ended up as etchings of verdant forests. She dotted them over mantelpieces or pinned them up against the walls, turning her neutral rooms into a wallpapered woodland paradise.

Reality felt easier to drop herself back into, shielded in the walls of her forest haven. Even so, taking the book out again and readying herself for the world felt like icy water slicing at her flesh.

Placing the book on the bed and sighing, she shuffled toward the washroom. After standing at the basin for a score of minutes, cleaning her hair and rinsing her skin of weeks-old grime, she looked up. The mirror above the basin framed a face that Einya didn't recognise; the flame that lit her reflection didn't reach far enough and sombre shadows clung to the edge of the looking-glass. Something had changed in her eyes, like a creature was trying to crawl out from behind the glossy veneer of her irises.

"What has happened to me?" she rasped, horror gripping tightly at her heart.

Hidden in the faded blue orbs staring back at her, there was a clear reflection of the Star-rock, stuck there like a piece of grit that wouldn't come out even though she'd rubbed at it until her eyes were red and sore.

The thrumming beats of the Stars trembled through her every thought and lingered in her awareness like a dream not quite banished by waking. Even whilst standing in front of the mirror, the lure of the words from the book was strong. *I could read a little more now, I'm better now*, she thought, and then shook her head to force the thought away. They had absorbed her entirely in a determination to understand as fast as wildfire rips through a forest, and it was increasingly difficult to fight the urge to be completely engrossed in her work.

A three-bell peal broke through her thoughts and rang out through the stone squares of Gemynd. An urgent summons, calling the Astrologers to the cavern. Dread plucked at her. *What now?*

Einya slipped thick gloves on, watching in twisted fascination as the starlight writhing beneath her skin was snuffed out by the dark cotton sliding over her fingers. The bells droned on as she readied herself to go to the cavern. The lingering whisper of the Star's voice still trailed her in the streets. Their voices felt like they'd fused to her vocal cords, as if speaking would bring forth their words too.

As she crossed the square toward the cavern, it wasn't clear whether the bells or the incessant thrumming of the Stars was louder. Entering felt like stepping willingly into a venomous snake-pit. There was a bustling as near a hundred Astrologers stood within the now cramped cavern. Sepult Disren had raised himself on a small set of portable wooden steps in front of the Stars.

He looked like a mouth as part of a withered face with two looming eyes over him as he stood between the twin Star-rocks. She jostled her way through the crowd to get closer. A bowl was being passed around with the colours of Astamitra churning within, not in its usual liquid form but rather the strengthened azure-dust that came in from Parlenta. What was happening, why did the Astrologer-Elect think this could be a good idea when none of them had tasted it undiluted before? His warning on overuse seemed empty now if he was just going to have everyone take it anyway.

Astrologers cupped great handfuls, tipping the powder into their mouths whilst the Astrologer-Elect spoke from his high platform. "Astrologers, friends—I am calling you here on an occasion I am deeply saddened by. The death of the Thennet boy might not just be one freak incident; there are signs of uprising."

Sepult Disren raised one arm to run his fingers over one of the Stars. "Some Raskians have decided our protection and the love of the Stars is not enough for them, may the Stars leave them in darkness. The Guard has found lies, inflammatory pamphlets, but furthermore, they have the names of those trying to unseat our star-blessed rule. I have asked the Constellan Guard to uncover this conspiracy and maintain peace in our land. There will be no more deaths of children, or anyone, at the hands of Raskians."

The Astrologer-Elect lifted a crumpled pamphlet, throwing it to the floor of the cavern. Einya felt as if something clutched her heart and brain in a vice grip, expecting the next words to be about Tollska, even though she knew it was unlikely. Could this be happening? Seeing only the reaction of Rask, but not the cause—it felt like a convenient lie to justify persecution.

The Astrologer-Elect spat out his last words, eyes wide in the half-light. "These lies will not go unanswered. Go to Rask, spread the love of the Stars and find me the names of those who speak against us."

"Will we be safe?" a shrill-voiced man asked from the crowd.

"Wait, this is wrong…" Einya tried to say clearly, but her voice was drowned by the mass of questions echoing around the cavern.

The Astrologer-Elect lifted his hands, reaching out to the Stars, and continued speaking over the din. "Yes, my friends. The Stars will protect us. Take the Constellan Guard with you. Be sure, my friends, that we will give the Stars the love they deserve. We will make Rask understand, or may we be shrouded in darkness too. Stars, give us your mercy. We will find names and add them to the testament of your will that will burn down all those who speak against your power."

It all happened so quickly, and a brief spike of panic grabbed Einya instantly. Before she could object again a rush of air hissed, pressure building to intense levels in the cavern. Einya flinched, covering her ears as a sudden wail pierced through her. Next to her, a man had collapsed to the floor, screeching in pain, with blood trickling from his ears. A crescendo of distress rose within the chamber as the thrumming of the Stars pulsed and ground noise through the cavern. Einya snarled, pushing through the pain, coldly angry with the Astrologer-Elect's actions. Why expose them like this, what did it achieve?

Many of the Astrologers gripped their star pendants and gems tightly, and those close to the Star-rocks threw themselves to their knees. The trembling whisper of the Stars began to echo, a slow dirge like a long, drawn-out organ note. All those around her had glowing dilated pupils and the gossamer blue powder residue clinging to their lips.

Panic rose in Einya's throat again in the form of acidic bile pulsing up into her mouth, burning as she gulped it back down. She grabbed a woman next to her, who was tearing the hem of her coat with trembling hands, her nails now snapped, revealing a bloody mess beneath them. Holding the woman still, cradling her almost, Einya pressed down the nausea writhing in her own throat.

She scrunched her eyes shut tightly, took a deep breath and forced herself to focus through the song pounding through her mind, before opening them again. Einya took the other woman's hands, stopping the fretful movements, smiling reassuringly. "Shh, shh. It's alright. What is your name?"

"Sundial. Sundial," the woman stammered.

"That's your—"

"My birth-Star. Uh, my name is Yathyen."

"Yathyen, would you like to leave here?"

The woman nodded, her skin pale and her eyes stretched unnaturally wide. "I want to see my children in case the Stars decide I won't awake in the morning for not realising Rask is rising up, for not trying to stop it."

Einya tutted, sucking air through her teeth. "That won't happen, I promise, the Stars are more dispassionate than that."

Einya put one arm around her, supporting the woman as they stumbled out of the cavern, up the winding passage and through the small wooden door. Once outside, she left the door ajar and scooped up a small handful of snow from the ground, which she used to melt over Yathyen's cut fingers and rinse away the blood.

"Go home, be safe."

"Thank you, thank you. Please, tell the Stars I am sorry."

"There is nothing to apologise for. Look after yourself, Yathyen."

Yathyen looked like she had tried to smile, but it was so faint, she barely moved her lips at all. She hurried away, leaving a deep track in the snow behind her.

Einya took three sharp breaths as she watched Yathyen leave. The fire of her own birth-Star kindled inside her, forming into an uncharacteristic inferno of anger. She stepped back through the wooden door, ramming it shut in its stone frame. The booming echo was satisfying, as were the sharp reverberations thundering through the heel of her boots as she strode back into the cavern. The dirge was gone now, and only her anger remained, hissing like a kettle boiling over.

The Astrologers were, for the most part, pressed against the Star-rocks. There was enough space for many of them to be pressing their lips to the floor beneath the rocks, whispering, crying, begging for guidance. They looked like wilting flowers cowering beneath an overgrown tree.

Sepult Disren sat cross-legged in between the Stars, tears streaming down his face. Einya didn't pause; she kept striding until she was in front of him, her anger raging within her now. She knelt, struck him round the face with an open hand and his white, unfocused eyes reclaimed their colour. He seemed dazed, and she'd have pitied him if it wasn't for his drugging the Astrologers with Astamitra.

"Furnace?" the man mumbled.

"My name is Einya, I won't be called by my Star. What do you think you're achieving here? I need to speak to you."

She didn't wait but instead yanked him up by one arm until he was forced to stand. He was a bony old man as it was, and his weight was nothing to Einya's strength. Keeping a vice-like grip on his arm, Einya called out in a voice that pierced the Astrologer's mumbled prayers and faint cries, feeling the strength of the Star's voice thrumming in her voice box once again.

"Astrologers. The Stars will forgive; go home and find the warmth in your lives. See your families, forget this happened." It seemed to break the maddening frenzy, and Einya realised the Star's dirge was no longer ringing in her mind. "Get out of here."

The words slowly seemed to permeate their awareness. A slow shuffle of feet heading toward the door out of the cavern began. Satisfied, Einya turned again to Sepult and nudged him up the stairs out of the cavern and into his manor.

The fire of purpose still flared up within her. Einya called to his servants to bring the Astrologer-Elect a glass of brandy and something to eat.

With the maid's help, he crossed the marble floor in a stupor, until he was ensconced in a deep leather chair with the glass of brandy clutched between his quaking hands.

"We need to talk," Einya spat, perched on the arm of one of the leather chairs.

"Einya?" He looked so lost that Einya felt a tug of pity, but she steeled herself again.

"What happened down there?"

"I was… so appalled that anyone could speak against the Stars. Raskians should be grateful. We have protected them for almost a hundred years."

Einya thrust her right hand deep into the pocket of her dress, fighting the urge to punch the man. "Were you so appalled, you thought you'd shatter everyone's minds with Astamitra, frightening them into finding you names of Raskians for whatever this is? Is it worth destroying people's minds with Star-blood? What's more, Raskians are starving. This goes both ways."

His eyes abruptly focused on her, it was sudden and surprising. She tried not to flinch as he spoke. "Never mind that. We have sovereignty; they are striking at our Star-given rights. Your mind isn't shattered, I note; it seems you are not concerned with Rask's uprising damaging Gemynd. So, I have to ask, why?"

Einya's heart stammered in her chest, sensing the approach of a trap.

A sharp look had crept into his eyes as he set his brandy down on the stone table. She scrabbled for a way to shift the focus from her. "Elect... Sepult, it was not just me. I am surprised it affected you."

"I didn't take the Astamitra; I need these people to bring me names for the testament."

"Then how were you so... entranced?"

"The Stars speak through me," he pronounced, so imperiously she almost snorted.

It was an obvious lie; he must have taken some of the Star-blood. But she glossed over it, her main concern burning in her mind. "You're going to tell me about this list, and what will be done to those on it."

"Einya, listen..."

"No, I won't let you charm your way out of this."

"The Stars spoke many years ago saying what they wanted from Rask..."

Einya bared her teeth. "I know—unlike others—that they are neither benevolent nor malevolent. They are historians. This list is nonsense; what will you do to the people named?"

Sepult Disren picked up his brandy again, regarding her over it before taking a deep swig. "It's there to deter; it's your cousin's initiative. She fears what will happen if peace is not attained. You spoke to the Stars, it worked? You didn't tell me."

Einya sighed. This wasn't the point she wanted to make. "I was waiting until I knew more, it's not really talking..."

The man leapt to his feet, grinning suddenly. "Wonderful! Einya, this will save important lives."

"Important lives?" Disgusted, she scowled. How could he value life so little?

"Yes, Gemyndian lives. But, never mind that, you spoke to the Stars! Let's not argue, let us celebrate."

The mood change took Einya by surprise. Had he forgotten, just like that? The Astrologer-Elect stood and seemed to dance over to her. His arms wrapped around her in a brief, awkward embrace before he called to the servants to bring a bottle of wine in celebration.

Soon, she was given a large glass, which she politely sipped whilst watching the unwavering grin of Sepult Disren shining across from her. "This calls for jubilance, Einya. Finally, we can know the will of the Stars through you. We can prove our star-given rights over Rask and end this tension, the lies and the killing."

She shook her head. "I don't think you heard me. It's not about hearing them speak about some divine right—they're impartial."

"Oh, don't tell anyone that, this is about *you*. The voice of the Stars! The bringer of peace."

Einya put the glass down, concerned that it might shatter under her tightening grip. "It's not, and you need to know that the Stars don't believe Rask should be thralls to us. It will change everything for us; we're building our settlement on a lie."

Sepult slammed his glass upon the table. "Nonsense. The Astrologers of old were wise; would you change our history?"

She nodded then, trying to steady her breathing. "If it was a lie, yes."

"We need Rask, they need us. That's all there is now."

"It's not…"

"It's politics. Don't ask any more. Now, let us celebrate. I wish to make you my personal Astrologer and my heir."

Einya glared at him but forced herself to grab the glass, sip it and close her eyes briefly to think of a political answer. "I believe, and correct me if I'm wrong, that this is not a question of heirs but of an election of peers, Sepult…"

"But it can be, and the added benefit is you're family of Pearth Arden. All in your favour."

The Astrologer-Elect produced from a bag a scroll containing details of the succession. He unfurled it, the crimson ink still freshly glistening on the page. This was going too far, too fast.

"Sepult, I do not want it."

"Nonsense. Sign here."

This had been planned all along. Realisation crashed into her, plummeting in the pit of her stomach: this manoeuvre to seal Rask's fate by making a voice for the Stars.

"I need to go." Einya stood. "Thank you for the wine, I have a duty I must attend to."

Surprise clung to her at the steel-like strength that had resonated in her voice. She left by the main doors and took the steps down to the street, two at a time.

"Einya, you fool," she muttered. "Stop giving them what they need."

She got only a little way across the square before a flurry of bodies crowded into it. A Raskian dressed in thick wool, but bare-footed, was tethered behind a cart, blood seeping from his exposed skin. Einya watched with an acrid taste rising in her throat at the trail of blood following the group entering the square. She looked the other way and kept her pace towards the towering manor she had once called home. This couldn't go on.

Chapter Twenty-One

To find a birth-Star, one must be pure of heart in the Stars, or the reading will latch on to someone else.
~ The original Testament of the Stars

Tollska sat in the large entrance hall of the Arden manor, listening to the pealing bells that had been ringing for what seemed like hours. The manor was strangely quiet, Pearth conspicuous by her lengthy absence. Her receiving a birth-Star had been the topic of their conversation for days now since she'd announced the idea to Tollska. Why the sudden urgency? Something was happening, it must be. Some kind of way to make her less Raskian, for some reason?

The late morning sunlight filtered into the room, showing the empty sheets next to her from where Pearth had already gone. A lavish breakfast was laid out for her and Krytha, the Arden Matriarch, joined her instead. More food than just bread, eggs and weak beer to breakfast was unusual. The strangeness of it added to Tollska's sense of unease.

This was made worse by being entwined in conversation with Einya's mother and she felt a sharp wave of relief when Prethi entered. The man slumped down silently in a chair nearby and made only passing attempts at conversation.

"Prethi," the matron began. "When did you return? You've been much absent of late."

"Visiting a sick friend, Lady Arden," Prethi mumbled, and then ate non-stop seemingly to avoid speaking.

Krytha turned back to her then, interrogating her on her ideals and hopes. An awkward exchange had endured, but Tollska had felt a cantankerous defiance pulse through her at all attempts to intimidate her. Krytha had insisted on Tollska calling her Star-Lady as the proper rank for one related to an Astrologer and continually asked Tollska about intimate details of her life, including what she thought her birth-Star would prove to be.

Tired of pointless small talk, Tollska eventually managed to make excuses that Pearth expected her to practice with her blade regularly. This placated Krytha, and Tollska hurried away to the courtyard where she diligently ran through the manoeuvrers Pearth had shown her. She flicked the light blade in arcs, undercuts and thrusts and let her mind drift away from the overshadowing concern at Einya coming to the manor to find her birth-Star. Bells were ringing somewhere in the distance, but she tried to tune it out and focus on her drills.

Prethi had followed her out and was watching, chewing a piece of fruit as he rested against the wall.

"You've got good at that."

"Not really. I've not had time to practice. Where've you been, Prethi? I saw you avoid that conversation; you been back with Luskena?"

"No, and I can't say more."

"Why?"

"Because I'm keeping someone safe, so please don't ask again."

"That I can understand; aren't we all these days?" She smiled, sheathing the blade. "I need to go anyway, good to see you safe though, whatever you've been doing."

She bounded up the stone stairs into the manor two at a time, before settling in the library where she tried to banish thoughts of what was to come by flicking through a tome on Raskian plants. Her nervous thoughts didn't go away: What was this going to be like? What would she say to Einya? Tollska had heard tales of the strange, more detailed, procedures required for finding the birth-Star of a toddler when they hadn't been gifted one at birth. What would the process be for a full-grown woman?

Outside, the bells stole the silence and shouts added to their cacophony. Tollska stood and stumbled her way across the flagstones, the train of her gown catching on the heels of her boots. On the other side of the large lead-framed windows, a commotion was rising amongst the busy crowd, the Constellan Guard in their radiant white uniforms crossing the square in force.

Pearth stood at their front, and a man hung limp behind her in the arms of the guards.

Tollska staggered again. *It couldn't be.* But of course, it was. It felt as if a blade had punctured her chest at the sight of the man in chains at the heart of the group. She lifted her skirt slightly and her heels hammered across the floor as she sped from the hall and into the street. She pushed through the throng, looking frantically around until she saw him. Gunsk's bare feet scraped along the cobblestones, and he was shouting something unintelligible around a tight cloth pulled across his lips. Tollska bit back a slight sob. *What have I done?*

She followed behind the group, unnoticed, until they reached the centre of the square. People were leaning out of the windows of the tall alabaster buildings surrounding the scene now, and Tollska crept along behind it all. It was only when she got close that she gave up on subtlety, taking six swift steps to where Pearth stood, ignoring the presence of the Astrologer-Elect who strode along purposefully beside Pearth.

"Where are you taking him?" Tollska demanded.

"To the tower." Pearth's eyes didn't even look towards her.

"Please, he's old..."

"Don't interfere," Pearth snapped, and then looked towards the Astrologer-Elect. "Many apologies for my spouse."

Pearth pushed past her, the glistening guards following after, in stark contrast to the bloodied man they dragged with them. Tollska looked around at the growing crowds with a creeping sense of dismay, even though she knew this might happen. In front of the latticed gate that led into the tower—and the dungeons beneath—the group stopped. A small group of Raskians had followed the crowd and were standing helplessly as Gunsk was stretched across the gate with arms held in place against the metal.

Pearth's outstretched arm pointed at the man's head, which hung low between his raised arms. "This man speaks against the Stars. The Stars will now speak against him, for eternity."

Tollska hurried forward again and saw Luskena amongst the Raskians present as she tried to bustle through to get to the man she'd known most of her life.

"Wait, Tollska, you ain't going up there." Luskena stepped across her path.

"Why aren't you helping him?" Tollska's words stabbed in staccato bursts.

"What would I do other than add myself to this example?"

"They'll kill him!"

"You knew this might happen when you agreed to give his name."

"I didn't know this would happen; I can't let them…"

The heavy grip of Luskena's tight fingers pinched Tollska's arm in their grip. She tried to pull away and toward the gate where Gunsk was tied, feeling panic surge up inside her as they ripped his tunic off his torso.

"Stop, you fool." Luskena's whispered hiss splattered Tollska's face in spittle, her eyes flaring.

"What are you doing?" Tollska snarled, still tugging against Luskena wildly.

"This is the spark we need. Imagine when we print this? Rask will rise up."

"How can that be all you care about?" she spat.

Over their argument, Gunsk howled as one of the guards etched the shape of a star into his exposed chest with a dagger.

Both the women's heads snapped around to stare. From where Tollska stood, she could see the movement was surgical and precise, and that they at least packed the wounds with herbs as soon as the cuts had been made.

Tollska turned back to Luskena with a cold rage in her eyes. "You let that happen—"

"We need to give people a reason to fight," Luskena hissed.

"We have enough reason from Rask's hunger alone."

"But this will start the flood like nothing before. I want this persecution, Tols, persecution is how freedom is won. Persecution shows the hidden injustices we've lived with for years."

"Your heart is made of ice," Tollska spat.

"We have both let people get broken for our cause, so don't pretend you're better than me."

Tollska dragged her arm free of the other woman's grip, conscious for the first time that the other Raskians were watching her with the look of people fearful of a wild beast. She turned on her heel and saw the limp body of Gunsk carried through the gates of the tower on a plank of wood. "This isn't the last of this, Luskena. Now they know they can do this and Raskians will stand by, what next?"

By the tower gates, the Astrologer-Elect stood, his eyes piercing across the grey square at Luskena and Tollska.

Tollska turned and used one arm to pivot Luskena with her. "The Astrologer-Elect is looking at us, and we mustn't damage everything we've achieved. He'll tell Pearth and we'll lose my links up here…"

Luskena chuckled darkly, sneering. "Yes, wouldn't it be terrible if your lavish meals and comfortable life was no longer possible? The Astrologer-Elect won't turn me in, not worth the trouble."

To Tollska's dismay, Luskena even waggled her fingers in a little wave over to the Astrologer-Elect.

Tollska pulled Luskena further away, her words tumbling over each other in haste. "What are you doing? Are you determined to make him think we're up to something? I'm going."

"Tollska, you're not the only one with connections here. How arrogant of you."

Tollska watched as the Astrologer-Elect looked away as if deliberately trying to avoid them now. She shook her head and looked at Luskena one last time; she seemed to have a self-satisfied smirk plastered across her sneering face.

Striding back towards the Arden manor, teeth grinding, she felt all the crystal clarity of why she'd come to Gemynd seeping through her thoughts. Her frosted breath came in short, spiked bursts like a bull huffing out its lungs before charging at its tormentor.

She weaved through the crowd as the Constellan Guard dispersed everyone and ran up the steps into the grand doors of the Arden manor. The banners of the family's birth-Stars hung over the doors. Would anyone see her tear them down? She stamped straight through the halls into her private rooms, then slumped down into a chair with her head in her hands.

It was like this that Pearth found her, her dress sleeves torn from the tussle and her face still smeared with Luskena's now frosted spit.

The head of the Guard took Tollska's hands in her own. "None of this now, come on."

Tollska bit her lip to keep from sobbing, not meeting Pearth's eyes. "I grew up knowing him…"

"I'm sorry, love, it is what must happen to maintain peace." Pearth's voice was surprisingly soft, which made it more infuriating.

"How did I not know?"

"Why would you?"

"I can't look at you."

"Then don't look, I know this is hard. I'm sorry."

"What will you do to him, and those on the list?"

"If peace resumes and these pamphlet writers stop, nothing. It is preventative."

Tollska glared out the windows into the square and felt, after a while, a warm damp cloth pressed against her cheeks to clear away the grime clinging to them. She flinched in surprise and looked at Pearth at last, whose eyes had a flicker of warmth dancing in them.

"I don't understand you, Pearth." Tollska's raw words scraped like chains grating against stone.

"I do what I must to keep those I care about safe. Examples have to be made."

"But…"

"I care about you, there. See? There's more to me than the Guard I have to be."

Tollska's breath shuddered as she tried to find the lie in the woman's eyes. Damn, this was exhausting. She rubbed her eyes roughly, focusing herself and regaining control. Fighting foolishly wouldn't get her anywhere. To lose control was to be little better than Luskena, she thought to herself, forcing a smile.

"Love," Tollska spoke haltingly. "I'm sorry, I was shocked by it all."

"I understand. Take the time you need, change your clothes. If you are still able, we can see about finding your birth-Star."

Tollska looked deep into Pearth's eyes. It seemed as if Pearth was a mirrored image of herself. Like they were two battling hawks with locked talons in mid-air. Each attempting to deceive the other at their ferocious game, each waiting to see which one of them bloodied their beak first. It was a long way down when you battled amongst the clouds.

Tollska smiled and leant close with a slow kiss, brushing Pearth's lips with a purposeful kiss. Her own lips were still flushed crimson from the icy winds.

Chapter Twenty-Two

The Astrologer-Elect must be chosen through the votes of their Astrologers.
~ The Testament of the Stars

Einya paced the length of the grand library of the Arden manor, feeling like a ghost within these halls. The familiar creaks of the wooden beams, the murmurs from the servants' hall, the service bell's tinkling in the hallway were all muffled as if heard through a half-awake groggy shroud.

One sound remained clear: the lyrical voice of the Stars singing in sympathetic harmony. Their words carved images of different birth-Stars in Einya's mind as she fumbled with the Star-gems in their pouch to distract herself from the cacophony of noises.

The small door at the side of the room opened, Pearth and Tollska entering with arms interlocked like chain links. Their slow approach felt like a ceremonial procession, and Einya found the

Raskian woman's face completely unreadable. Tollska's fine burgundy gown was laced at the front and her neck adorned with a silver torque glinting in the sunlight.

Einya's legs trembled as she stood, gripping the corners of her skirts and dropping into a deep curtsey.

"Cousin. I'd like to offer my congratulations," Pearth said, her bright words clipped and forced.

"Congratulations for what?"

"For your confirmation as successor to the Astrologer-Elect," Pearth said, her teeth brimming into a smile. It spiked Einya with a dreadful sensation as if she'd tumbled off a cliff.

Einya blinked twice, lips slightly parted. Of course, Pearth knew; this was all sealed before she'd said yes. "I haven't agreed."

"The Stars have spoken, especially since you have ears for them."

"We should focus on the matter at hand."

"Not yet. You and I must speak first. Privately."

Einya nodded, letting Pearth lead them, glancing briefly back to where Tollska stood in the room, frowning after them.

They stepped out of the large room onto the balcony overlooking the stone turrets of the tiered settlement beneath them. Pearth placed her hands on the smooth balustrade, fingers splayed across the marble surface.

Einya rested her elbows on the stone, leaning forward across the balcony. "What's this about, Pearth?"

"This is about what Gemynd becomes. Things are changing, Einya. My guards are being attacked by Raskians, more of them are dying, and we are blind to external threats because of what is happening here."

Pearth turned, propping herself up on one arm, eyes wide. Her long hair had fallen from her tight bun and she almost looked dishevelled. "Parlenta knows much more about the Stars than we do, Aisren as well. We're being outmatched, Einya, and we need to catch up. The Astrologer-Elect clings to the old ways, but not me."

"Outmatched, how?"

"They've worked out how to use the Star's energy, so Parlenta claims. But they've mined it extensively. What happens when they run out? They'll come for our Stars, and we don't have the knowledge they do."

Einya shook her head, disbelief simmering through her. "The Elect told me about the mining, he said it was a secret. Why are you telling me?"

"Because I need you on my side, I need you to be the next Astrologer-Elect. I need strength and innovation. I think you can bring that. I don't trust Sepult Disren, he's buying so much Astamitra from them that each Myndat we pay brings us one step closer to their coming to take our Stars. Our claims of sovereignty from our twin Stars aren't enough anymore. We need to evolve, too."

Einya swallowed and ran one hand over her eyes. The puzzle kept getting more complex. Could Pearth really be right in all this? She sighed. "What do you suggest we do?"

"Use the Stars like Parlenta does. The Stars' energy, you have it, and you can use it against them if the time comes."

"How do you know?" Suspicion crept over her.

"Septult told me, naturally," Pearth said. "Look, rub Star-blood into the eyes of others, it pushes their influence straight into the soul of their victim, I'm told. Do this, and people will follow you then. You're close to the Stars, use it."

"And do what?" Einya said slowly, deliberately. She'd read this in the book but had dismissed it as barbaric and moved on. Had Pearth read the book too?

"Use those others to fight for Gemynd. They will serve you, laced with the power of the Stars, but under your control."

Horror gripped at Einya, and she strode away a few paces and turned back with her teeth bared. "Like thralls? Bound to the energy of the Stars? No. We've built our settlement on Rask's servitude; maybe if that's the only way out, we deserve everything we get."

She saw rage flicker in Pearth's eyes then as the woman began to speak, voice raised slightly. "Rask is part of us… see past your blindness. This is bigger, we need an edge."

Einya clenched her fists tightly inside their thick leather gloves. "How do you know all this anyway?"

"It's what Parlenta is doing; I've had spies there for some time. We need to be strong, be a deterrent, to show them we can do the same."

Einya shook her head. "I won't exert this power over anyone. It's mine to use how I see fit. It was granted it by the Stars, and I'll not use it to hurt anyone."

Pearth reached out, the woman's rough fingers gripping Einya's wrist. "Cousin, they will do the same to us. I need everyone together, fighting to keep our freedom. Don't be like Briarth. Be on my—our—side. I'm trying to keep us together at all costs… or we're going to fall, divided. Please, I need you to understand."

Einya turned her head away, ripping her wrist free. "I can't, you fear becoming the victim whilst content to play the role of persecutor. It's disgusting."

Pearth sighed. "You're just like Briarth, you'll see us all destroyed over your morals. I need to end the conflict in our settlement, with Rask, or this is going to go badly for us. That just means blessing a few rebels with the light of the Stars to show we can to Parlenta. It will stop the conflict; we won't be divided, and we'll look strong externally. Please, Einya. They have Bri, and I'm trying to bring him home… you owe it to him to try or who knows what they might do to him?"

Einya's sharp-nailed fingers rose, clutched Pearth's jaw and gripped tightly until her cousin's lips pursed apart with the force. "You *lie*; there's no lie you won't tell. Why would I believe you about Bri?"

"It's not a lie…"

"You'll say anything to get me to adhere to your horrid plan. I will proceed with the star reading and leave." Einya's eyes lay fixed on Pearth. "I won't help you with this, never ask me again."

Pearth stepped so close to Einya then that their noses almost brushed. "You will regret this choice, cousin, when they kill you as a rival power and control the rest of us."

Pearth raised one hand, gesturing toward the doors inside. As they entered, the Guardswoman's iron-like mask of certainty slipped back on. "Tollska, are you ready?"

Tollska nodded, crossed the room with a subtle sashay accentuating her walk. "What do I need to do?"

Tollska extended one hand towards Einya, who took it on instinct. Einya thought this smooth and deliberate gesture must be an act to conceal her nerves.

The soft skin of Tollska's hands was enough to distract her. Those bright questioning eyes, so hard to ignore.

"Sit, please," Einya mumbled, avoiding Tollska's eyes as the woman sat down in front of her. She still trembled, the previous conversation reverberating through her thoughts.

Kneeling on the floor, Einya kept her gaze on the intricate pattern of the terracotta tiles—better than losing herself in Tollska's beautiful eyes again. She felt the needle-sharp points of the Star-gems digging into her clenched fist around the pouch.

The first scatter across the floor left the gems far apart and unaligned to any pattern. Gathering them up, she looked sideways at Pearth.

The guard's stare was hard as marble. "Will it work?"

"Time will tell."

"Einya, look at me," Tollska's quiet voice whispered, irresistible and warm.

"Yes, Lady Arden."

The Raskian's eyes seemed to her like a sunrise, scarlet and fresh. Her scent was its usual musky blossom scent of a summer dawn. It all just reminded Einya how hollow life was without Tollska.

"Try again," Tollska whispered.

"I am trying to see clearly. I am waiting for them to find me."

Einya chose her words with care, hoping but not knowing whether the meaning she desperately wanted to convey had laced itself into her words. She cast the Star-gems again, this time keeping her eyes bound into Tollska's gaze. They scattered; this time the pattern lay clear as they glinted on the midnight rug.

"I need to be sure..." Einya mumbled, casting them across the rug again. They settled identically. Einya looked up again, daring to smile. "The scales of justice, Lady Arden."

Tollska stood, and Pearth wrapped her tightly in an embrace, whispering in her ear. Einya watched, aching and disbelieving. Tollska's eyes didn't leave Einya, who remained kneeling on the floor. A flick of movement out of one eye lured her eyes away from Tollska back down to the Star-gems. The pattern had changed, and they rested glittering in the winter sunlight. It couldn't be. As if things couldn't get worse.

Einya recognised the new symbol instantly. A drowning, limp-winged phoenix: the symbol of destruction.

Chapter Twenty-Three

There are good Constellations and bad. Those that are bad will
curse a life forever.
~ The Testament of the Stars

It was early in the morning and the sun hadn't risen yet. A loud knock sounded at the door, and Tollska sat up instantly. In Rask, hammering at the door spelt bad news, and it took a few moments to remember she was in Gemynd. Pearth wasn't beside her; instead, the three small dogs were curled up, snoring softly. How did she get here? She remembered Einya had left abruptly after finding her birth-Star the previous evening.

The rapid gathering up of the gems had surprised Tollska, and Einya hadn't even looked at her. Not even a shred of warmth had passed between them.

Pearth had then invited friends, family, guards and all sorts to well-wish Tollska as one of them. Her wine glass had been constantly filled up, and music had played loudly into the night.

None of it had distracted her from the sense that shadows shrouded Einya. *Nothing to worry about now, nothing to be done anyway.* She'd told herself that repeatedly, but everything had still seemed empty. So she drank a bottle of wine, and then drank even more, until the evening had become a blur.

A renewed knock bashed against the door, hammering in her head as well. She swung her legs over the side of the tall bed and lowered herself to the cold slate floor of the chamber.

Wrapping herself in a coat, she went to the door, tugging it open. It was Astrologer Derana. She remembered him as plum-like with hued purple-red cheeks from when he'd married her to Pearth, but now he looked more skeletal and a strange pallid green.

"The Astrologer-Elect wants an edict signed, he asked for you personally."

Tollska said nothing for a moment whilst wakefulness caught up with her, regarding the man's eyes that looked like eclipsed moons in his eye-sockets.

"Why me, and what's the edict?"

"I don't know, he simply said to fetch you."

"Well, I will be there. I'll dress first."

She shut the door in his face, relishing in the joy of having the small power of making him wait, and took her time to select a robe simple enough to button herself into. Tugging on fur-lined leather boots, she left a note on the bed and headed out into the hallway.

Derana tried to shepherd her with a light touch to the small of her back. Frustrated, Tollska turned to him. "If you want my attendance, then allow me to walk without your assistance. This is my home. I don't need your help."

He looked away, and they walked in a spiky silence with their mutual distaste for the other evident on their faces. The feel of Derana's clammy hand on her skin lingered, triggering her memories of his slimy condescension from the wedding day. At every door, she forced herself ahead of him, letting them shut on his fingers. The pang of guilt at the man's frail condition tugged at the edge of her conscience, but she ignored it, remembering the moist feel of his sweat-coated hands. Her head still pounded, and that left little room for kindness to this man.

When they reached the Constellan Council chambers, she mounted the steps at a deliberate slow pace, as a sheen of black ice coated them. Turning the large door handle, she stepped into the fire-lit halls, feeling the instant broiling heat from the fires as she stamped the ice off her heels onto the stone floors.

The Astrologer-Elect sat on an ornately carved chair by the fire. Tollska had only seen him a handful of times. It was only now as he turned to look at her that she noticed the long straggling grey hair with black streaks through it. It seemed dull compared to his bright and piercing eyes.

He didn't stand. Derana, who'd entered behind her, simply gestured for her to approach. Breathing deeply, she reminded herself that she belonged in these halls and that this gave her some degree of power. *But what do I say?* She forced a smile, trying to shake off some of the nerves.

"Astrologer-Elect, how can I help?"

"Councillor Arden, I have an edict and I need it passed. I thought given your dear Pearth is out doing her good work, you might welcome the distraction."

"I will do what I can."

"Good."

He lifted a heavy parchment that lay across his lap where he sat and passed it to her. Tollska felt the rough edges scrape against each other as she unrolled it. In the corner of her eye, Sepult Disren's fists were clenched tightly in dissonance with his attempted relaxed demeanour. Neatly looped crimson writing stood out on the scroll.

"The Testament of the Stars?" Tollska murmured, leafing through the paper and seeing a long list of names written in delicate curved script. "Might I read it first?"

"Sign it," he said, spittle splattering from his lips.

Tollska shook her head, frowning and anxious. "There will need to be a vote."

"Not for this."

"There's always a vote."

The Astrologer-Elect rose and suddenly stood in front of Tollska as if a strong wind had blown him over to her. "Listen, Raskian, let's be clear. You are here because I told Pearth to get a

Raskian spouse; you are here to clear my laws. You will sign it, or you will end up on the list."

"I am upholding your rules. A vote."

"Do you imagine a vote would deny it? There'll be a vote before it's activated anyway, you are just here to agree the names."

"It would be fair to vote."

"You picked a side when you came here. If you don't sign it, someone else will."

Tollska looked through the edict again to buy herself a few precious moments. Was this the bridge to burn on, or was there a bigger battle to win later? She looked up again, preparing to lie. The inevitability seemed to scuttle closer, spider-like.

"Astrologer-Elect, please understand, I am worried I'll lose my rank if I don't uphold the rules."

"If you keep me on your side, that will not happen."

"Then I will sign if we can avoid death. If this will restore peace. Please."

The Astrologer-Elect's jaw slacked from its tense grimace then. "Gentle soul, of course."

"Can I ask why now, what's happened?"

"They are moving against us. We need to defend ourselves. Agree this list, and it will be used to bring peace if we ever need to activate it. We need to clear the streets of these rebels."

"What have 'they' done?"

"Trade wagons have been burnt on the promontories into the settlement, guards murdered brutally and so much more."

"More? Is that crime enough to condemn this many Raskians?"

"Rask will push us into a war, and I've found out something interesting—the name of their leader, Oenska is it? Familiar to you, I gather. Sign or your mother will be the first of these names I bring here when I get this sanctioned."

Tollska sucked air into her lungs in shock, coughing slightly. "How do you…"

"We have ways. Sign, and I'll make sure others go first when the time comes."

Tollska stood and crossed to a table nearby, placed the scroll down and scratched her name across the rough surface with a quill. The ink seemed tinted red to her eyes.

Sepult Disren snatched it up and passed it away to Astrologer Derana before turning back to her. "It speaks highly of you, Tollska, that you care about people's lives. I will try to remember your reluctance is compassion, not disloyalty. Stars watch you, dear one."

She forced a smile and said nothing, feeling only a clenching around her heart. After the two Astrologers left, she finally spewed out the words she'd bitten back.

"Freedom. I care about freedom."

Tollska didn't wait, she didn't even think as she rushed toward the doors out of the Council building and slammed them shut behind her. She ran to the stables and saddled her horse, before realising that would be a very unsubtle way to travel to Rask.

In the end, she hurried through the streets and down a few alleys toward the winding steps, into the pits of Rask, where she hoped the streets wouldn't be filled with guards already. It must be where Pearth was, after all.

When she reached the streets of Rask, understanding dawned. Burnt out buildings, blood on the streets and bodies lined the alleys. The truth of it cascaded over her like an avalanche. *Damn. It's already happening.*

Fragments of wood and stone paved the barren street she found herself standing in; a building to her left had been painted with Gunsk's name over and over. The building had been a guardhouse between Gemynd and Rask but now was a fire-ravaged husk.

A trembling silence filled the road, unusually so. She shuddered as she heard only her footsteps, twisting round a corner into a wider street where carts, tables and chairs had been stacked up high and towering as tall as a building. The wooden clutter blocked everything beyond.

"How did I not know it had started?" she spoke to the emptiness, running one hand through her hair and raking it out of its tight band.

Tollska twisted her way quickly out of the road and hid in a narrow alley where she threw herself down in the sludge, where mud and snow had mixed. She rolled around, coating her fine grey robe in as much of the dirt as possible. Anyone dressed as a Gemyndian would be ripped apart, she knew, even if she looked obviously Raskian.

Covered in mud with her hair hanging loose around her shoulders, she wove her way through the narrow alleys of Rask to find her mother. The sun was flowing through the gaps between the buildings now, a crimson tapestry looming over the Raskian fields.

Chapter Twenty-Four

*The Star-blood seeps into the victim's very soul if applied through
the eyes. That is how controlling a star-struck is possible.*
~ On Astamitra: a Parlentan research paper

Bri's shoulder still ached, even though he'd grown mostly
used to having his arm lodged in the star's bore hole. How had they
even achieved that? He'd tried to wrench it out many times now,
and each time, it hadn't worked. One time he'd managed to get it
half-way out through an extended period of painful wriggling
before the custodian saw and stopped him. There was a handle,
struck deep in the rock, that made it somehow easier to keep it
there even though it meant his fingers were numb from being stuck
in a fist around it.

The miners hustled around him, as the hag-like custodian
sat on a stool by the cavern entrance and smoked a clay pipe. He
grew to hate her and laugh at her, at the same time. *Only way to*

keep sane, he would tell himself as he made up grotesque stories about the type of life that he imagined this woman had.

The business of the mine continued daily. Even in the harsh storms that lashed the mountain, the miners came. With long thin metal straws, they spent the day sucking the strange blue liquid out of the star and spitting it into a large cauldron-like bowl, which would be taken away at the end of the day.

Then, like clockwork, when the miners had left, the custodian hobbled over, unscrewing the small black pot. Her gnarled fingers swirled inside the crusted dust, before pulling the bottom curve of Bri's eye down to reveal the red lining and rubbing the sapphire powder along it. It burnt fiercely, and he squirmed as she rubbed the powder into his other eye. He had come to dread it, and to his shame, his voice screeched a little in fear of the nausea and lack of control he knew would follow.

Please, no. He squirmed as she placed her finger at his hairline, running it down his forehead and to the tip of his nose. Almost immediately, he flailed against the rock until he fell into a strange, dream-laced sleep. Mist-shrouded figures flitted in and out of his thoughts. Einya and Luskena mumbled rhythmically with inaudible words. Einya's eyes shot through with rivulets of blood, staring up at him, her skin marred with a phosphorescent glow. He wanted to reach out to them. Were they real? They felt real. But the haze did not last long enough for him to find out, the custodian always made sure he didn't stay 'sleeping' too long.

Today, the wakening felt like a knife thrust into his gut, and the custodian was standing in front of him as he opened his eyes. A stabbing gasp spluttered from his lips, choking out words with difficulty. "How are you doing this? How are you keeping me tamed to your whim?"

"Curious." The withered woman sipped from a vial of the Star-blood and ran one gnarled finger down the bridge of his nose.

The strange calm melted through him again. "What is this? When will you be done with me?"

"Oh, little boy, when you die or go insane. You see, the Queen wants to know how much Astamitra one can take until it is too much. She wants to know if her theories on the Star's energy, and control, are true."

"She takes it then?"

The custodian chuckled. "Naturally, it's the finest."

"Probably should've learnt about its qualities first…"

"Quiet, boy."

Bri sighed. "Listen, hmm? I have people to help, as your Queen won't listen to me. I need to go."

"Tell it to the miners." The custodian took a small scrap of meat from her pocket and stuffed it into Bri's mouth before she hobbled away on her stubby feet and began scribbling in a book in the corner. "You'll go when the Queen of Parlenta has learnt all she needs."

He chewed on the meat, absurdly grateful as his stomach rattled with hunger. She left him for another day then, and he tried to sleep slumped against the star. It was difficult, as the miners returned in the morning and began chipping into the rock again.

That night, after the miners left, the custodian rubbed the Star-blood tincture in his eyes as usual. It was the only way he could be sure of the time of day. He blinked as hard as he could to keep some of it out. When the custodian had left, he spat on his spare hand, rubbing the spittle into his eyes, but it wasn't quite enough as he felt quickly like his feet weren't connected to the rocky floor.

"At least I am conscious this time," he mumbled.

He soon wished he wasn't. Needle-stabbing bursts of pain ripped at the inside of his fingers, tiny fissures opening in his skin as sharp bone poked through their tips. What was happening? He panicked, seeing the bone poke further out. *That's it, I've gone insane.* He found he was laughing manically but stopped quickly when the sound of crunching stone grated behind him. He twisted around as far as he could, dread grasping hold of him. The Star-rock seemed to be bubbling as if a volcano was beginning to erupt. The surface was icy cold, and instead of molten lava tumbling out of the cracks forming in the Star-rock, there was a strange ice-like substance starting to slump out through the gaps in the stone. Panic made his tongue feel warped and mutated in his mouth as he struggled into action.

His wrist stung as he tried to pull his arm free of the bore hole, the creeping frost reaching for his fingers as well. His icy breath punctured the darkness, struggling until a stillness took him as the slow flow of ice welled up inside the rock, engulfing his arm. Raw energy surged through him, and he heard the warbled sound of his voice crying out in pain. He pulled harder then.

The shaft of the Star-rock finally cracked apart, releasing his arm, which had turned from its usual tawny tone to a deep frosty azure. Was the star attacking him? He desperately scrabbled away from the rock, but the icy membrane spread further over his skin. Horror gripped him. Reaching his hands up to his eyes, he realised he couldn't see properly. The cave was blue-hued, like it was underwater.

"Let me go, not like this," he mumbled. Someone was close by, he realised, and he stumbled toward them.

"Listen to him babble. He's had enough then." The old custodian's voice tumbled through his distorted senses as he tried to reach out to her with his bone-claw grip. The stone had continued to protrude into claws from his fingers.

"You have had him as your specimen long enough, now we will take him back as an example," a voice said.

Bri looked up. The man was wearing drab grey colours, but with a gold ruff. An Astrologer. Next to him stood a man with a bright gold star emblazoned on a velvet tunic and the unmistakably Gemyndian trait of a slightly bucktoothed mouth.

The custodian huffed, hunched over Bri where he'd slumped against the wall and ran one hand down from his hairline to his nose. "Shame, he'd melt like butter for the queen now."

"That wasn't the intention or agreement," the Astrologer spat.

"I am aware, thank you. Tell your commander she should reconsider our offer, messenger."

Bri stood between the custodian and the messenger; sanguine, acquiescent. The star's frost felt like it had clung to his heart and ceased it from hammering fretfully against his ribs. He tried to move, but couldn't. In front of him, the Star-rock now seemed husk-like and empty as he stared down at the shards of stone, his sight slowly returning. Something in the darkness still writhed, unfurling from the fragments of the Star. His own voice screamed: *run*. But he still did not move, screaming internally as he just watched the glow from the Star drift toward him. *Could the others see this?* With the strange calm keeping him steady still, he felt the glow wash over him like icy water as he stood there helpless.

"What now?" he whispered, breath frosting on his lips. His voice scraped up his windpipe and rasped out into nothingness, the frost clustering within his throat. It didn't take long for bright sparks of light to burst within his eyes as he slumped to the floor, feeling the hiss of air suck back into his lungs and a strange comforting emptiness as he plunged into darkness.

A gnarled hand rubbed over his face, brushing the stubble of his beard in the wrong direction. Was he soaring upward, or was he being lifted? The clattering of a carriage, slowly winding down the mine ramp, lulled him into nightmarish sleep as he felt the icy mountain winds rip across his sweating skin.

Chapter Twenty-Five

No quarter, no mercy. We have starved, now we'll make them starve.
~ Luskena of Rask's words in a pamphlet

The streets through Rask were scattered with debris from the building of barricades. Tollska ran. On the looming promontories above the settlement, fragments and splinters scattered down and shouts could be heard. She shielded her eyes, the flakes of wood drifting down like snow from above, and hurried further into Rask. Squashing down her surprise at the number of barricades built in such a short space of time, she pushed herself onwards. The sharpening of metal grated as blades were dragged across whetstones and songs of bravery drifted out of taverns as she ran.

Reaching the cottage, she squeezed through the door without pausing. The little room vibrated with activity, leaving her unnoticed for the time it took to breathe in the atmosphere. The printing press stamped out page after page with a furious regularity, a man and woman loaded and re-loaded the tray and lowered the stamp with excited fervour. Luskena was stacking up a pile of swords in the corner. *Where did they get those?*

Her mother was deep in conversation by the fireplace, purple streaks of hair hanging loosely about her shoulders.

Tollska remembered dying those streaks of hair with crushed berries when she was little. She longed to hold her mother close despite the chaos around her.

"Oi, look who it is. Our beautiful Gemyndian gem." It was Luskena who saw her first, shouting across the room. The grinding gears of the printing press ceased, and all eyes turned on her.

"Luskena, she's still one of us." Her mother's words; sharp, quick and authoritative. "What is it, Tollska?"

Frantically she spoke. They had to know, and quickly. "The Constellan Guard, they're coming. There's an edict, the Testament of the Stars they're calling it. They made me sign it. I'm sorry, but I had to come and tell you. You need to hide…"

Oenska stood. "We wanted you to know their first move, so you could tell us. You have done well, Tols. We've been waiting for this moment since we built the barricades. We will not hide, we are ready."

"The Astrologer-Elect said some trade wagons had been burnt?"

"I did that." Luskena grinned, her eyes wide and bright in the dully-lit room. "The guards didn't smell nearly so fine as the sugar burning in the cart, but it was splendid all the same."

"We knew since they took Gunsk that this was coming, and now we know when. We will secure the last blocks in the road and take more trading caravans." Her mother was pacing in the tight space around the fireplace. "And this time, Luskena, we will keep the food and not burn it. I will not allow senseless killing. It makes us no better than them."

The room plummeted into a tense silence for a moment, Luskena's eyes narrowing and her teeth bared slightly. "I am not free of their taint, as you know, Oenska…"

"Quiet! You bring this up as a war wound every time, and I'm tired of it."

The uneasy silence held for a moment longer, narrowed eyes brushing awkwardly over Luskena but not looking too closely into her ferocious gaze.

The woman at the printing press spoke, breaking apart the quiet. "What now, Oenska?"

"We keep to the plan; it's time we called on Einya to speak to the Astrologers. Then we will be ready for when they come to the barricades."

"I'll go find Einya," the woman at the press, Skren, said. "I'll go after I've put the pamphlets out."

"Thank you, Skren. Be careful, take some of the fine clothes from the crate over there."

Skren nodded, lifting a huge stack of pamphlets off the table by the press.

Oenska stood, ushering people towards the door with a few warm words as they departed. "Everyone should prepare and spend some time with their family."

Soon, the room was empty except for Tollska, Oenska and Luskena.

Tollska watched as her mother sat on the edge of the printing press wearily. She reached out, gently grasping Oenska's shoulder in support.

Luskena stood with a blade in one hand and a pamphlet in the other. "Let me go speak to Einya, make her see what's needed."

"No." Oenska glared back at her. "Einya will do what she needs to without your help."

"You care too much about her. She needs to be made to give them our message."

"She will give it in a way that doesn't get herself killed or exposed by your unsubtlety," Tollska spat.

Luskena dropped the sword on the pile, causing the blades to rasp against each other. She crossed the room to Tollska. "She's just a tool, like these swords. She's one of them. Who cares?"

Tollska struck her with the back of her hand, full across the smaller woman's cheek. "Get out of here, Luskena. You didn't care about Gunsk either. Leave."

"Tollska, stop now. I need to speak to you both. Luskena, bite your tongue."

Tollska bit her lip instead, only just stopping herself from spitting out a string of insults at Luskena. Although not quite held apart by Oenska, who stood between them, an uneasy truce prevailed.

The older woman continued, ignoring them both. "Here's what we'll do. We want them to see our plight. Einya will go to them to tell them of the injustice we face. Tollska, you will go home to Pearth. Don't draw attention to yourself. If they ask you for more names, say you can't get into Rask, it's blocked up."

"I will take the latest pamphlet, just in case Pearth wonders where I went."

"Good, yes. Let's hope they listen when they realise their food is no longer arriving from Rask, let's hope they hear reason."

"If they listened, we wouldn't be here. I wouldn't be scraping two Rask pennies together to try to spark a fire in the back of the Mule. I wouldn't see children sent to the inn to keep safe and dry because their home is freezing, and what crops their parents have left for food are being burnt as fuel because no one in Rask can afford to buy it off them and no one can afford an axe to cut down wood for fire even though the forest is on our doorstep."

Luskena spat on the floor, pausing in her rant. "If they listened, I wouldn't have been turned back down to rot in the streets by the Gemyndian who claimed to love my mother, but cared nothing for me once she died…"

Oenska held one hand up to stop the tirade. "Bloodshed won't help, reasoning with them will."

"This will end in blood. Our blood, in the rivers of Rask." Luskena's last words were cold and gravelly before she turned and stamped towards the door.

Neither Tollska nor Oenska stopped her leaving. Luskena grabbed two of the rusty swords and headed out into the streets.

Tollska heard her mother sigh, a heart-wrenching exhalation of a little more of her life. "I must go, there's a revolution to plan."

Tollska took her hands. "Ma, is there no one else who can do this?"

"None that won't just pursue violence like Luskena. I'm pulling at the reigns of a raging beast, and the straps are snapping."

"Let me do it, please Ma."

"No. I want you safe in Gemynd."

"But you should leave... They have your name."

"No doubt, it was going to happen sooner or later. You should go home, petal, they'll be filling in the entrances to the steps back up."

Tollska pinched her lips together, holding in a torrent of words. This was draining her Mother... "My home is here. How can I help you if I am not with you?"

"And one day it could be again if you choose. You help me in everything you do, and just by being alive." Oenska kissed Tollska's hair, holding her tight for a long moment. "Go. Don't worry about me."

Tollska straightened up from where she rested against the table as Oenska stepped away from their embrace. She felt humidity clinging to her as if a thunderstorm was about to crash around them both.

She walked to the door, despondent, turning to look back at her mother. "You drew the path of my life, Ma, carved me out of oak, and my boughs will never break. Never forget my love for you reaches deeper than the roots of our trees." A smile clutched at her lips as Tollska committed the moment to memory. "I will be the earth that grips your roots, Ma, the grass for you to grow from." She turned and pressed through the door before regret could hold her there any longer.

Tollska ran through the streets, keeping to the shadows. How had it come to this? Shouts and the smashing of wood on the great causeways towering above her echoed down. Falling sleet stung against her skin amongst the few droplets that tumbled from her eyes.

She reached the jagged stone wall around the edge of Gemynd and found a set of steps. Crowds of Raskians were already prying up loose stones from the streets and stacking them in the narrow doors. The guards lay dead at the bottom of the stairs.

"Let me through!" Sprinting full-pelt towards the nearest spiralling staircase, her shout cascaded around the small courtyard.

Twisting through the tight-packed bodies, someone jostled her, and she struggled to keep her footing on the slick stones.

"Where you going? The fights are gonna be here," a man said, eyes-wide and gaunt-faced.

"I need to go up there, I'm…"

"I don't care who you are." The man grabbed her arm, and she tensed.

"That's Oenska's daughter, she's the one who made the sacrifice," a young woman said.

A silence descended over the crowd, and they watched her closely as the man released her arm.

"Be careful, sacrificial Tollska." The young woman gripped the hem of Tollska's sleeve as she spoke. Tollska nodded and passed through the crowd.

The Raskians brushed their hands along her shoulders in a strange ritualistic act as she moved. Their whispered words of praise and hope seemed strangely distant. She swallowed, unsure of the odd way they looked at her like a prophet.

She took a few steps up, turned her head back and saw expectant faces looking up, the way she imagined Astrologers looked at the Stars. She spoke simply.

"Freedom will be ours."

Tollska looked up into the skies of Rask as she took the steps two at a time, a flock of birds circling the stone turrets of the settlement. That was the last she saw of clouds and birds before the fires began.

Chapter Twenty-Six

The previous Astrologers believed the Stars to be passive, but
Gemynd will make them so much more.
~ The original Testament of the Stars

Einya went straight to the caverns after leaving Tollska, the pattern of the drowning phoenix Constellation still etched into her mind. Why she did this, she didn't know, but she flitted back to her rooms briefly and strapped her fine filigree short blade to her hip before leaving.

She'd stayed enshrined in the darkness of the cave for at least two days after that. Somewhere, she'd lost track of how much time had passed, having asked the Stars again and again about the phoenix's meaning at this time.

Their whispers still buffeted around the walls of the cave, surrounding Einya with their thrumming hurricane of noise, but there was no clarity amongst the cacophony. Instead, mutated forms seemed to be clawing their way from the shadowy arêtes of the rock.

Einya stood with her hands slotted into the deep grooves of the Star-rock. She ignored the brusque footsteps ricocheting around the cavern of someone coming down the carved corridor towards her.

This time, it was a familiar guard, Malthis, who Einya had awkwardly befriended in the darkness for some company.

"I brought you some food, Astrologer Arden," he mumbled.

Einya sighed, arms sagging by her side. "Thank you. It's time I stopped, anyway."

They both sat down to eat, Malthis only a breath away from Einya in the half-light.

"Fighting has begun," he said, eyes bright. "Raskians are stopping the food from coming in."

"In Rask?"

"Yes, they've built barricades... but don't worry, Astrologer. We'll keep Gemynd safe."

Einya let him prattle on, unaware of her growing tension. Where was Oenska in all this? Were the roadblocks on the promontories connecting the farms to Gemynd still in place? What was Pearth doing now? All these thoughts were footnotes underneath her main thought: Tollska.

After they had eaten and Malthis had left, Einya threw aside the plate of food and picked up the book. A scribbled note in the corner of a crumbling page said: *for forcing a change in views*. She re-read the page over and over, soaking up the words that suggested thoughts could be changed using the memory of the Stars. She had avoided the harsher sounding uses for the Stars but, even though the thought appalled her, maybe now was the time?

She shook her head. "Let me just ask you first," she mumbled.

Gripping a crevice in the stone, she pressed her head against the rock and felt the familiar sensation of listening to the Star-rocks creep over her. She'd not taken any Astamitra from the large bowl this time or drunk an undiluted vial of the powder. Not worth the risk of taking too much. Plenty must still be flowing through her blood, and it didn't feel like it would run out. This time, instead of asking, she focused on an instruction: *Show them the truth.*

A single, clear and bell-like voice sliced through the whispered echo. Lips forcibly parted, the words flowed through her. *"We are only memories; you are the future. Decide based on the histories we show you, or show others the memories instead."*

After the Star's hissing voice faded from her mouth, for the first time in many months, Einya was left in silence. No soft songs twittered in her mind, luring her to speak for them, and all the half-heard words from ghostly voices reverberating around her skull had faded.

She gathered the book back up, stowing it in her leather bag, before trudging up the sloping corridors to the rickety door that led outside. What now? There was no choice really. She would have to follow the instructions in the book, despite the consequences. A strange loneliness clutched at her and she felt as if she hadn't breathed properly in months. Pushing open the small door, she pressed forward over the step into the street. There was no welcome fresh air, just gusts of wind laced with burning wood. Smog-like clouds concealed the winter sun, seeming like broad smoking arms reaching over the settlement.

Although only a short walk away, Einya felt like it took a long time to reach her rooms. Lots of people bustled this way and that. Soldiers strode through the middle of crowds wearing the distinctive black breastplates gilded with the golden Stars of the Constellan Guard, carrying large pikes. As she battled through the main square and finally reached the door to her rooms, she paused. Was there never any peace? The lock had been forced and hung loose in its casing. Einya drew a short blade from the sheath at her side, shoving the door open with the heel of her boot.

"Who's in here?" She raised her blade alongside her face, ready to thrust it swiftly into the eye of anyone who rushed at her.

"Oenska sent us," a voice whispered.

Einya breathed a sigh of relief, glancing at the hiding place with Bri's plans sealed up beneath the floorboards. She rounded the door. A woman she didn't know and, regrettably, Luskena awaited her. The first woman was huddled on the edge of one of the chairs by the fire, but Luskena had reclined on the bed with her boots and outside coat dropping mud onto the sheets.

"My name's Skren. Oenska says it has started, and that now is the time to speak to the Astrologer-Elect. It was meant to just be me, sorry; Luskena followed me here."

Einya ignored the last. "Thank you, Skren. How did you get here, can you get back?"

"There's a route, right at the back of the settlement, for our return." Skren smiled.

Luskena sat up and stretched in a mock-wakefulness. "So, when will you do it?"

"Do what?"

"Speak to the Elect, obviously." Luskena stood and ran her hand along the walls, disturbing Einya's mural of trees, watching as some fluttered to the floor.

"When it's right." Einya's teeth clacked together as she spoke, as she fought back a glare.

"And when is that?"

"When I decide."

Skren stood up, fidgeting with the cuff of her sleeve. "Luskena, we should leave." She said it over and over but her words found only deaf ears. Einya pitied her a little, dealing with that firebrand.

Einya took a deep breath, forcing herself to think about how this must seem to Luskena.

"Look, I have some evidence that the Stars don't care about the control of Rask, but I alone have heard them say so. The Stars don't really speak, it's just energy and intentions. I need to find another way to get the Astrologer-Elect to hear it too. I have one plan, but if that doesn't work, I will need to keep looking for an answer."

Luskena stopped circling the room, her eyes pinned on Einya now. "Power concedes nothing without demand, Einya. Remember that, instead of using your fancy diplomatic ways. Tell them if they don't give us liberty, they will starve, like *we* have starved because of *them*."

Einya sighed, feeling the weight of not having slept much in countless days dragging at her. Her words sounded spiky to her ears, but she didn't care. "They will call you traitors and rip you apart if I do that. We need to make them see the truth. I have a book, it has ways of speaking to the Stars in it and ways to use their memories to shape the views of others. If the Elect doesn't listen, then I'll try more and more of those ideas. Happy now?"

Luskena shrugged. "Come on Skren, stop lagging around. Let's go."

Einya ground her teeth with a burning frustration after the Raskian women had left. She pinned back up her drawings of trees, checked the cubbyhole to reassure herself that Bri's message was still there, and lastly, swigged at a strong wine straight from the decanter. She took one last look around, trying to imagine she was standing within the woods she used to run in with Tollska and not in the stone walls of her lonely house. Shouts began to rattle in her ears and she headed to the door.

In the streets, a thick smog infused the air. Across the square, a wooden-beamed manor house smouldered, licked with rising black-red flames. People scattered through the stone courtyards, throwing buckets of water unsuccessfully onto the spiralling inferno.

The putrid ash prickled in her nostrils, coating her throat until she wretched. In the distance, the fleeing form of Luskena and Skren briefly emerged before being plunged back into the shadowy smog spewing from the burning building.

Chapter Twenty-Seven

The average Raskian is better for having their wares managed by those who have a superior education. The Stars know it, and so do we.
~ The original Testament of the Stars

Einya tried not to think too much about what came next as she headed to the Astrologer-Elect's manor. Rehearsing her words whilst walking left no room to worry. The bell-pull chimed their sounds high within the manor's tower and was answered quickly.

As the door was tugged open, surprisingly it was Sepult Disren himself who answered. His beard was unkempt, and the ruff usually neatly pinned with a brooch at his neck hung loosely around his shoulders. She was ushered in quickly and she stepped inside without saying any words.

"Einya, I am pleased to see you. Have you heard? Rask has risen up; they're killing guards on the streets of Rask. But, worse, they've been here—they've burnt a manor house."

"Yes, I know. It's why I am here."

"Where have you been? I have not seen you in a week, maybe more."

"Seeking answers."

"Good, excellent. Tell me what you know. Tell me how we can end this."

Einya slowly crossed to sit in a plush chair. It seemed strange to relax in luxury now that civil war had started. Sepult Disren followed closely, perching on the arm of the chair opposite her.

"The Stars have no opinion on Rask," she said simply, observing as the Astrologer-Elect twisted his hands in strange anxious contortions.

"How can that be? Everything we know says…"

"If you will take the Astamitra, you can hear their words, I can show you how and teach you to hear the truth. I need you to stop my cousin seeking unity through fear. There are better ways."

Einya watched as the man stood up and paced, his face set with a forceful grimace in a schism from his previous nerves.

"I don't like this either, Einya. I have never seen the future path I should take from them when I have taken Astamitra; I need you to find the future for me."

"They only tell the past, Elect."

"Then tell them to learn the future."

"Elect, they are just historians. This fighting with Rask, it could end without all this grappling with the Stars."

"How?"

She paused, running her tongue over her chapped lips. "Treat Raskians as people. If you treat them as beasts, then beasts they'll be. Give them freedom to trade their own goods, and then trade with them instead of taking their food."

Sepult Disren paused in his pacing. "Einya, you mean well, I know you do. All of that we can look at later. Right now, I need to be able to say the Stars have agreed their Testament. I need that, so we can end this fighting." The man's eyes were wide, several tears bursting the banks of his eye sockets. "I know you want to save everyone, but I can't help you. For that, and what follows, I am truly sorry."

What did he mean? Einya tried to calm herself, but her heart hammered too quickly in her chest for that. The Astrologer-Elect went to a bell-pull by the fireplace, and a faint tolling sounded somewhere else in the tower. Einya had to force herself to stay seated as surprise gripped her when the door opened and Pearth, accompanied by two guards, entered.

"What is this, Elect?" she asked, forcing herself to recline and cross her legs nonchalantly. She wondered if he had control over any of this, watching the slightly hunched figure of the elderly man leaning over the fireplace.

Sepult Disren looked away, stooping deeper over the flames.

"Cousin." Pearth wore a tailored gambeson, Stars embroidered across every scrap of it, and atop that sat boldly engraved pauldrons with the Arden crest of two stone turrets upon them. Her hair had been tightly braided back, pulling her face into a severe grimace.

"Pearth, surprised you aren't at the barricades." She drew her words slowly with the affectation of relaxation. Her cousin stepped sharply over and stood towering over Einya.

"We have burnt one on the main promontory, and now fiery splinters rain on Rask. The rest is only a matter of time."

"I am pleased you have it under control." Einya smiled, certain it didn't reach her eyes.

An uneasy silence held for a few moments, Pearth still staring down at Einya.

"I have something I need you to do, Cousin," Pearth began, and the guards stepped up behind her. "My soldiers saw that woman in Gemynd a few days past, the one Briarth slept with a few times. No sign of her having left again. Let's be thankful your brother is no longer able to see her. I wonder if she has another contact here. I need to know who."

"What would I know if she did? I have been with the Stars for days." Einya tried to slow her hammering heart, forcing a ghostly smile. Sepult stood nearby, his emerald doublet tight across his bunched-up shoulders.

Pearth seemed to ignore the Astrologer-Elect. "I have people for that, it's not what I need from you. I want you to sign

175

the succession, and as your first role as the next Astrologer-Elect, renounce Briarth from our family. State that anyone who consorts with a Raskian rebel listed in the Testament of the Stars will be killed along with the Raskian they have been with."

"Why would I do that? The military decisions are for you. That distinction has always been clear."

"If you do not then I will bring Briarth back here as one named in the Testament of the Stars, and he will be the first example."

"If you can find him," Einya spat. It felt like she was being swept down a river and couldn't grab at the banks. "I don't want the succession, and I won't say you got any of these names from the Stars. I know well the Stars didn't give them to you."

Einya saw Sepult Disren look at her, almost pleadingly, but she said nothing more.

Pearth nodded slowly, their eyes still locked together. "Guard, remember the order on my desk that acknowledges my dear spouse as a spy? Take it, rip out her tongue and bring it to me."

The guard started to leave, and Einya found she'd reached out one arm and grabbed Pearth by the edge of her tunic. Her teeth were bared as she glared at Pearth. She wished she could wrap her fingers around her cousin's neck.

"You are a cold, wretched, woman and no cousin to me. *You* asked her to spy." Einya's heart plummeted as her words tumbled from her lips and she gave herself away.

Pearth's twisted smirk told her all she needed to know. "For peace, you know this. Sign, renounce your brother in the name of the Stars and save the woman you love. There's no choice, really, is there?"

Einya trembled, not being able to control her quaking legs brushing against each other. She struggled to get her mouth to speak coherently. How had it come to this? "I will sign, and then I never want to see you again. There is nothing in this world you haven't taken from me."

Pearth said nothing. She held her hand out and Sepult Disren hurried up behind her carrying the succession scroll and a quill.

"You will publicly denounce him in the name of the Stars, make it clear it's their will. Bring us peace," he said, but Einya kept her eyes on her cousin, as it was very clear who was the wolf and who was the rabbit out of the pair. There was no choice, she had nothing to fight back with.

As Einya signed, she thought of Bri, likely in a tavern somewhere and completely unaware of the war in Rask, singing the songs of their youth as he laughed the nights away with whoever would keep him company. Guilt gnawed through her heart as the neat swirls spread from the nib of the quill.

Chapter Twenty-Eight

*Build barricades, hold back our produce, but do not kill them. I
won't be made a murderer by Gemynd.*
~ Oenska of Rask, writing in a pamphlet

Tollska found her way to a part of Gemynd she'd never
been in before, where the cobbles started to rise into the long
promontory descending into the northern part of Rask. She ditched
her muddy coat in the alley and rounded the corner. The Constellan
Guard were lined up, firing arrows into the fiery haze.

Ahead, a large burning barricade blocked the way, and
Constellan Guards with pikes were spiking at bits of burning debris
and hurling it over the sides into Rask. Smoke stung the inside of
her nose as she ran towards the fire, searching with streaming
smoke-filled eyes for Pearth. Below the walls, the burning debris
had caught on the thatched roofing of some of the hovels and was
now beginning to spread like little bonfires far below.

A supply line had been formed some way back from the barricade, and runners were fetching more saltpetre powder kegs to roll down the promontory to where fighting was expected. Tollska guessed they must plan to smash barricades down with canon fire if they could. She tried not to think of the devastation that would bring. Two guards at the supply wagon stopped her. "Eh, what are you doing here?"

"I'm looking for Pearth Arden, I'm her spouse."

"She's isn't here. You shouldn't be either. It's not safe."

"If she arrives, tell her I was here."

Tollska took one last look over the side of the high roadway and turned back towards Gemynd, wiping away the acrid fluid dripping from her eyes. She had to find Einya, as much as the feeling of guilt chewed away in the pit of her stomach at the thought.

Running back toward the heart of Gemynd, her long gown billowed out behind her as she sped along, scanning the streets in vain. At least they were mostly empty, most Gemyndians choosing to hide indoors rather than see the reality of the smog over the settlement. Those few out on the streets looked at her suspiciously, but Tollska barely noticed. The cobbles stung the soles of her feet as she ran, searching desperately for Einya.

Moving from the heart of the settlement to the edge, she eventually reached a towering wall and followed it around the circumference of Gemynd until she found what she was looking for.

Sat on the edge of the wall, with her legs hanging over the side, was Einya. The woman watched intently over the smoke-clogged Raskian districts as Tollska stepped tentatively up behind her. "It should be a good view, all the way to Aisren."

Einya turned, surprise etched on her face for a brief moment before turning back to look away over Rask again. "What do you want, Tollska?"

Tollska slumped down beside Einya and swung her boots over the side of the wall despite her slight uneasiness at the plummeting edge beneath them. "This has gone too far. We need to find a way to end it."

"You're not wrong," Einya mumbled.

Tollska dug her nails into her other hand as Einya looked at her, noticing for the first time her once-lover's tired features: deep circles under her eyes and a skeletal frame to her face.

As Einya spoke, Tollska thought her voice had lost its once musical tone. She watched as Einya inhaled sharply and sighed again.

"I can't do anything, Tollska," Einya said. "Your beloved spouse has seen to that. They've all but chained my arms."

"What do you mean, Einya, tell me what you mean?"

"They know where Bri is, and if I step against them, Pearth and the Astrologer-Elect will kill him."

Tollska said nothing for a long moment, instead reaching one hand out and tangling her fingers with Einya's. "I'm sorry, Einya. I'm sure he's being careful."

"I'm not sure of that, or anything."

"So, you won't help my mother, then? Einya, they have a list, with so many names on it. What will you do when they start taking them?"

Einya turned to face her, a fire burning in her blue eyes, making Tollska want to flinch backwards. She'd never seen Einya so angry.

The woman's words were laced with such fury. "How can I, Tols, how? It's all so clear now; they only gave me the book because they knew they could control me when the time came. I've already asked them to stop this."

"Wait, a book? What book?"

"On how to influence the Stars and speak to them. I was meant to find out the truth, but only to reinforce their *truth*, because they knew they could hold me on a tight leash. So how can I go to them now and tell them to give anyone their freedom? I am only a pawn in this game of Chess. You and Pearth are the warring queens; I can't act while you're here. You're in too much danger. We could flee together…"

Tollska squeezed Einya's hand tightly and whispered: "You aren't a pawn, you know, and we need to resolve this. You have a light within you, a determination, that's burnt bright for all the ten years I've known you. Is a little wind gonna blow that out?"

"My life has been akin to a hurricane since you left," Einya murmured, her voice fading into a whisper.

"I love you still, Einya, your strength is a beacon."

"If you loved me, you would have told me everything and we would've found a way."

"Would we? You wouldn't have hated the game I played as I used you whilst I learnt about what Gemynd planned to do against us?" Tollska whispered back.

"Not at all."

"That's easy to say now."

Einya looked away again, and Tollska felt as if one of them might as well be at the bottom of the wall and the other at the top for all the distance that now stretched between them. "My home burns, Einya, and I had hoped you'd help me like you said you would. I'll be locked up if I tell them anything or campaign against them to stop this fighting."

Einya's jaw tightened, eyes squinting slightly. "Why?"

"Because I'm Raskian, and my mother is on that list."

"That is not a revelation. I know when you are lying. So, tell me, why?"

Tollska bit her lip and then began. "I've been spying on the Raskian rebels for Pearth. But also telling my Ma what I can about the Guard's movements."

"You are insane to continue this, it's too dangerous…"

Tollska squirmed a little at Einya's incredulity. "I had no choice, it's the only way."

To Tollska's surprise, Einya lifted her spare hand and cupped her face gently. She leant into the warmth instinctively as Einya spoke, even though the woman's sapphire eyes burnt fiercely. It was almost like they were lovers again. Almost, but not quite.

"They will destroy you, and your mother, if they find out," Einya whispered.

"It's a risk worth taking, and here's why." Tollska waved one hand over the burning settlement. "They have burnt our homes. Please help us, Einya. Help me."

Einya shook her head. "I have to be careful or whatever is planned with the Testament of the Stars will be done to Bri too…"

"If they find him."

The smoke was rising now behind them, and Tollska could only see Einya consumed amongst the smoke wisps that floated in the wind. Tollska kissed her, fully and with a passion she'd never felt for Pearth.

Tollska felt the tugs of a smile at the edge of her lips as she sat back, watching Einya. "Remember the fire, the strength, the fervour you had for life. Then fight."

Einya sighed and leant her forehead against Tollska's shoulder. "I will do what little I safely can. I want to help you, believe me. If I can do more, I will."

Tollska breathed out a smoky sigh of relief and kissed the top of Einya's head. "I'll always have thanks for that, I promise."

They sat there as an icy breeze blew clear some of the smoke, revealing the green fields beyond the settlement and the tall trees woven into the distant horizon. Eventually, long after the sun had dropped over the edge of the trees, the pair reluctantly unhooked their hands from each other and, standing, stepped away from the edge of the wall.

Tollska gently ran one thumb over Einya's lips. "You should go home, Einya. Not least because you smell!" She laughed at Einya's shocked face.

"Do I?"

"When was your last wash?"

"I have been in the Star cavern for a few days, I suppose."

"There we go. Washing! You need to. Let's take you home." Tollska grinned, pleased to see Einya couldn't resist smiling back.

They walked through the streets in the dark, Einya guiding the way. For those brief moments, it felt like a vague memory of old times, and Tollska felt the flutter of hope tremble through her. The feeling went as quickly as it came.

When they rounded the corner, Tollska sharply gripped Einya's arm to steady herself. They stood there in the street clutching each other, trembling hands shaking in tandem.

Across the walls of Einya's home, huge numbers of the pamphlets from Rask were plastered, covering every spare space. Tollska recognised the latest words instantly, blocky words proclaiming the injustice against their compatriot, Gunsk. Across the black and white papers, bold red letters stood out. They simply said:

Do something
- L

Tollska clenched her jaw and pulled Einya by her hand into a narrow side alley in case anyone saw them together.

Einya's teeth bared as she spat her words. "She's forcing my hand, Tols, my choice is gone."

"I get that. Luskena has been angry that we're not doing more. But, here, act sensibly, don't be rushed."

"You need to leave; they cannot see you here. You'd be put on this list too," Einya whispered. "Go."

Tollska's jaw locked tightly, teeth grinding together even though she knew Einya was right. "I can handle this, believe me."

"I do, but please—don't make survival harder for yourself."

Shouts were starting to ring around the square in front of Einya's rooms. Tollska tried hard not to worry about what would happen now, as she lifted Einya's fingers and kissed the tips gently.

"I'll see you soon, Einya. I'll make sure of it."

"Go, after everything I couldn't see it end like this for you because of me."

As Tollska backed her way up the narrow street in the darkness, she kept her eyes on Einya for as long as possible, watching Einya's silhouette sag against the wall, head tilted up towards the Stars.

Tollska finally turned away and ran the circuitous back routes she knew to return to the Arden manor, hoping desperately that Pearth hadn't noticed her absence.

Chapter Twenty-Nine

We must sanction the sending of spies to Parlenta and Aisren, lest
we lose our edge in this cluster of island settlements.
~ Commander Arden addressing the Constellan Council

Thick dripping rain woke Bri as it splashed on his forehead, large drops spattering on the rough stones around him. He pushed himself up from where he lay, looking around. How had he got here, and where were the guards? It seemed only moments ago he was in the mine with the Star. There was nothing to be seen in the grey morass of the stone plain; the clouds drifted low and pinned in his vision to the small area around the cart.

Rips of screams sounded from within the fog, and Bri sprung up into a crouch with some surprise that he could move freely again. Frantically he held up his hand, remembering, expecting to see the long claws bursting through his fingers still. He sighed, relieved. His skin was undamaged and had taken back its usual hue and, although still damp, at least he was no longer cold. He picked up one of the guard's swords, which lay beside the cart. In the grey clouds shouts still echoed, and he clambered up to the seat of the cart, intending to drive away whilst the chance was there.

"Help me, help me please." The rattling voice of one of the guards stung his ears with its high pitch.

Bri sighed at himself and jumped down. One day, it would be lovely to be less selfless. The grey cloud swarmed around him as he stepped into it.

Sharp blue glowing orbs illuminated the way, just above ground level, and he pressed towards them. Curious, as well as anxious, about what the strange lights would turn out to be. If it hadn't been so dark with the rain pelting down on him, he might have laughed at what he saw when he got closer. The guard was running, his face slowly turning white with ice. Chasing him was a little fox, whose eyes were the source of the azure glow in the murky shadows.

The growling fox huffed out icy air from its little lungs, the misty breath clinging to the outstretched hand of the guard. His bright eyes pierced the murky half-light as the trembling guard backed away with sword raised, sagging against the side of the cart.

"What're you worried about? It's just a fox." He bit his lip on a laugh. "Come on. I'm trying to help you, for some reason."

"Get away! It did something to you—like it ate some light that came from your mouth or took your breath out of you or something. We're supposed to take you back, with the messenger, but just take the fiend away… it ain't natural."

Bri paused. "Messenger?"

"From Parlenta, with some message for Commander Arden. He sat with you in the carriage. He took our horse and fled when the fox came…"

"Wait, what? Why would he do that?" Bri stepped forward so their faces were fractions apart.

"Please! No closer, no closer. I'll tell you. We followed you to Parlenta. That's it, that's all it is. We were meant to bring you back as you're on the list of rebels and traitors. We were meant to tell the commander how Parlenta used the Stars against you. The messenger wants to make some deal, he had Parlentan soldiers with him—we had no choice. We're just escorts for the Astamitra trade."

Bri blinked, brushing the rain from his eyes. "I'm on a list of traitors? Figures."

"I've told you all I know, please just leave me be."

Bri looked down at the fox, which was panting next to him with an ephemeral glow around the tips of its fur as it glared at the guard. It had slumped down on its haunches next to him, which seemed strange—but it wasn't the strangest thing he'd seen today.

"Come on Bri, leave while you can," he muttered to himself.

Frost crisped over the edges of the guard's skin even as Bri straightened up and ran past. He grinned and bowed a little to the man on the floor without stopping. "Thank you for your hospitality," Bri mumbled.

Just then, a guard with a crossbow emerged from the fog of the rain clouds. Bri slammed his feet into the ground to run faster, hearing the shouts from the guard who tried to follow him into the swirling grey clouds.

Bri pelted onwards, even though he could feel the cuts of stone stinging his nearly bare feet as his battered shoes finally disintegrated. He ran onward dizzily into the rock-strewn plane beyond Parlenta. A gentle tinkling cadence twittered in his ears. He realised he was giggling to himself as he fled into the wilderness, frost still clinging to his skin.

"You're still mad, then," he mumbled, and somehow speaking to himself just made him want to laugh more.

He stopped eventually, the blood streaming from his feet as sensation crept back into them. The clouds were frittering away now as the sun rose across the plain, which was barren except for the trees in the distance. He sat, exhausted, vaguely wondering what he would do now when a noise behind him made him jump.

The glow-eyed fox padded up to him where he'd sagged down on a nearby rock. The ice-tinged russet critter slurped its rough tongue over Bri's feet, which at least soothed the wounds enough for him to continue walking.

Bri heaved himself up again, feeling a stab of hunger. The fox nuzzled at his ankle and trotted off towards the trees, yowling a little as if to say to follow him.

Bri sloped along after. "No better plan, I suppose."

He walked for a day until rocky plains blended into rolling grasslands. Bri smiled, hobbling to a little stream in a meadow to drink and wash his cuts. The fox clambered onto his lap as he sat on the shore, its eyes still glowing with something that felt familiar. Realisation hit.

"You took the Star in, didn't you?" Bri whispered, feeling a strange glowing link between him and the fox as if the fox was willing him to understand something. It felt like the Star-rock reaching out to him again. He sighed. "You and I are in such a quandary then."

The fox chittered a little and rolled over on his lap. Bri tentatively rubbed the little creature's chin where the fur blended from orange to white. "Little star-fox, can I call you Quandary? I'd be honoured if you would stay with me awhile. It's lonely here and I'm bad without company."

Quandary chittered again, brushing his tail against Bri's bare leg. Little huffs of icy breath emanated from his mouth, leaving frosty droplets on his russet fur.

In the river, a shoal of slow-moving fish sloped through the water, and Bri eyed them greedily. After a few attempts, he stabbed one through with the sword he'd taken, sliding it off the end of the blade in front of Quandary before going back to catch another.

At last dropping into a crouch beside the fox, Bri tentatively pulled the bones from his smaller fish and nibbled at the meat. Gagging on the taste of the uncooked fish, he threw the rest to the star-fox and instead gathered a small handful of berries from a nearby shrub.

They settled for the night. Quandary curled up on top of Bri, one paw stretched across the man's knee. It took a while to get settled, the fox chirruping irritably if Bri shifted too much, but it was all too strange. Bri sighed again. He had to sleep, but the gravitas of everything that had happened kept demanding his attention. With one hand resting on Quandary and one hand gripping the sword, Bri eventually drifted to sleep with the sound of the river churning by next to him.

Chapter Thirty

Do the Astrologers really understand the use of Astamitra?
Can the Astrologer-Elect confirm to me he understands the risks?
~ Lord Hyther of the Constellan Council, speaking in the
chamber

Einya stood in the narrow alley beside her house, an icy
wind biting at her skin as she tore thought after thought out of her
mind, trying to think about what she would do next. Drawing in a
deep breath, she rounded the corner and strode towards her door.

There was a small crowd outside, including a minor unit of
Constellan Guards. The woman at the head of the guards separated
herself from the crowd, the Stars etched into her breastplate bright
and clear even in the darkness.

"Astrologer Arden, this is your house?"

"It is."

"Do you know who did this?"

"No, if you find out I would like to know."

The guardswoman huffed slightly. "Raskian scum. I'm sorry this has happened, Astrologer."

Einya said nothing and went to open the door. She made sure she hadn't been followed in, then went straight to check the floorboard hiding place. It was undisturbed. She slumped in a chair with her eyes closed for a mere moment, relieved and exhausted. *Can't rest for long*, she thought. As soon as the voices faded into retreating footsteps outside, she sprang up with an energy that surprised her given she felt so tired.

She went to the small chest with the undiluted Astamitra stashed inside. Grabbing a few of the vials, she was sure some of the blue hues of the crushed stone fluctuated under her skin as well.

"You're going mad, Einya," she muttered, standing up.

Taking her coat from the hallway and buttoning it tightly around her chest, she headed outside. The heavy weight of the star-book in her leather bag bashed against her hip as she walked.

The Astrologer-Elect's lavish door with ornate carvings had become so familiar to her now that it didn't seem strange to her to be knocking on it loudly after midnight. The Raskian butler answered, and she pushed her way in. "I need to see Sepult Disren. Tell him. Please."

She strode in and sat down by the fireplace, although it had burnt down to just embers. It would have to do, she was still frosted to the core and struggling to steady her trembling hands. The fluctuating colours oscillated just beneath her skin again. It was mesmerising, but she drew her eyes away at the scrape of a door opening.

Sepult Disren wore only a nightgown, and an expression of nerves and irritation, when he entered. She didn't let him start the conversation. "Sepult, they are burning Rask. Do you think they will send goods after this? How do you think this will end?"

The Astrologer-Elect rubbed at his eyes as he approached. "Einya, I know you mean well. It is not as simple as that. We require their goods. Without them, we will starve."

"Surely we can buy all the goods we need."

"We make nothing, we build nothing—where would the money come from?"

"Is that all this is about? What about their lives?"

He rubbed his eyes again, sitting down wearily. "I am going to summon the Council to sign an edict about the future of our relationship with Rask. I will try to put something in that."

"Like what?"

"I don't know, how can *I* know what they need? This is to ratify the Testament of the Stars. Then we can show Rask that it's more than just a political whim; the rest is detail."

"Have you *asked* what they might need?" Einya watched as he scowled like a petulant child. "Have you asked the Stars about their will for the people of Rask?"

"You ask them again, but be sure to get the answer *I* need."

Einya almost marched out then but forced herself to stay seated. In her head, the scene of Rask burned away, sparking at her anger. She could hear the whispers from the Stars below, like they were bursting out of the floorboards beneath them, reaching out to her.

She shook them out of her head with a small flick. "If this is about peace, then listen. Why do you think their answer will be different? Sepult, they are part of history."

"History can be sculpted to suit our needs."

"That's one decision you could take," Einya spat. "The only reason Rask is lesser is because of decisions Gemynd took a hundred years ago. You don't want them to die, do you?"

It was then that the Astrologer-Elect stood, pitiable and pathetic as he hunched over. He seemed like he might disintegrate at the slightest touch as he gripped the side of a dresser to steady himself. "You don't understand."

Einya stood to face him. "I will go back to the Stars, but you won't like what I find."

She took the winding stairs down from the entrance hall in the grand manor, straight into the Star cavern. It didn't take long to tip the contents of her bag over the floor in a habitual and well-practised ritual before grabbing the book. Leafing past the page of the usual communication ritual, she paid it no mind at all as she headed deeper into the book. The different ceremonies felt so familiar now, but she still shuddered at the descriptions of some of them.

Here it was, the right ritual for the situation. She'd tried to reason, at least. So maybe this really was the only way. Einya set the book down so it was propped at the base of the nearest Star-rock. The torches were already lit around the cavern, casting a scattered umber pattern across the stone floor. She grabbed some tall pillar candles, lighting them from the wall sconces and placing them around the base of the Star-rocks.

Once these were in place, Einya knelt amongst the flickering flames, breathing in deeply. She'd read about the other rituals in the book extensively but had never considered doing any of them. The page the book was parted on now suggested that after performing this ritual, you could twist the views of others by holding them in the light of the Stars still in the sky and whispering truths to them.

The book had instructed that much more of the crushed Star-stones were needed to complete this. She plucked one of the small vials of undiluted Astamitra from the pocket of her coat and, without any ceremony this time, tipped all the colourful liquid down her throat and swallowed before she could pause to think.

It struck at once. Einya felt instantly as if she knelt on a ship, the ground beneath her swelling on the tide. The torchlight had faded, and only the bright glow of the Stars shone through the shadowy room. The only other light was the glow of her own hands, which gleamed effervescently as if her blood was fluctuating colours underneath her dark skin. She tried to focus her memory on the tasks required as written on the pages, even though her vision swam and she couldn't see the writing anymore.

Einya took up her long dagger from the floor of the cave, dug the point of the blade into a crack in the Star-rock before her and prised a loose piece of it away. As she removed the small chip, she felt as if she was tugging a heavy memory away with it, like dragging an unconscious body across the floor. She focused on it as the Star-stone grew hot in her hands. In her mind, the memories of the Stars emerged as vividly as if they unfolded right in front of her.

An old Astrologer-Elect was writing at a desk with the words clear to see in their black ink: *The Testament of the Stars: Splitting our settlement into farmers and nobles.*

In the pit of her stomach, she felt the stabbing guilt as if she'd done something awful. She could sense the same Astrologer nailing the edict to the Star-rocks, and guards began ushering Raskians away from them. Raskians rushed forward, trying to speak to the Stars, praying and begging.

Then the wall was built. The newly crafted cavern closed the Stars off as guards escorted Raskians away into the streets beneath Gemynd, some of them in chains.

The whispers from the Stars turned into deep howls, and Einya fell backwards over her feet where she knelt as the sound sliced through her hearing. The memory faded as she tumbled backwards, tears streaming down her face. *Loss.* The Stars felt loss when the settlement had been ripped in half by the greed of a few. Now she felt it too. Einya clutched the small fragment of Star-stone in her hand. It felt like a jagged pebble weighing heavily between her fingers.

She stood carefully as if she carried a dead body; picking up the book took excruciating effort and it felt like she was wading through a rising tide as she slowly walked away from the Star-rocks. It felt like little insects were landing on her shoulder, like hands emanating from the Stars were tugging at her ankles to pull her back toward them.

Snarling, determined, she pushed hard in her effort to drag herself away through the gravity-like tug. The Astamitra tingled inside her as it twisted through her veins, and it was like the Star-blood's strength was the only thing fighting the grip.

She gasped for air as she finally reached the door, her lips cracked and dried and her hair hanging limply over her sweaty face. Out in the fresh dawn air, she slumped to her knees in exhaustion, one arm clutching the book and her other hand pressing the fragment of Star-stone painfully into her palm.

Looking at her quaking hands, Einya could see a gossamer phosphorus glow emanating from underneath the skin on the backs of her hand. She knew what she needed to do next—when the shadows of night descended again.

Chapter Thirty-One

If we do not wise up to their politics, then we might as well roll over.
~ Commander Arden addressing the Constellan Council

The trees crept up ahead of Bri, drifting branches on a misty horizon that seemed an uncertain distance away. They'd started walking at dawn, and it had been a long trek. This final stumble toward the woods felt arduous, and he'd stopped regularly to try and bind his feet with strips of cloth from his trousers, which were getting rapidly shorter.

Quandary snortled and snuffled around in the undergrowth whenever they paused, looking expectantly up at Bri if he didn't follow him. His eyes still glowed, and if it wasn't for that detail, Bri would have struggled to think of him as anything other than just a fox.

"Are you more fox, or more Star now?" Bri mumbled softly, reaching one hand out to Quandary's tousled fur. The star-fox skittered a little away and then returned to tentatively sniff at Bri's palm, tumbling over his own paws a little as if uncertain how to make the body move.

"You'll get there, little fox," he giggled. Quandary chittered lightly, rolled over next to Bri and slopped his tongue over the man's hand.

When he stood back up, Bri winced as the cuts on his feet stung even in the long grass field. As they walked slowly onwards, Quandary stayed close, his large tail swooshing against Bri's legs every so often.

When they finally reached the line of trees, Bri paused and ran one hand over the tightly woven bowers of wood that blocked their path. It was like the woods had built themselves into a dense wall, and Bri turned to walk along its length.

After a while of running his hand along the wood and the leaves, he started to wonder if there was ever going to be a parting in the trees. Then he saw it, a small opening a short way ahead where the weaving branches parted into an archway. At the woodland-forged doorway, the ice that clung to the road melted away suddenly, and inside the forest, summer reigned. Bri stopped abruptly, jaw hanging slightly open in awe—how could this be? It was winter.

Musky purple flowers wove around a natural arch, twisting through the bower into a scented canopy. Beneath the flower-roof, a winding earthen road delved deeper into the wood with little crofts and avenues meandering off to the sides.

He stood there gaping as goldfinches flitted through the air around him. Their minuscule wings beat tiny gusts of air into his face as they flew close enough to touch. Quandary yapped at him and nuzzled against his grazed ankle, before dashing away after something that had snatched his attention.

A man with braided lavender hair, with skin smooth like the birch bowers around them, had emerged from one of the dens off the edge of the path.

"Did you mean to come here? Not many visitors in Aisren." The man's head tipped curiously to one side, his braids slumping over his shoulder asymmetrically.

Bri saw that his pallid blue eyes were dappled in the sunlight spilling through the canopy as he reluctantly turned his eyes away from the clusters of birds flitting around.

"Not exactly." Bri tried to smile, but he felt it only half emerge on his lips. "I am not really sure what I'll do now. I've never been here before, and don't know what to do. How is it summer here?"

"You'd better follow me. My name is Shrynaid." The man reached out and clasped his hand on Bri's shoulder before looking him over, and Bri let his question go ignored. "Can I offer you some clothes, maybe some boots?"

Bri just nodded and allowed himself to be led along a bark-strewn path to a lavish gatehouse with timber beams between wattle and daub panels. The house blurred in with the trees, for little leaves—tender and yellow-green—clambered over every surface and even wound their way over the roof on delicate little vines. "This is your house?"

Shrynaid nodded and ducked in through the low oak door, leaving Bri to marvel at the perfect blending of leaves around the criss-cross windowpane as Quandary swatted his paw at a fuchsia butterfly fluttering nearby. The little fox didn't seem so unusual here, and Shrynaid certainly hadn't said anything, which Bri felt grateful for since he had no good explanation for the glowing-eyed critter.

The man returned with an armful of linen clothing and a supple pair of leather boots, which he held out to Bri with an appraising look. "These should do you, yes, I think they should fit."

Bri took them, knowing there was no point in procrastinating when his shoes hung like embroidered ribbons round his ankles.

"Thank you, can I pay you something for this?" He slipped on a less tattered tunic and enjoyed the cosy comfort of fresh, warm clothes clinging to his skin.

Shrynaid only shook his head. "Coin goes nowhere in these woods."

"How is that so?"

"No one uses money. We just barter, so if you're staying here then you can pay me somehow one day."

Bri managed to smile then and bowed with only a little awkwardness, an idea fluttering into his thoughts. "Can I ask for help, actually? Who should I speak to?"

"Help?"

"For Rask. I'm from Gemynd."

"Gemynd. Well." Shrynaid frowned, and a fiery light pulsed through the man's blue eyes in that moment.

"I am no friend of theirs, but more an exile," Bri said hurriedly, remembering his political ineptitude with a fresh stab of inadequacy.

"You need to speak to Breyneda, and I will take you there. Follow."

Shrynaid turned and led him up the sunlit forest path deeper into the wood, but Bri felt now like the grey clouds from the jagged rock plane still drooped low around him.

Curious faces of children watched him as they gathered berries from unkempt hedgerows, and all sorts of linen-dressed people looked on with summer's joy dancing through their eyes as they sat by moss-banked rivers.

Despite the sense that once again, he might soon be a prisoner of his political failings, he couldn't help but think of Einya, imagining her radiant joy at the forest as she splashed through the river, laughing like she hadn't since their childhood.

They crossed a quaint wooden bridge that arched gracefully over the banks of the river. Little lanterns tethered to low hanging branches guided their meandering route to what felt like the heart of the woodland. As they walked, Bri saw more and more illustrious beamed houses, taverns and all sorts of buildings crowned with ivy and flowers that mantled every scrap of stone and timber they could cling to.

Quandary, who had been padding along behind despite occasional distractions, darted off into a shrub-line. Bri sighed a little. He would miss the little fox.

A winding path took them round the edge of a glade and into a small canopy of trees with a tiny hut hidden amongst the thick foliage. Many lanterns hung here, brighter now it was getting dark. In the dusky shadows beyond the hut, a larger glade with a light he couldn't quite make out glistening within it cast obscure patterns across the forest floor. Just beyond the forest threshold, an expanse of cliffs could be seen in the dimming light. The sound of waves crashed against them.

Shrynaid looked back at him, and Bri felt tenseness grip at his muscles as the smile that reached him wasn't as bright as when the man had greeted him first. The man's hand softly tapped at the door, which was laden with little trinkets of shells, driftwood, acorns and much more. "Breyneda, there's someone here you should see. From Gemynd."

The door opened almost immediately, and a woman with forget-me-nots braided into her brown hair stepped barefoot out into the glade. Her eyes were brown, but a golden glow burnt deeply within their shell and Bri felt as if the Aisrenese house-vines had also snared around his tongue.

Chapter Thirty-Two

*Parlenta has offered us more than Gemynd ever did, what does
that tell you?*
~ Raskian pamphlet

Hammering knocks battered on the library doors. "Lady
Tollska?"

Standing, she cast her book on the plush chair and strode to
the door. "What is it, Irinsk?"

Irinsk's hair hung loose as if she'd tugged it roughly out of
her bun in a moment of tension. "A man from Parlenta is here, he
insists on talking to Lady Pearth but I can't find her. He's got
soldiers with him."

"Soldiers?"

"Yes, they're in the hall… shall I serve them something?"

"Uh, no need. I'll see the messenger, show him in and then
find Pearth. She'll be at the promontory closest to here with any
luck. Take my horse, go quickly."

"Thank you."

Irinsk quickly hustled back towards the door and peered around it, admitting the visitors before slipping away.

The Parlentan messenger, dressed in slate-coloured clothes, stepped into the room first and sat on one of the large chairs without a word. A drably attired soldier in a grey chest-plate with a large primitive musket clutched in both hands followed the messenger in. Tollska raised one eyebrow, nervous and surprised. Despite the inaccuracy of the newly invented powder weaponry, it certainly leant status and wealth to the visitors, even though bows were still more effective.

"Can I help you?" Tollska said, moving slowly to sit opposite him, hoping she sounded powerful and strong.

"I'm here from Parlenta."

"I know that. How did you get through the barricades?" She leant towards him.

The man grinned, raising his hands as part of an elaborate shrug. "With words. I told the Raskians on those barricades that if I get what I want up here then Parlenta will give them what they want."

"And they believed you?" Tollska scoffed.

"What choice did they have? My small guard is more than a match for all of them with their rusty swords, and they surely can see my offer has merit. Luskena of Rask sends her greetings, by the way."

"I…" Tollska sucked in a deep breath, her hand pressing painfully into the metal spike on the end of her rapier's hilt. What offer did he mean? "I hear you have soldiers here."

"Yes, but they are just protection. The outcome will be the same, though, whether I leave safely or not. So, about what I want…"

Tollska stood and went to ring a small bell on the mantle to stall for time. "Can I fetch you some drinks? You must be tired from your travels, perhaps this conversation can wait until…"

"I will not wait."

"Whatever business you have with my spouse is not with me."

The man leant forward, smiling. "I come from the Mineral Master of Parlenta. About your Stars. We can use them; if your spouse were to consent, we would use them for greatness."

"At what cost?" Tollska spat.

The door slammed open and Pearth strode in.

"My answer is still no." Pearth's words rang clear as she crossed the room toward them.

"We would pay for the honour and make Commander Arden great," the Parlentan said, turning to Pearth.

"Pearth Arden doesn't want your glory," Pearth spat. "She just wants her homeland. Get your soldiers out of my settlement."

The gold-clad guardswoman crossed the room, mud-coated boots and blood-splattered tunic still clinging tightly to her sweat-soaked body. "No one invited you here."

"We heard there was a war… we thought now might be the time to reconsider our offer."

"How did you hear of the war?"

"Your cousin kindly told us. I had hoped to return him to you, but alas that was not to be."

Pearth pulled away, pivoting on her feet to hide the scowl on her face, but Tollska could still see it. She reached out to Pearth, but the woman turned back, a steel-glint in her blue eyes.

"Again: my answer is still no," Pearth growled.

"But consider…"

"No. Maybe if you had not mined your Stars so relentlessly, you would not be in this situation."

"Even in the tumult of a war, you would deny us?"

Tollska flinched when Pearth's strong fists flashed out and gripped the man around his neck. "These are *our* Stars. This is *our* home."

The Parlentan's voice still croaked out his words. "Consider, Commander Pearth, that your war means you will not stop us just taking what we want by force. We have offered twice politely, our third won't be so kind. Our armies are already on their way here, your small guard won't stop us."

Tollska stood. "Wait, you won't win favours by treating us like this."

The man turned to her, a twisted smirk on his lips. "You're a Raskian, yes? They tell me the head of the Guard married beneath her, but even so, you would stand with the woman who pushes your people into the mud to prevent us taking the Stars that they use to oppress you?"

"I would stand against oppression of all forms, and this is just another brand of it."

Pearth shook her head. "Leave it, sweet love. This man knows what he wants, and I will give it to him."

The guardswoman crossed the room, ringing the bell on the mantlepiece above the fire. Moments later, the doors to the library slammed open, brass handles bashing against the ornate wooden bookcases. Ten Constellan Guards pressed into the room, bows notched with arrows and raised. Outside in the hall, more could be seen surrounding the handful of Parlentan soldiers.

The grey-clad Parlentan dropped his unprimed musket, raising his hands. The wood and metal clattered to the stone floor.

Pearth crossed back toward the messenger, speaking to her guards. "Take the soldiers away."

"Come now, will you turn this into fighting so easily? We could resolve this with words." The messenger's arms were delicately raised above his shoulders and a slight smirk was on his face.

When the soldiers were gone and the doors shut, Pearth pulled a small pot from her pocket. "Tollska, hold him."

"What? Wait, why?"

"Just do it, or they will do the same to us."

"Do what?

"We are losing here. We need to send a message."

Tollska gripped Pearth's arm. "You'll send the wrong message if you hurt him."

"If our Stars are what he wants, then I'll gift it to him. Tollska, just hold him," Pearth demanded.

"But…"

"Do it, and save the lives of many here."

Tollska stepped forward, reluctance making her feet slow. She held the man against the fine chair he sat on. Pearth screwed open the little pot, tipped a small amount of a blue powder over her hands and rubbed it into the man's eyes.

"What are you doing?" Tollska started to say, but her words were quickly drowned out.

Even as the Parlentan thrashed and howled, Pearth pressed her hands against him to hold him down in her vice-like grip. The man bawled, but still managed to scream the words: "Your Stars will be ours!"

He froze still then, glass-white eyes staring at the ceiling and a sapphire froth spewing from between his blackened lips.

"What was that?" Tollska asked, her breath snagging as she spoke.

"That's what Astamitra does when used as a weapon, that's what they've done to others who stand against them. I have a good spy in Parlenta, she tells me all I need to know."

Tollska gripped Pearth's wrist tightly. "This has to end, this ain't right."

"Yes, and this is why I need peace. Parlenta will come, and we'll end up like this foul man if we don't do something about it."

Tollska gripped the other woman's wrist tighter then. "Why not say that, why not win peace with Rask that way? All we ever wanted was fair treatment and not to starve, give us that and end this madness."

Pearth ripped her wrist away from Tollska's grip, pacing the book-lined room. "What then? Say that this is what we've become—prey for a neighbouring settlement? That our Astrologer-Elect weakly opened our bellies to them by trading on their terms, that my cousin told Parlenta we were amid a civil war, so they knew they could come here and rip us apart to get to the Stars? There would still be panic, we would still be weak. It would fix nothing."

Silence hung there for a fraction of a moment.

"What will you do?" Tollska's heart clenched with tension.

"Force peace any way I can, then turn our armies towards the Parlentan threat. We will need to use their own weapons against them."

Tollska clutched again at Pearth, briefly halting the woman's steps. "There has to be another way."

"There isn't. Don't tell anyone how far we've fallen, please. I'm sorry it has come to this, sweet love, I do cherish you so and wanted to avoid this."

Pearth strode from the room, leaving Tollska there with the man slumped in the plush chair. A short while later, two guards came and dragged the man's limp body through the doors into the main hall and down the steps outside into the snow-lined streets.

Chapter Thirty-Three

Our coffers are emptying to buy Astamitra, our trade exclusively
with Parlenta. We are slaves to this trade deal.
~ Lord Hyther speaking to the Constellan Council

Snow permanently clung to the ground of Gemynd now, and the heart of winter was fast approaching. Behind the usual noises of the settlement, the cacophony of fighting in the streets echoed. A ripple of tension coursed through Gemynd, heightened by the awkward attempts at normality. The Arden household had thrown banquets two days in a row that, while widely attended by the nobles hoping for a distraction, were unusually sombre occasions.

Einya had mostly avoided these, except for one where she sat silent for the entirety. She'd instead spent the time creating a haphazard laboratory in her rooms. Vials, flasks and distillation tubes were set up with more determination than skill. In the centre of them sat a stone slab, which Einya had used to set a small fire on at the instruction of the book. She'd finally plucked up the courage to follow the next steps set out in the tome and sat with her back resting against the wall, grinding the Star-stone she'd chipped away into a thin powder.

It'd taken her two days to get the right glassware set up. She'd managed to find an alchemist who'd accepted an inordinate amount of money to let her take the flasks and vials she needed away with no questions asked.

Einya took a deep breath and pushed herself up from the wall, taking care not to spill any of the powder tumbling around the mortar bowl. When she tipped it into a small flask and rested it on the tripod above the flames, she stepped back quickly.

The warning in the book was accurate: the star-powder glinted brightly and blazed piercingly whilst the liquid began to drip through the tubes into the flask. She looked down at her own hands, which seemed to match the blazing brightness of the flask, so much so she now wore gloves to hide the glow whenever she wasn't alone.

She cleared away the flasks and tucked the book under the bed just in case but left the small fire simmering down into nothing. Once the liquid was bottled, she set out immediately with the still warm vial clutched in her hands.

Outside the manor, Einya waited to see the torches doused out after Sepult Disren returned. She let herself into the Star cavern and headed straight up the winding stairs to the manor. It felt as if the Star-rocks tore into her with their eyes, if they even had eyes, committing to memory every aspect of this moment as she passed them by.

Up inside the manor, it was silent and Einya slipped her boots off so she could pad up the stairs into the tower, unheard.

She'd never been this far in before and found there were a lot of twisting passages and strange angles to the corridors as if it had been built by a madman. Opening door after door by slight cracks, the shine of her hands illuminated the shadowy rooms. Einya eventually mounted a final winding staircase, which was lavishly carpeted and led to an ornate door.

"Am I ready for this? Best not to think," she murmured, padding softly down the hallway.

The door creaked on its hinge when she pushed it gently, revealing a grand four-poster bed, and all the trappings she expected of the master bedroom. She tugged her gloves back on, plunging the room back into the half-light of the moon, and tentatively stepped inside. Grand portraits of previous Astrologer-Elects hung on every wooden panel in the room and Einya felt them watching her unexpected deception intently as she stepped up to the plush bed, wondering who she'd become.

The vial stung the inside of her frosted palm with its lingering warmth, as she reached out with her other hand to place her fingers over Sepult Disren's mouth.

He woke with a start, and Einya hushed him instantly before tentatively removing her hand. "Shh, I have your answer."

"You do?"

"I thought you would want to know straight away, and your servants are not awake." She shrugged as if it were the most normal thing in the world, breathing deeply to keep the tremor from her voice. "I went back, found what the Stars think about the people of Rask. You can take a bit of the rock, press the thought into a stone and then crush the stone into…"

"I don't need to know how. You said I wouldn't like it." His eyes dug into hers and she felt the scrutiny as if it were an insect crawling over her face.

Swallowing, she tumbled through various thoughts, feeling each fragment of time escaping her. "This echo of their thoughts won't last long. The book says you need to drink it whilst it's warm. Thoughts go cold, and they cannot be found again."

He sat up in the bed, suddenly attentive. "Where is it, then?"

"Here." She opened her hand, and the vial glowed in the half-light of the moonlit room.

He regarded the vial for an extended moment. "It is beautiful. Such an honour."

"Very much so."

"Oh, Einya, I am glad you have brought me this. I thought you were turning away."

"How could I? You made me your heir." She forced a smile, which the man meekly returned.

"Should I drink it now?"

Einya just nodded, biting her lip on any words. She uncorked the small vial and placed it in his hand, watching him raise it to his lips with a reluctant curiosity.

The wrinkles around his eyes crinkled in joy as he downed the entire vial.

Ferocious convulsions began almost instantly. She pressed her hands down on the man's shoulders, tempering the violent thrashes that coursed through him. The frame of the bed rattled, his body twisting frantically. The scraping cries of the Astrologer-Elect tore at Einya's eardrums. She pressed one hand over his mouth, whipping around to look at the door, expecting guards or servants to run in at any moment.

After a fraught, flailing moment, she felt the Astrologer-Elect's body slump against her, his eyes a muted white and pupils faded of all colour. The man's mouth hung open and was burbling something. His skin seemed warped, wrinkled and twisted, like melting wax, in a way she was sure it hadn't been moments before. Guilt coursed through her: what had she done?

"Sepult?" She prodded his shoulder gently and then shook it. The man's body suddenly tensed, his feet jerked at unnatural angles and his fingers bent like snapping twigs. When he spoke, his voice rasped like metal screeching across glass.

"They lied, and I did nothing about it," was all he said. Over and over, he repeated it, thrashing his head from side to side.

Einya took a deep breath, then grabbed his shaking hands. "You can make it right."

The man twitched, his still colourless eyes roving around as if searching for something.

"Who's there?" he demanded in an imperious voice. "Am I dreaming?"

Einya froze for a moment, her lips parted, ready to answer and then a thought wriggled into her awareness and she dropped his hands instantly. She tugged off her gloves awkwardly, and the glow of her hands burnished brightly as she raised her hands towards his eyes.

She hadn't expected they'd be this bright, wincing slightly at the twirling blue shades emanating from her dark skin.

She scrabbled together her thoughts and spoke firmly. "You dream, Sepult Disren, of life-ripping lies that destroyed the happiness of many generations. You dream because you can repair this and right a century of wrongs."

Tears tumbled out of his eyes suddenly. That didn't help her feel less guilty. "What must I do?"

"Right the wrongs of a lie. Set history straight. They will be free and equal, and you will not stop them."

He sobbed, then, deep and painful sobs that tore at Einya's heart as he coughed out his tears. She was surprised to find her pity burnt as brightly as her hands and wrapped her arms around him for a brief moment.

"Why do you cry?" she whispered.

Around the sobs, he choked out a cluster of words that seared anger on top of her pity. "The Testament of the Stars, I can't change it. I would if I could, but Pearth holds the keys to everything. Stars, if I follow your words then… then I don't know what will happen to me. She made me do all this. Forgive me, please."

"Made you, how?"

"Star-struck Einya, I have a daughter. I love her dearly, though I've been parted from her for many years. Now she is being added to the Testament of the Stars because not even love can stop the Star's retribution."

Einya swallowed, feeling her understanding force itself around this awkwardly. "Who is she?"

"A Raskian… her name is Luskena."

Einya gripped tighter, tense and with teeth bared. "I need to leave now," she said. As she stood, Sepult Disren tried to clench his hands around her.

"Please, don't leave me. Don't leave me; protect her, Stars. Please. I never meant to not listen. Pearth has held my hand to the fire over my daughter, and I have been thoroughly burnt."

"Why didn't you fight for her, why didn't you try to stop my cousin?"

"I just wanted peace, not to harm anyone. I just wanted my daughter and wanted to be a good leader. I didn't want any of this."

"Good people get ravaged by politics if they don't fight."

"And here I am as a result. Help me, please." Tears dribbled down his cracked, wrinkled cheeks.

Einya let herself briefly be pulled back to sit on the side of the bed. "I'll protect you as best I can," she mumbled, her cheek pressed against his silver hair as she held him close, rocking him like a child. This was unexpected, but what else could she do?

She hummed a song she remembered Bri singing to her when she couldn't sleep as a young girl. As he fell asleep, she tenderly lowered the man to rest on his pillows before covering him in a thick blanket.

Einya gently padded to the door, looking back at the man who seemed so vulnerable cocooned in his bedding now that she knew the truth. She pulled her gloves on with a sharp tug, dousing their glow, before she opened the door and sneaked her way out of the manor. Hot, angry tears ran unchecked down her cheeks.

She inhaled icy air and raised her arms, howling out a fierce bellow that rattled her ribs. Tearing down her arms from the sky, she twisted around on her still bare feet and slammed her soles into the snow as she strode away into the night. It was time to make her cousin pay for all of this.

Chapter Thirty-Four

Killing while citing divine right is still murder.
~ A Raskian Pamphlet.

Tollska bounded up the steps to the side door of the manor, hearing shouts within the building. Doors were slamming shut, Pearth's voice echoing somewhere distantly. As softly as she could, she opened the simple wooden door into the kitchens, finding scattered dishes and broken eggs strewn across the floor.

She quietly walked up the stairs into the main house, dreading finding Pearth. She rounded the corner of the stairs and bumped straight into Prethi.

"What's happening?" She frowned at the short, dishevelled man.

"Pearth is angry. It's something to do with Einya," Prethi whispered, pulling Tollska away from the bustling staff who looked their way slyly. "You should go to Pearth, but you need to know Bri is trying to get help for Rask from outside. I couldn't say before when others listened. But, listen, something is going wrong. I'm not sure what. I've not seen Pearth lose her patience like this. Well, you've seen the mess."

Tollska nodded. "Thank you. I think I know what it is. Keep safe, alright?"

She huffed one steadying breath out and headed up the servant's stair into the main dining chambers.

Pearth was there, papers crumpled in one hand. She marched up to Tollska, her lips peeled back into an artificial smile. "Where have you been, Tollska?"

"Just in Gemynd. I would like to go to Rask for more pamphlets," Tollska responded, deliberate and slow.

"I have more than enough, and you shouldn't go any more. It isn't safe."

Tollska tilted her head to one side, feigning ignorance. "How? Where from?"

"My cousin's rooms, all over the walls. It's left some awkward questions."

"Is she alright?"

"I haven't seen her, but she usually is."

Pearth leant in and kissed her cheek awkwardly. "Tollska, if you find out who might be here putting out these pamphlets in Gemynd, will you tell me?"

"Of course." Tollska brushed her fingers over Pearth's sharp jawline. "Let's go somewhere private."

To Tollska's surprise, Pearth let herself be led away from the grand stairwell of the manor and into their private rooms. They both slumped down on the chaise lounge.

Pearth stretched out as Tollska rested against her. After a long moment of nauseating silence, Pearth began to whisper in her ear. "My cousin had a lover from Rask. I think it led him astray from his family."

"Did he?"

Pearth ran one finger up and down the curve of Tollska's neck, kissed her cheek and continued. "Yes and, you know, I think she is in Gemynd. I think she burnt that manor and put these on Einya's house. I'm hoping you're about to confirm it."

Panic spiked through her, but she pushed it away. "As I say, I'm not really aware of her. Her name is Luskena. That's about all I know."

Pearth leapt up from the chaise and began striding around the room, her heels stamping on the stones. "I don't blame you, Tollska, really I do not. But you see, there are two ways this can go and Luskena seems an obvious option…The Astrologer-Elect needs an example, *we* need an example to try and end this conflict, and I cannot find Einya to ask her about this. So, the question is, did a Raskian do it or did Einya put these up herself?"

"Why would she?" Tollska stood as well, gripping her hands behind her back to stop them trembling.

"She's been making pleas to the Astrologer-Elect for the liberation of Rask. Like her brother, I wonder if this woman that he took up with has gotten to her, too."

Einya or the Raskians. Not this, not this choice. Tollska forced herself to take a deep breath and slowly meander over to a decanter on a nearby table. She poured some amber liquid—it didn't matter what it was—into a glass to stall for time whilst she desperately scrambled her thoughts together. The eyes of her spouse drilled into her back.

Sipping delicately, she turned back to Pearth and spoke intentionally slowly. "Luskena used to distribute pamphlets. That's all I know. Perhaps she still does?"

"Interesting." Pearth's eyes were raging.

Tollska met her gaze but felt she'd revealed more than she thought she had.

Pearth frowned. "Very well. She will be the first we take from the list."

"But she's a figurehead to Rask. If you kill her, she'll be a martyr."

Pearth took Tollska's hand, kissing the back of it with such tenderness that Tollska might have almost forgotten they were warring with words. "Thank you, sweet love, if she is a figurehead then it should end this war before it's too late."

As if a weight had been lifted, Pearth ordered food brought and they spent the rest of the evening cocooned together in the bedroom with a decanter of heated wine passed between them, ignoring the world outside.

Tollska plastered on her best political smile, masking the hollow dread that now churned in the pit of her stomach at what was to come.

Two mornings later, as sleet battered against the windowpanes, Tollska awoke with a maid's hand jostling her shoulder. "You've been summoned to the Council; I made you a flask of something warm to take with you."

Tollska groggily slid out of the bed, feeling the cold slabs against the soles of her feet. This was the first time the Constellan Council had met in weeks. Why now? The fighting had distracted Gemynd from all its usual business. She sidled up the winding stair to her usual seat at the rear of the chamber.

Tollska watched the entrance intently, and the minutes stretched out long and slow as Councillors arrived. The carved door finally opened fully after an hour of the Council waiting, and the Astrologer-Elect entered with a few clerks bustling in behind him.

"I will not keep you long," the Astrologer-Elect's voice boomed out. Tollska almost snorted in laughter at Sepult Disren's ironic words, as absurd as it felt to be laughing then. She hid her mouth behind her hand and allowed herself a mischievous smirk. It quickly fell away at his next words.

"The Testament of the Stars is set to mandate peace, revising that which was agreed when Rask became part of Gemynd. You will all sign. Please. Rask will be given freedom to stop fighting. In exchange for higher trading rights for Gemynd, we will free them to have any other rights as they wish. As long as they give up the named agitators in our Testament of the Stars. Then this war will be done."

A man at the front of the chamber cried out. "Should there not be a vote? You've as good as condemned these Raskians anyway, why come to us now unless you need our agreement for something already started?"

The Astrologer-Elect's eyes reflected the flicker of the tall candles in the head-height candelabras. "We need this to bargain for the lives of our people. Once those on the list are gathered, there is no need for this senseless war."

A man stood that Tollska had never seen in the chambers before. He began shouting. "Votes are mandatory. Rask will never give you these people anyway."

"Votes are advisory, Lord Hyther, as you should know from when you forced through your amendments to several edicts of mine without a vote. What is one edict, if peace is what it brings us?"

Several Astrologers filed into the room and ferried the Councillors towards the large edict scroll set on the centre table. Tollska stood, seeing Einya shuffling in at the back of the crowd of Astrologers. The woman's hair hung loose, seeming to have silver streaks laced through it that bounced the bright morning light spilling into the large room.

Tollska saw the simple black gloves and thick wool coat Einya wore, covering her arms fully despite the several roasting fires lit in the chamber. She didn't have long to dwell on the strangeness, as the situation mutated again.

The Astrologer-Elect rested a claw-like hand on Einya's shoulder, who stepped forward.

"There is a further edict," Einya spoke clearly so that the whole assembly could hear, her voice dull and steel-like. "My brother, Briarth Arden, is a traitor. He is no longer recognised as Gemyndian; he will be returned here and face the justice of those added to the Testament of the Stars. I also sanction the arrest of his lover, Luskena of Rask, who will be made an example of and taken to the tower lockups. I place both of them on the Testament of the Stars, as decreed by the Constellations."

Tollska sat lightheaded and panicking until the ushers came for her, pointing her toward the edict to sign. She made a messy scribble of her name, roughly written under the eyes of the Astrologer-Elect who, to her surprise, looked like he might weep at any moment.

Einya stood there too, watching passively, no emotion showing in her grey lifeless eyes.

Tollska ached to reach out to Einya and breathe some colour back into the woman's life. Instead, as Councillors flowed out of the chamber, she numbly allowed herself to be dragged along with the tide of people until she was outside.

In the street, guards were mustering, cleaning blades and stringing crossbows. In the centre of the street, a large vertical beam had been raised on a platform in front of the Constellan Council chambers. Two guards were securing the pillar in place. Spiked through the timber were thick-cuffed chains at both the top and bottom. A sign had been crudely painted in crimson with the words: *Luskena of Rask, the first blood taken for the Testament of our glorious Stars.*

Tollska swallowed, a brittle cold grip tightening around her heart. The control she thought she had was crumbling away.

Chapter Thirty-Five

The truth is something I thought I knew. Now I have no compass to guide me.
~ Astrologer-Elect Sepult Disren

Einya's feet trailed blood into the alabaster snow as she ran through the backstreets of Rask. Every time guards fighting Raskians came near, she would bundle herself into an alley or down a set of stairs to a basement door to some house or other, Mud and grit now clung to her hair and skin from casting herself into the dirt to hide from skirmishes.

She was barely armed, only carrying her short rapier and a hammer she'd stolen from a blacksmith's shop and couldn't risk running into a fight. She'd used the hammer to bash a small hole to squeeze through in one of the stone blockages at the bottom of the stairs. Now she ran full pelt, ignoring the pain, towards the blue-door cottage at the edge of the settlement. Bodies still scattered the streets—it looked like no one was bothering to clean up the Gemyndian guards—and they just rotted where they had fallen.

By the time she'd reached the cottage, her black dress hung loosely from her shoulder, the lacing having parted at the back. Her hair was roughly coiled up still, but thin wisps tumbled over her face.

Oenska sat alone, and the Raskian woman quickly stood when Einya entered.

Two quick strides forward, and Einya wrapped her arms around Oenska. "I've done it."

"Done it? Done what, sweet one?"

"Given the truth to the Astrologer-Elect. I cannot wait here long—I need to go back. I promised I'd help him…"

"Help him? You're babbling." Oenska pulled Einya over to sit by the fire. "Tell me what you mean."

"He's being controlled by Pearth. We were looking the wrong way. The edict activating the Testament of the Stars, it's been signed by the Constellan Council. They'll be coming to take people away. You need to get out of here."

Oenska's hands tapped out a pattern on the table as her expression twisted with different thoughts. "Go back, Einya."

"What, why? I need to…"

"Go back. I need you to look after Tollska if this is true."

"Will you be alright?"

"Don't worry about me. I'll hide in the woods. Go to her. One of our barricades has fallen. If the guards are taking people, you need to get out of here. We can only fight them for so long, since we've no black powder weapons and only a few old bows."

As if to sketch out the urgency of Oenska's words, shouts could be heard down the street. "If you're found here then you'll never get them to listen."

Einya nodded numbly and stood. "How will this end?"

"In truth, I don't know, but if the Elect listens then maybe we will find a way."

"I'll try, but we need a plan for when it doesn't work. I need to get to my cousin."

"Tell all who might listen."

"I will…"

"Go quickly, Einya. Aisren have sent soldiers here to help us, but not many. We don't fully know why, but they will push up a promontory with us. We'll be in Gemynd soon if it works. Now, get out of here, Einya. Take my love with you."

The younger woman stood, and her gloved hands gripped Oenska's fingers tightly for a fragmented moment before she slipped away into the streets.

The warrens of Rask welcomed her, and she pressed herself into the shadowy walls of buildings as Constellan Guards ran by. Screams wailed through the streets as children were torn out of their homes. Men and women bound with coils of rope were dragged towards great wagons. It seemed one of the promontories had been cleared, as the guards moved the wagons away towards them.

One wagon ahead was being filled with Raskians, with only two guards shoving people in through the rear door of the carriage. Bare-footed people pulled from their beds, still wearing their nightclothes, shuffled toward the carriage.

Several deep breaths, staggered in gasps, burst from Einya's lips as a man's tunic was ripped away from his flesh when he tried to fight. The two guards clutched at the man, jostling him toward the carriage. A woman and two children were hurling stones at the guards.

Einya's hand pressed around the wooden hilt of her rapier, its criss-cross imprint digging deeply into her palm as she strode across the narrow street. The first incision, unexpected, thrust deep into the guard's lung. The man spattered blood from his lips instantly and crumpled to the cobbled street.

The children cowered away, but their mother surged forward and tore at the other man's hair. She screamed with sharp, stabbing fury burning in her eyes as she tugged the guard away from her husband.

Einya tore her blade from the cavity it had plunged into, warm blood slipping it around in her grip as she turned. The guard twisted to strike her, hurling her backwards and bashing the back of her skull against the wood of the carriage. A brief spike of noise slipped from her lips. The guard's fingers grasped at her neck, tearing away the neat lace ruff until it lay in tatters on the ground, the white lace soaking in the crimson puddle.

Bright ruptures of light pricked through her vision, but she leant forward anyway, pressing into the tightening fingers around her neck until the point of her blade pushed seamlessly into the guard's gut. In the hectic moments of panic that followed, Einya felt the vice grip tighten on her throat briefly, the man scrabbling at her bare skin.

He then fell back, panting on the cobbled floor, blood flowing over his doublet. The mother's arm, still outstretched, held the other guard's sword and had thrust it in and out of the man's back. A moment of uncertain silence followed, but shouts and the clatter of wagons sounded with an echoing tremolo in the narrow street.

"Come with me," Einya said, her voice rasping as she tried to drag in enough air to speak.

The woman with the sword nodded, and the small family huddled close as they pattered out of the alley together. They ran for a while, towards the buildings abutting the fields of Rask.

Curving her way around the corner, Einya pelted into a Constellan Guard in full armour. The force knocked her to the snow-mud ground. A small group of Guards had a Raskian man tied to their carriage, he was sobbing, a young girl lying loosely in his arms.

The guard looked surprised, and then something dawned on him. "You, you're from… wait! What are you doing down here?"

Einya didn't wait; on instinct, she ripped off one glove and in one fluid moment stood up, thrusting her hand against the guard's eyes. The permeation of light from her skin in the dark alley flooded the soldier's vision, and Einya stole the moment to whip her rapier up and skewer it straight through the man's neck.

As he collapsed to the floor, a shocked look in his eyes, Einya tugged the blade free, feeling the disconcerting sliding of the edge against meat. Sheathing the rapier, she slipped the glove back over her hand to hide the glow.

The now small crowd of Raskians huddled with her in the alley, untying the man tethered to the carriage. He clutched the small girl back to his chest, rain-like tears smattering his face.

"What was that glow?" he murmured, blinking as if the light still stung his eyes.

"Explaining would take too long. We've got to hide you somewhere," Einya said, frantically looking between the nearby buildings as she helped the man stand up.

She beckoned them on; the nearest large building was painted in fire-red paints and had white words of wisdom neatly arced on the side. The faint smell of spice mingled with the acrid smoke from the promontories. Inside the temple, deep bowls of incense carved with words still simmered away in the ombre light.

"Anyone here?" Einya hacked out three deep coughs after she spoke, the smoke bristling in her throat.

The mother with the sword pressed in further, finding a small ring pull in the floor that she tugged up and opened into a cramped earth-damp cellar. "In here. This is where the Word-Weaver goes if she needs to."

Einya dragged the concertina doors to the street shut as the Raskians clambered down into the musky cellar. Quickly striding back to the hatch, she leant in. "I'll cover the door with a rug, stay quiet."

She'd dragged one close by, ready to drop the hatch shut and cover it, when a hammering at the door tore through the room. Tight, frozen fear pressed into her heart and she stood with a vacant expression. A hand grabbed her wrist from within, tugging her down into the cellar. Stumbling, Einya's face landed in the dank earth, plastered with mouldering soil.

She looked up, dazed. Two Raskians dropped the hatch back into place. In a tight, crawling procession, the Raskians made their way along what looked like a narrow tunnel into the rear of the underground hovel.

She dragged herself along behind them, feeling the sodding soil soak into the knees of her dress. When there was no more room, they stopped, each of their stifled breaths grazing the neck of the nearest person.

Above, heavy booted footsteps stamped across the wooden floor and the sound of smashing urns crashed onto the ceiling above their heads.

An unknown hand gripped her fingers tightly and, in the darkness, Einya gently clung back.

Chapter Thirty-Six

*They still fight us, even when their power is crumbling. What fools
lead us now?*
~ Raskian pamphlet

"You're from Gemynd," the woman spoke with sharp
words.

Bri had been ushered to sit beneath the lantern light at the
side of the glade, and the birdsong still loudly struck at his hearing
even though he knew he should listen to the people. A small
huddle of Aisrenese folk had gathered around, and Shrynaid had
been whispering in the woman's ear. She nodded once and brushed
past the man.

"I want you to know the warmth of our woods, stranger, so
tell me your name."

"It is Briarth Arden, lady, and I meant no offence here. My
words are too honest, my mind is too simple."

She smiled at that, the golden glow still prickling in the depths of her eyes as she leant over him a little where he sat. "I am called Breyneda, and if this place you find yourself had anything like a leader, it would look like me."

"You speak in riddles, lady."

"I enjoy games, gentleman."

She straightened up, looking around the glade at her people. "He seems honest enough, simple, despite his fine words. I think he does well enough by our standards—even if he is from Gemynd."

"Such dislike of Gemynd?" Bri mumbled.

"We have reasons."

"I do not doubt."

"So, what help do you ask for?"

Bri swallowed, wondering if this was one of those moments to be circumspect. But, predictably, he spoke anyway. "I am no friend of Gemynd either, despite my blood—which is half Aisren, by the by. Anyway, I ask you to help Rask. Gemynd has broken them over their knee and holds power over them. I want that done and gone."

Her eyes stayed delved deep into his with mesmerising scrutiny. "Why?"

"Because I fight inequality where I see it and champion everyone who needs it."

"A brave fool, then," she cried out to the assembled people, and a ripple of laughter mingled with the birdsong. "Tell me more."

"Gemynd controls them, rips apart their people's lives."

"Very dramatic. Tell me specifics, not frivolities."

"Gemynd is using the Stars to hold power over them, and it will mean many deaths."

Bri saw the woman smirking, and he looked over his shoulder and saw that, behind him, Quandary had padded back out from somewhere and was stretched out by a fire.

"Gemynd does not understand the Stars. He does though," Breyneda said.

The people gathered around the fires seemed to break into little conversations, leaving Bri and Breyneda to talk.

"He follows me here and there," Bri muttered, gesturing back to the fox.

"He is star-laced, as we call it."

"Star-struck?"

"Yes, taken on by a star to move around. I think you might have known this."

Breyneda reached out one hand and Quandary padded up to her. "When the Stars fell, it took them a long time to cool, and then they pushed their energy around. This is how we have our forest haven."

Bri raised one eyebrow. "A star did this?"

"Yes, just like one pushed its energy into this fox."

Bri almost laughed. "I don't really have any words for that."

"Wonderful, isn't it? Better than keeping them holed up in a cave, or whatever it is they do in Gemynd."

Quandary had padded closer and was now squirming his way around Breyneda's arm. "So, Rask…"

Bri nodded, feeling a gentle stirring of regret in his heart. "My sister is there."

"In Rask?"

"Gemynd."

"She is part of the oppression? Is that why you left?"

The little fox shuffled from Breyneda's lap onto his, his small glowing eyes beaming up at Bri. He fussed him a bit, and then looked back at Breyneda. "She is an Astrologer, but no. She has a good heart. I left because I did something foolish that would endanger her. I spoke against Gemynd. Rask is starving at the hands of Gemynd after years of oppression in the name of the Stars. They plan rebellion, maybe it's already started, but I fear it will be short-lived. They have no black powder or canons in Rask, but in Gemynd they certainly do. This is why I am asking for help. Not just for my sister, but for the Raskians.

"I see. The Astrologer and the rebel, a good story, don't you think?"

"As long as it ends well."

"I'll do my best; we are no lovers of star-gotten power." She winked. "We'll go, but you must stay."

Bri shook his head. "No, I must return."

"It wouldn't be wise."

"Wisdom is not what I do."

"Then let me educate you in it. Think, Briarth—"

He grinned, lopsidedly. "Call me Bri."

She smiled, and nodded gently, before continuing. "Think, Bri, if you go back, you will likely make things worse for both you and her."

"I need to help her, help them—"

"Then trust her. If you want our assistance, then you will stay. It's my only condition."

Bri sighed. "Well, there's the end of my saga then."

"Oh, don't be so melodramatic. Better to have a good end to your saga than to die."

"You make a compelling point. Can I ask, when did this all happen?" He waved his free hand at the trees. "Can I see the Star?"

"One day. For now, I insist you break bread with me."

"No choice?" He grinned.

"We run a barter system, and this is the price for my help."

Bri let himself be led amongst the crowds and, as the evening drew further on, sweet, warm wine was brewed up in large cauldrons. Flutes and lyres strummed, and Bri found a joy in the simplicity that he'd never found within Gemynd. As he drifted to sleep, curled up on a soft moss bed with Quandary nested next to him, he thought of Einya and hoped she was still alright.

Chapter Thirty-Seven

We banquet so that we can look the other way while atrocities happen in our name.
~ Lord Hyther speaking to the Constellan Council

The streets were empty as Tollska crept away from the Arden banquet early. It was a few nights after the testament was ratified. The fighting in Rask had intensified in contravention of all expectation and hope. The noise from the lower settlement had pinnacled into an ongoing chorus of wails and shrieks. Banquets were thrown every night to drown the desperate clamour and hide the guilt in vats of sweetened wine.

Pearth was still out fighting, making it easy to slip away. There were only so many times Tollska could hear praise of the new edict for how to deal with Rask before she was sure she would claw someone's eyes out. She walked along the streets of Gemynd, her blue gown with sapphire gems encrusted into it blending her in with the icy-blue snow that reflected the pale moonlight.

Amongst the towering stone buildings, she felt more out of place than ever, knowing the conflict still continued in Rask but not knowing any more than that. Tollska thought most of her mother, praying that she would be alright.

She rushed through the quiet streets. In the distance, the moaning, wailing and shouting of fighting droned ever on. Tollska found what she was looking for quickly enough; the post in the ground still stood in front of the Constellan Council building.

She pressed her back against the corner of the nearest building and furtively looked around. There was only a pair of guards by the wretched figure still chained to the post now. Luskena hung low, her wilting head lolling on her chest where she had sagged forward.

Tollska stepped sharply into the street from around the corner of a building, swinging her arms purposefully as she approached the guards. "I need to speak with the prisoner."

The guards swapped tense looks. Both were carrying crossbows, with the insignia of the Constellan Guard emblazoned on their breastplates. Tollska stared at them sternly down the bridge of her nose, a hard look of petrified rock in her unrelenting gaze. "I am to find out if she will tell us more about the rebellion, and who is behind it. Or should I tell Pearth Arden you denied me?"

The guards nodded, taking one step away from the post to allow Tollska access. She smiled, thanked them with a saccharine sweetness and stepped up to Luskena. Forcing her anger and dislike of the woman away, she lifted Luskena's head with both hands. "Luskena—"

The woman croaked, it sounded almost like a twisted laugh. "Sacrificial Tollska. Do you know they call you that as some sort of accolade for all you've done? What about sacrificial Luskena? I've lost everything, too."

"Be quiet." Tollska looked around at the guards, who were thankfully talking between themselves.

"At least you're not freezing, and starving." Luskena coughed raggedly.

"I need you to tell me who else is leading this in Rask." She spoke loudly and then softened her voice again. "I need to know what is happening, I need to find something I can do."

"Destroy the Stars," Luskena's voice rasped, and she lifted her head just enough that Tollska could see her bloodshot eyes burning intensely.

Silence held for a brief moment. Tollska chewed her lip until it split and stained her teeth red. "I meant something that would stop the fighting."

Luskena spat on the stones. "Wouldn't it? No Stars, no power over us. No fighting."

Tollska huffed out a heavy sigh, uncertainty clinging at all her thoughts. "How would I even do that?"

"You'll find a way, Sacrificial Tollska." The hollow cackle of Luskena laughing sounded like the grating of iron rasping against iron. "You'd better. They are tearing down houses in Rask; how long until they tear down your mother's?"

Tollska pressed closer to Luskena, wrapped her fingers around the other woman's throat and squeezed slightly. "Chew your tongue rather than spit poison, shrivelled leech. It's because of you I'm in this bind; without you, I could do what was needed with no suspicion."

Tollska threw the other woman's head back so it bashed against the post. The guards looked over and Luskena groaned. When she raised her head, her eyes had melted into raw pleading with soggy drips seeping from her tear ducts.

Luskena splattered blood across the stones where she'd bitten her tongue. "I am not your enemy. You need to do something. Do something, Tollska."

"You risked exposing me and Einya. If it wasn't for you, I'd have the luxury of time. But you think with a fool's passion and consider only yourself. Enjoy the tower dungeons."

"Tollska, wait, please."

Luskena's words snagged at Tollska and she paused in her turn to leave. *Curses.* "What?"

"They're taking Raskians up the promontories and into Gemynd. No one knows what they'll do; I was one of the first they found. Everyone has scattered, some have even run into the woods."

Tollska nodded and whispered. "I will do something; you can be sure of that."

She strode away, not pausing to leave her parting words with the guards. "She won't speak."

There were many hours before dawn, and Tollska's forming thoughts bubbled into a strengthening idea in her mind. She kept on ploughing through the snow in the roads where it hadn't been fully cleared, focusing her mind on her plans. The moon reflected in every window she walked past, its great orb-like eye glaring at her as she walked by. A thought struck: the book Einya had mentioned. Abruptly turning, she headed towards the square with Einya's rooms on.

No light burnt inside those dark rooms. The pamphlets hadn't been removed and they flickered in the icy wind, plastered over the windows and blocking all light from outside. Tollska didn't pause, she stepped brusquely up to the door and twisted the handle. Feeling it click as the locked barrier didn't budge, she paused, taking her rapier from the carved scabbard at her hip. Placing her shoulder against the frame, she shoved hard and felt the door give way.

As she stepped inside, an acrid scent pricked at her nose and she choked down a hacking cough as the smoke filled her lungs. Tollska saw the simmering embers of a fire, burning low on the stone slab in the centre of the room and saw the low hanging cloud of smoke as the moonlight spiked through it in surreal rays of murky light.

What have you been doing, Einya? She wondered, searching quickly for the book she had come for.

Having no luck with the cabinets, she got down onto all fours and scrambled around the floor, not caring as the knees of her dress tore on the wooden floorboards. Eventually her fingers closed onto the smooth leather she wanted to feel, tugging the heavy book from under the bed as it hissed along the floor. She quickly wrapped it up in a thick scarf and headed back out into the street.

Lightness crept into in her heart as she left, glad she might be able to influence the Stars. Stronger than that, a warm hope that Einya would be free of the dangers this book held bubbled up within her, eclipsing all thought of herself. The pale-eyed visage of the woman she loved still hung within her vision. She hoped freedom from the Stars would bring some brightness back into Einya's life.

Chapter Thirty-Eight

Peace is now required to protect Gemynd, it must be achieved at any cost.
~ The new Testament of the Stars

"Is there a way out?" Einya whispered.

The boots had faded across the floor as guards had stamped above their heads and away, dust sprinkling down and into their eyes. At the back of the hovel, one man was fumbling with the planks in the wall.

Then light burst through the dark pit, the rattling of the brass ring-pull chiming as the hatch was cast aside.

"Anyone?" A voice—Pearth's voice—echoed in the little box under-room.

"I'll check again." The tap-tap of footsteps sounded as the glowing circle of torchlight carved the darkness away.

Einya felt tight breaths expand the ribcages of the two people bunched either side of her, pressing into her in the narrow space. When the torchlight fell on their faces there was a strange silence; no fuss, no shouting, just a moment where both sides regarded the faces of the other.

She turned her head to one side, showing only the mud-caked cheek.

"Raskian vagrants, Commander, curled up in the mud."

"How many?"

"Ten, Commander."

Sharp steps again, then Einya heard her cousin's acidic voice spit words. "If they burn us, we burn them until they see that ending this rebellion is the only way."

"But with them in there, Commander…"

"Do as I say."

The darkness this time was not silent as the hatch slammed back down. The man at the rear of the hideaway, no longer gentle, felt the panels but then bashed them with his fists. Children sobbed in the darkness, and Einya's voice was lost in the cacophony as smoke started to seep into the small room.

"Move, move faster," she tried to shout, voice still hoarse. She stepped on ankles and tangled in legs, trying to crawl to where the man was scrabbling with the planks. She banged her head on the ceiling above her as she moved, which already began to smell of burnt cedarwood, its scent mingling with the musky soil.

Finally, at the back, she pushed the man aside and shoved the tip of her blade between the planks. Tears and voices tore through her senses as she prised away one after the other until fresh-tasting air flowed into her lungs. She threw the planks onto the earth ahead of her. A dim light flooded through the undercroft. She moved to one side.

"Go, get moving!" Einya shouted.

The scramble to crawl through the narrow gap began, a few people crawling ahead of her, and Einya leading the rest of them through the confined earthworm-lined tunnel as the light grew and they reached a small opening in the middle of a field of crops. She slumped out onto the earth, sprawled star-shaped amongst the maize as she counted the Raskians clambering from the hole. *How had it come to this?*

After a few scant moments of dragging air into her smoke-scorched lungs, she stood. "Everyone here?"

Silent nods. All were looking back to the burning word-temple, which painted the grey sky with crimson flames. She turned to leave, sharp tears pulsing out of her eyes at the atrocity. Her cousin's order still resonated around her mind.

One hand gripped her wrist. It was the woman with the sword, her eyes warm despite the ragged collection of Raskians with singed clothes. "Thank you. Thank you for all you did."

"I..." Einya stopped and simply knelt before the woman. "I'm so sorry... for all that we've done to you."

The sword-woman shook her head, her thin robe still clung around her with words stitched into it. "Them. Not you. You will never be part of them."

"You're..."

"Jesk, the Word-Weaver. Yes."

The Word-Weaver's spare hand reached into her robes, pressing an ash-covered slate pebble into Einya's grip. "This is for you. Your new future."

The slate, warm in her frosty hand, swirled with crimson letters that pushed through the murky cinder-dust covering. *Ash-born.*

Two strong hands hooked beneath her armpits, and Einya was hauled to her feet by the Word-Weaver. The woman laid one hand gently on Einya's cheek. "Make them pay."

Einya nodded before turning to push through the tall crops away from the circle where the Raskian families clutched each other as if they would never let go again.

She made it to the winding stair back to Gemynd via an extended route to avoid the fighting, breathless and covered in blood. Her rapid ascent made her wheeze, but she didn't let it stop her despite her icy feet, which seemed to be tinged a faint hypothermic-blue.

She didn't pause at the top, rushing through the streets until she burst into the halls of the Arden manor. The rough stone floors scraped abrasively against her cut feet. Jagged breaths snagged in her throat.

Prethi was there, with a lopsided grin. He hurried over, tutting at Einya with a twisted smile still etched on his face. "Einya, it's been too long. Look at you! Scruffy as you were when we were children together, having mad-cap adventures."

Einya huffed out one further heavy breath and forced a rickety sort of smile. "Prethi, I'm so glad to see you. Is Bri hidden…?"

"As far as I know, he made me leave when he was in Parlenta."

"But Parlenta is against us…"

"I know, we'll just have to trust in his ability to survive."

Einya nodded, tearing a few strands of hair from her head as she raked her fingers through her brown curls. "Listen, I'm trying to find Tollska. Is she here?"

"Not for some days." Prethi knelt in front of her then, his warm brown eyes flitting over her cut and battered body. "Let me clean you up, at least I can do that. Look at the mud on your face, and the blood on your feet! I don't know what you've been doing, but it won't go well if you're seen like this. Your cousin was raging last she was here because something has gone wrong. No one has told me what."

Einya winced, her words rasping from her smoke-dried throat. "The unity of the settlement is broken beyond repair, and she's frightened. Parlenta wants our Stars, and Pearth will do anything to stop them."

"So, what'll happen now?"

"I don't know, but I want to stop Raskians being used as a weapon in this. Let's get out of here in case she comes back."

Prethi led her back to her old rooms in the manor, which had been left much as they had always been except for everything Einya had cleared out of them when she had moved. It felt strange, sat on the edge of her fine silk chaise longue in the opulence she'd all but forgotten she'd ever had.

Prethi went to the nearby chamber and came back at length with a bowl of steaming water, which he set down on the wooden floor.

As a gentle trickle of warm water tumbled over her feet, padded away by the soft cloth in Prethi's hands, warmth kindled within her.

She was almost loath to break the companionable silence. "Can you tell me, has Tollska been alright here?"

Prethi smiled sadly up at her as he squeezed bloody liquid from the soft cloth he held. "I've not been back long enough to say, but listen, I know you loved her and probably love her still, Einya. You were always one for unwavering loyalty, but please don't do this to yourself."

"I have to know." She felt her voice choking slightly on the words. "I've seen her a solitary handful of times, and I haven't been able to read her face."

Prethi gently squeezed his slender fingers around her ankle in a soft affectionate press of one old friend to another. "Pearth treats her well from what little I've seen, I wouldn't question it at all."

Einya leaned heavily against the post of her old bed, relieved. "It feels like I don't belong here anymore."

"In the manor?"

"In Gemynd."

"You could have left with me and Bri, at least you wouldn't have been alone."

Einya ran one hand through her hair. "Too late now. Do you think he's still in Parlenta?"

"I don't know, Parlenta has some link here. We saw trade shipments coming in from Gemynd. We didn't really get a chance to talk after that, but he sent me back here to warn you."

"The Astrologer-Elect has unwittingly traded with them, so they know we haven't used our Stars in the way they want to. You should've stayed with Bri." Einya pulled her foot away from him, even though it stung her tender skin.

Prethi smiled, not warmly, but regretfully. "Where are your old boots?"

She pointed to a large cabinet.

He returned with old soft-leathered boots and then fetched a bowl of warm water. After washing her feet, Prethi placed the sopping red cloth down in the bowl, and with a painstaking tenderness, took up a towel again and patted down Einya's feet. The man's pale fingers were tinted red. He then carefully eased Einya's feet into the worn boots.

"I know that I should have stayed with Bri, but he told me to leave. He needed you to know the danger here, that's all. Bri gave me little choice," Prethi eventually spoke.

Einya shook her head vigorously. "I keep thinking I have understood this madness, and then something else sends me spiralling. I need to find Tollska."

"Then let me come with you now and help you find her," he said, smiling. "We were always close; you, me and Bri. Let's not lose that, in these broken times."

Einya smiled, nodding, having barely comprehended until that moment how much she had ached with a quietly persistent loneliness, which Prethi seemed to be brushing away like a cobweb. He insisted on bringing her some food, and they ate a small selection of cold meats and warm breads together.

After they'd eaten, Prethi briefly stepped outside whilst Einya picked out an old, slightly moth-eaten dress from the clothes she'd left behind and slipped it on. She slid the bloody rags of the fire-damaged dress under the bed and strode towards the door.

They left the manor by the side doors out onto the balcony, hurrying down the steps into the gardens where she'd last seen Bri. They hadn't changed, except for one crucial detail that stopped her in her tracks. The three trees she'd planted there had been hacked down to their stumps and had been taken away, leaving only their wooden discs buried in the small patch of soil. Unable to stop herself, she ran to them, brushing her fingers over the concentric rings within. The sap was still drying on the bark, showing they'd only been removed recently. She tried to calm her breathing as Prethi stepped up and gripped her shoulder tenderly. What had she done to deserve this? She bit back a sob.

"When did this happen?"

"I don't know, Einya. Come on, let's go."

"Each scrap of my world here has been ripped apart. I loved these trees."

"I know, come on. We'll plant more one day, I promise," Prethi said urgently, tapping her shoulder and nudging her to move.

She nodded, numb, and her knees clicked as she stood sharply upright. They took the small circular stairwell down into Gemynd's streets and began their search for Tollska.

The Constellan Council building was locked and the two guards who stood out front told them no one was inside. Einya paused as they left; the post where Luskena had been chained was ominously empty and blood splattered the cobbles beneath it.

Prethi tugged her away again, and they slowly walked to the wall overlooking Rask, near to where Einya and Tollska had sat together.

Smoke billowed over the settlement. Like little crumpled matchsticks, collapsed huts and housing scattered the whole of Rask. The promontory in this section had been cleared, and large carriages were moving slowly from Rask up into Gemynd. Einya sighed and stepped away from the edge of the towering wall. She led the way, finding her pace slowing now, as they bee-lined straight for her rooms.

The lock on the door had been left in shattered fragments across the stone steps, and Einya felt a dangerous spike of hope pierce through her heart to think that Tollska might be waiting for her here. She pushed the door open eagerly and saw the scattered remains of her work still strewn on the wooden planks.

Prethi moved in past her quickly, his rapier drawn. "What happened in here, Einya?"

"Finding ways to speak to the Stars…"

Prethi tutted. "You've really lost yourself to the Stars, haven't you? Just like Bri and I feared."

She couldn't find anything to say to that and instead looked around the rooms, feeling a creeping disappointment at their emptiness. "She's not here."

Einya kicked aside some of the papers of her notes as she moved around. "They must have taken her, they must know she was…" Einya bit her lip suddenly, imprisoning her words within her mouth.

"She was what?" Prethi asked. "You can trust me. You know I always liked Tollska."

"She's been helping some… friends, to get some information, that's all."

Prethi's eyes widened. "What are you mixed up in, Einya?"

"I want to end the division. I'm not lost to the Stars," she spat, finally finding her words. "I am using anything I can to save those I love."

"How?"

"The Stars don't care about the control. We created this conflict. I know that because they told me."

Prethi raised both eyebrows. "How can you be sure?"

Einya nodded. "There's a book, it helped me know what to do with the Astamitra, to hear something of the will of the Stars. You have to believe me."

"I do." Prethi smiled. "The Stars caring about that always seemed an aloof, distant concept anyway. Like your brother used to say."

Einya made some noise of agreement, but her mind had drifted to the book. She skipped over the detritus on the floor clumsily and crouched on all fours, reaching into the dust carpet under the bed.

When her hand met only air and grime, she choked on a gasp, a sickly panic prickling in her throat and mouth. "It's gone, the book's gone."

Prethi looked under the bed too, as if to be sure. "Is it important? You've already spoken to the Stars, you said."

"Someone else might use it against Rask, somehow, say they can hear the Stars and then lie…" Quickly checking her hideaway, she noticed they hadn't taken all the Astamitra, just the book.

Einya sagged down onto the edge of the bed, forcing her brain to rattle through thoughts and solutions. All she could think about was the trussed-up image of Tollska, locked within the deepest parts of the Gemynd tower dungeons and branded as a traitor.

Prethi sat beside her and she slumped slightly against him while she planned what to do next. Out in the courtyard, the carriages returning from Rask began to clatter across the stones, which had been freshly cleared of their snow-blanket coverings.

Chapter Thirty-Nine

They said they would not take us, yet look at what is happening now!
~ Raskian pamphlet

The euphoria of her plan snuffed out like a fire being doused by a lashing rainstorm as Tollska realised she had no clue how to proceed and few options open to her. She had read through some of the passages, the processes seemed densely written and the only concrete point was the use of the crystal it called Astamitra. Not daring to take the book back to the manor, she had read it by moonlight in alleyways. But the fleeting nature of this meant she had not been able to fully take it all in.

Tollska froze in place in the night-shrouded alley for a breathless moment, and then turned on her heels, heading towards a small alleyway at the back of the Constellan Council chambers to find the rear door. While the front was always guarded, this small entrance was never really used. Nearby, she knew there were two huge crates where all of the used papers from the Chamber were thrown. She lifted the lid of one and tossed the bag over the edge. Looking around quickly, she then hoisted herself over the side and settled on the rustling parchment bed.

Fumbling around in the leather bag, she took out a candle and a box of tinder. It took a while, but she eventually got a spark to hold the candle in, before quickly stamping it out as it landed on a piece of parchment and began to simmer dangerously.

Tollska rested the book on her bunched-up knees and flipped it open at random, finding a page marked with a scrap of fabric.

"Transmute the will of the Stars," she read out loud, running one finger down the strange text line-by-line to familiarise herself with the process. She read through three times before the candle began to burn low, and she was sure there couldn't be too much more of the night left either. A sharp puff blew out the candle. Gathering up her belongings in the darkness, she ran her hand over her face twice to snap herself out of the vague sense of surreal disbelief that clutched at her.

Nerves accompanied her with every step towards the Star cavern, struggling to keep a brusque pace. A guard stood at the door. Resting her hand on her dagger, and slinging the bag over her shoulder again, she paused at the corner of the opposite building. Taking a deep breath, she didn't let herself think and sprinted at full pelt at the guard.

"Help, you must help. Pearth says for every guard to go to the nearest promontory, Raskians are breaking through!" she cried.

The guard didn't shift. "How? How can they be?"

"I don't know, she just said go."

"If they're breaking through, I should guard the Stars…"

Tollska shifted her weight on her feet anxiously. Then she saw her opportunity. The guard, despite his diligence, strained his head to the distance in vain to see if he could see the fighting. In a clumsy moment, she struggled to quickly unsheathe her blade, but she thanked her luck he didn't notice until she thrust the tip of her rapier against the small of his back. He yelped like a surprised dog as the tip of her blade spiked into his flesh.

"Open the door." She grabbed his hair with one hand, awkwardly steering the man.

"What, wait…"

"Open it, and I'll let you leave when I am done."

The man whimpered a little and fumbled for a set of keys on his belt. He was young, and the realisation spiked a wave of guilt through her which she quickly pushed aside. She made him step inside first when the door was open, kicking it shut behind her before guiding them both carefully down the unfamiliar corridor.

The cavern emerged, the sconce-torches flickering against the towering Star-rocks. She gulped a little then, understanding for a brief flash of a moment the majesty these inspired in the Astrologers.

Grabbing the man's hair tightly, she dragged his head up. "Take off your sword belt."

The blade clattered to the floor, and Tollska awkwardly kicked it to one side. Then, taking a moment's risk, she dropped her blade, grabbed the belt from the stone floor and quickly used both hands to tighten it around the man's hands.

Picking up her rapier again, Tollska gestured to the Star-rock closest to her. "Stand there, keep quiet."

The trembling man moved toward the Star-rock, hands half-raised.

"Please, I won't interfere," the guard mumbled.

"I won't hurt you, just keep quiet and I'll be gone before dawn." Tollska forced a ghostly little smile. "Promise."

She went about her preparation as far as she could remember from the book, flicking her gaze between the book to check her accuracy and the guard to check he hadn't moved. It took her what felt like an hour to be confident that she'd set the candles in the right place, emptied the bag of all she needed and understood everything the book required. Even then, she was far from sure, but what choice was there? It was as if she was being swept away to the bottomless sea by a pernicious tide.

Tollska shoved away the thought that her mother would be found and killed if this didn't work and wondered how long it would be until Luskena gave up locations and names.

Placing a long taper in the nearest torch-flame, it flickered into a small glow and she carried it to the candles in the circle she'd set out.

The guard watched in fascination as she blew the flame out, having lit the candles.

She lifted the small vial, hoping it proved to be the undiluted Star-blood mentioned in the book. The torchlight glimmered through the concentrated Astamitra with a shimmering light, casting the crystal-dust in a temptingly beautiful azure glow. It was a risk, but what else could she do?

She flicked the small cork off the top with her thumb, tilted her head back and tipped the entirety of the Astamitra onto her tongue. The strange fizzing sensation was instant, causing her to wretch, but she managed to force herself to swallow.

At first, the only sensation she could feel was the dragging of the gravelly crystal-dust down the inside of her throat.

Then, with a sudden tearing like a waterfall tugging someone off the top of a slippery rock, the cavern dissolved away. A cutting light poured into her eyes. Black dots drifted through the light like spirits that seemed to hover within the silhouettes of the Star-rocks. Tollska couldn't tug her eyes away or force them closed.

Suddenly, it felt like a claw had latched around her thoughts, wrenching them from her as she scrabbled to hold onto them. It was then that she lost all sense of her physical body and could only feel the black fissures in her eyes like grit stuck within them.

Her mouth was open, lungs pushing air out like she was screaming, but she couldn't hear anything other than the sudden sense of the Stars' silken voices seeping into her thoughts. It felt like warm liquid poured over her, or like a feather brushing softly over her skin. There wasn't one voice but many, clashing timbres chiming across different notes, laced with a deep rumbling thrum that scraped over her senses.

Her lips formed the same shapes over and over, against her will. "Free Rask. Free Rask."

Tollska struggled, energy slowly building pressure within her as if something might burst. It felt as if something was trying to escape into her. The light had faded, and the cavern came back briefly into focus.

Rippling nausea flushed through her, and it seemed like many days might have passed. Stabbing throbs lanced through her temples, and she tried to remember what her body felt like. It was as if she had never occupied it before.

A slithering sensation slipped around her as if a snake encased her ribcage. Flailing with her hands, she felt the stones morphed cage-like around her body, holding her high against the largest Star-rock. Weightless, she thrashed, terror coursing through her in feverish waves. Her hair felt hard, solid, fused against the Star-rock.

The last thing Tollska remembered was looking out across the cavern as the torches burnt low. The strange euphoria of falling, the giddy feeling of unbridled joy, blended with a breathless feverish tremble.

The guard ran from the cavern. Time seemed to twist into itself like the vagueness of a half-asleep, half-awake stupor. The last scrap of her memory was of a gentle hand stroking her face as obscurity and darkness took her senses.

Something lanced into her awareness, a malicious sense of someone's intention stabbing at her like hailstones lashing her face. The guard had left the door to the cavern open, and she could see a small part of the settlement.

This is the last time I'll see daylight.

The thought resonated with a certainty she couldn't shake. Outside, the crimson sun flowed over the horizon and bathed Gemynd in blood-red winter sunlight.

Chapter Forty

There is no return from failing the Stars.
~ Sepult Disren, Astrologer Elect

It didn't take long for Einya to assemble a new idea out of the chaotic web that spun through her mind. She'd absent-mindedly bit down hard on the insides of her cheeks, and a metallic blood taste accompanied her thoughts. She searched a final time for the book, tipping out contents of cabinets and scattering the bed covers over the floor. The last thing she did before she and Prethi left the rooms was to find the loose floorboard, lifting it away with a habitual protective glance at Prethi, who waited in the corner.

The crumpled card that Bri had given her those many months before was still nestled there amongst the dust.

"We need to leave." She snatched up the note and tucked it into the buttoned bodice of her gown, before moving to a table near the window and lifting her rapier from it, before strapping it around her waist.

Prethi wordlessly tailed after her as she strode toward the door. She kept a rapid pace, her heels tapping a regular drumbeat on the stone streets, guiding them via the nearest promontory. A regular tide of carriages clattered up the promontory and flowed into Gemynd. Einya ignored them and strode on, thinking only briefly that a barricade must have crumbled.

Prethi stumbled over his feet trying to keep up as he breathlessly tried to speak to her. "Where are we going?"

Einya didn't pause. "To the Star chamber. If someone has taken the book and the Star-blood then it's for a purpose: they mean to use it against us. I need to stop them."

It didn't take long to reach the door to the Star chamber, and Einya saw from a distance that it was clustered with Constellan Guards who stood blocking the doorway. The door itself had been torn off its hinges and lay abandoned in the snow by the steps to the manor above the cave.

"Step aside." Her eyes flashed hot like the blue of a carbon-lit flame as the guard didn't move. "I am an Astrologer."

"No one is to enter, there's been an accident."

"An accident? I am an Astrologer, and you must let me enter. By the will of the Astrologer-Elect."

"My orders don't come from him."

Einya stayed staring at him for a moment, hand clutched on her dagger as she considered forcing her way in. It was only when Prethi mumbled some words of sense and guided her away by her elbow that she broke the frozen gaze she held on the guard.

Carriage after carriage filled the square as they watched. Not the lavish carriages usually seen in Gemynd but looming white carriages with no windows and large padlocks battening down the rear doors. From around the corner, Einya and Prethi watched and saw the doors opened on the carriages nearest to the Star cavern.

Raskians were dragged out of the doors, bloodied, in chains, and thrown to the ground. Guards were grabbing the chains around their feet to tow them into the cavern.

"What's going on?" Prethi choked out. "I didn't expect anything like this… I hate it here; I wish I'd not returned."

"I'll get you out again one day, I promise. Come with me."

She pushed off the wall and set off at a half-jog, straight for the steps of Sepult Disren's manor, Prethi close behind her. This time, there was no pause to ring the bell; she just wrenched the door quickly open, stepping inside and thanking her luck it was unlocked. It slammed shut behind them, the frosty air of the manor clinging to their skin. No fires were lit, no torches were burning.

"Sepult, get down here!" her voice howled through the manor.

Silence was the only answer, and Einya yelled two more times before mounting the stairs. Each room she slammed the door open to was empty. She rushed through them, tearing down curtains and looking inside the large walk-in wardrobes in case he was hiding anywhere. But the place was deserted.

She returned to the entrance hall where Prethi waited, and she stormed past him.

"I hate this weasel of a man!" she exclaimed as she pounded toward the small door down into the cavern.

She was grateful, in the long run, even though she struggled at that moment when Prethi grabbed her with both arms. "Breathe, Einya, calm down. Bri wouldn't forgive me if I let you get killed."

He tried to smile, but she saw it die somewhere on the way to his lips. Einya gulped in three deep breaths, gathered her thoughts, and turned the handle to the cavern door. She saw Sepult Disren cowering on the top step, his eyes flooded with tears. She heard Prethi's exclamation of surprise, but Einya focused only on the Astrologer-Elect.

It took her a moment to find some coherent words.

"What are you doing?" she whispered, crouching beside him. "Can't you see they're taking Raskians into the cavern?"

The withered man beckoned her closer, and Einya could smell the acrid tang of strong alcohol on his breath.

"I have no power," he rasped. "I cannot stop them."

"Have you tried?"

"Quiet, please, please keep quiet."

"We're going to stop them doing whatever they are doing. You know the truth; you need to tell them before everyone regrets what is done here. Killing Raskians isn't the way to keep harmony—and loyalty—if that's what they care about."

Sepult Disren sniffed and wiped his nose on the back of his hand; his words were almost whiny in tone. "They won't *listen*."

Einya rolled her eyes. "They certainly won't if you don't try. When did you become so pathetic?"

"I just wanted you to broker peace," the man mumbled, trying to curl away into the stone again. "I didn't know it would work. I thought the book's rituals might just be symbolic. Something I could use as proof we were right. I didn't expect any of this to actually work."

Prethi pushed himself into the tight space of the spiral stairs down to the cavern, jostling against Einya. "Einya, we need to leave. If they find us here…"

"I'm not leaving, I am stopping them, so draw your sword." She turned to the Astrologer-Elect. "And you're going to help me."

Even to her own surprise, she shoved Sepult Disren and he staggered upright, extending his legs to stop himself from falling forward down the steps. It didn't take long to cajole him down the stairs in whispers and jabs with the hilt of her dagger, which she'd drawn ready.

Prethi walked closely behind her, constantly whispering in her ear and trying to persuade her to leave. Einya ignored him and strode on. As she took the steps down, Prethi's whispers grew fainter as once again, the constant purr of the Stars rose in a crescendo until it was all she could hear.

Their voices, as always, twisted around each other and twined together in a strange musical lilt. Behind it was a gurgling mess of noise that sounded like pain, even as their words spewed from her lips. *"Star-listener. Star-listener. Use the light that you took from us. Look at what they've done. We're withered to nothing."*

Three sharp breaths stabbed in her side like they had punctured her lungs as the voices laced through her mind.

They strode further down into the Star chamber. Wails, screams and groans rippled around the Star cavern. Darkness clung to the walls of the hewn-out rock underbelly, and only in the light spilling down the corridor to the outside square could Einya see the ghostly outlines of figures pinned against the twin Star-rocks. Chains rattled against the Stars.

As she tugged off the gloves, a painful flare of light burst from her hands and spiked through her eyes. The shocked remarks from Prethi and the soft moaning sobs from Sepult Disren clashed dissonantly. She ignored them, desperately trying to see through the bright flaring light into the depths of the cave.

The cavern refocused, flickering torchlight focusing her eyes on the two Star-rocks with close to thirty Raskians chained around each. Large spikes drove the rattling chains into the Star, and blood splattered down the grey stone.

In the centre of the cavern, Pearth stood, with a long rapier drawn, the tip dug into the greying flesh of Tollska's face.

"Step closer, and I will push this blade into her beautiful brain." Pearth's face was blank, unreadable, calm in contrast to Einya's heart, which struck hammer blows against her ribcage. The light from her hands illuminated Tollska, part-submerged inside the Star-rock, with only her face and limbs hanging out loosely like a rag doll. *No, please, not this!*

Einya's hands trembled, horror pulsing through her mind, the shining rays emanating from her fingers flickering across the cavern's walls. "This isn't you, cousin. You said yourself, you care for her. And all these people, what about them? Do they deserve this?"

"A small handful of lives to save us from Parlenta, Einya."

Einya lurched forward, heart frozen in terror, rapier raised.

Tollska's grey eyelids were unmoving, crystalised by the stone fragments that crusted them shut. The haunted faces of the Raskians watched her with an array of tense expressions, all of them avoiding looking at the shadow-clad figure of Pearth Arden.

"Now, cousin," the guardswoman spat, "you will help me defend our settlement."

Chapter Forty-One

*We never truly understood the Stars. This never truly stopped
powerful people from using them as weapons, political or
otherwise.*
~ Einya Arden

Einya pressed her teeth down into her tongue, slicing into
the flesh. The metal rapier hilt dug into her clenched palm as she
glared across the cavern, feeling more than seeing the light from
her hands flaring brighter as her rage boiled over within her. She
tried to hold it back. "Stop this."

Pearth's blade still pressed into Tollska's forehead, a rivulet
of crimson running down Tollska's stone-hued skin. Guards were
gathering around the woman in a semi-circle facing away from the
rock.

"Einya, really, I wish that you would understand. I truly
do."

"Understand what, your desire to push me around as your toy? Your desire to destroy lives?" Einya spat, feeling the starlight bubble up angrily within her. She couldn't hold it, and spikes of light burst across the cavern from her hands.

"What is this?" someone, presumably a guard, shouted with a shrill panicked voice. The guards huddled closer to each other, just small specks in the brightness flooding the cavern.

Einya watched her cousin step away from Tollska, even as she shielded her eyes from the light.

"How are you doing that, cousin?"

I don't know. Einya bared her teeth. "It is the light of justice, come to tear you down for all you've done to Rask."

"Justice? All this weakness that you'd have us preserve will just make us subject to a different settlement." Pearth flicked the blade of her sword away from Tollska for a mere moment, pointing at Sepult Disren scrambling into a corner.

"His mind is threaded into nothing. How can that be leadership?" Pearth snarled. "We needed Rask, we needed peace. Just a few sacrifices to show our strength, Einya, that's all it was. But it's too late for that. Now Parlenta comes, and we've no choice. You have the light of the Stars; you could help us."

"No, I won't be part of this."

The anger erupted, she had nowhere to hide it anymore. Starlight burnt through her, searing through every pore in her skin and flooding her with fear of its power. Einya charged across the floor, thrusting her light-brimmed hand at her cousin's eyes. Scraping yelps of pain tore from Pearth's lips, starlight burning her eyes and twisting a warped joy into Einya's heart. The guards scattered, shielding their eyes as the burning light flared again and again in white pulses.

The next thing she felt was the heavy weight of her cousin, flailing wildly, striking back against her in a chaotic frenzy. As Einya staggered sideways she saw guards cowered in the corners, howling in pain as light washed over them in the waves bursting from her skin.

With her energy sapped, Einya stumbled in shock against the Raskian chained closest to her, throbs of blood tipping over her hands. Pearth's rapier had thrust deep into her side.

How did I not notice?

Pearth dragged the blade back out again. The woman blinked sharply, trying to clear the light from her eyes. "Damn you, Einya, damn you and your birth-Star. I thought you would understand, I made you the next in line for power. We were going to ensure peace together, you and I. Protect us from control from others."

Einya reached down to the seeping cut at her side, the light of her hands refracting off the glistening blood. She spat on the floor, rasping heavily as the pain flooded through her as her adrenaline crashed.

"I don't want it. You're no family of mine; you didn't do this for me. You didn't do this for the settlement. Let these people go. This isn't the way to secure power. I'll help restore peace if you let them go, but not like this." She looked around the terror-filled cavern. There was fighting now, the light from her hands having dimmed. It slowly came into focus, but specks of light still floated in her eyes.

Prethi had charged as well and now lay sprawled on the stone floor with a guard standing over him, cudgel in hand.

"I looked in the wrong direction when I thought I could trust you," Pearth spat. Bloodshot rivulets had scraped deep red rivers into the white of her eyes. The guardswoman stroked one hand over Tollska's limp ankle before moving cautiously away, with her blade still raised, toward the cowering figure of Sepult.

"Stand up. You understand me, Astrologer-Elect. Help me, now; let's end this war and have some semblance of a force to fight Parlenta when they arrive," she commanded.

The frail man pressed his hands against the wall of the cavern and lifted himself slowly to his feet. Outside, the dull hammering of blades on steel armour rattled around the courtyard, and Pearth briefly glanced up towards the entrance.

The small man whimpered and curled in on himself as best he could. "Let me go, please, haven't I done enough?"

"Not yet. One more thing, one more thing." Pearth gently stroked his back where the man now feebly stood; almost tenderly, almost caring. "Then you can retire to somewhere filled with sun and peace, how does that sound? Taking your daughter with you, perhaps."

The man nodded, almost leaning against the Guardswoman.

Pearth unfolded a coarse parchment, pressing it into Sepult Disren's hands. "Do it quickly."

Einya watched, disgust carved into her face as her lips curled downwards, breathing heavily still as she tried to summon the strength to move. *But what can I do? The light has faded.* She felt sick, and the room seemed to spin around her. She pressed harder onto the deep cut in her side, feeling Tollska's slender foot against her cheek with a lingering residual warmth. Managing to push herself up off the Star-rock, she limped towards Pearth. "Don't do it, please, don't do it… Pearth, let him go."

The Astrologer-Elect's whole body trembled, and he looked to Einya with a pleading expression that sagged like melted wax.

"Please, don't do it. Think of their lives," she said again, but then a guard ran down the corridor towards them, fracturing Einya's attempts entirely.

"Commander Arden, the Aisren army have filled the square. We're surrounded."

"Sepult, do it now," Pearth spat.

The Astrologer-Elect read the parchment, which seemed to have a Parlentan seal stamped upon it. His face slackened, hung in rough misery.

"In their eyes?" he asked, expression full of horror.

"Yes, in their eyes," Pearth spoke, distracted for one moment.

Einya grabbed her opportunity, ripping her rapier from her sheath and thrusting it at her cousin's neck. "Pearth, let them go. Even if you do this, there will be no guarantee it will help against the Parlentan threat. How would you live with yourself after?" The tip of the blade wavered slightly; she struggled to keep it steady in her hands as the pain ached in her side. "Let them go," Einya rasped.

Pearth scowled, rubbing her hand over her bloodshot eyes. "Thrown in a cell by Aisren, enthralled by Parlenta? There's only one choice, Einya. We need to defend ourselves."

Shouts outside rose in a crescendo. Pearth's reddened eyes were wide, the woman's hissing breath ragged and unnatural. "Sepult, do it, and do it now or we'll all die."

Einya staggered forward a little more, as best as she could, rapier pressing at the edge of Pearth's neck. The pain leeched further through the side of her torso, the Stars whispering comforting lullabies in her ears. "Cousin, let me fix this… it will save lives. Isn't that what you care about?"

"Be quiet."

A guard ran at her from the shadows then, and Einya twisted around, excruciating fire ripping through her wound as she thrust her blade clumsily through the approaching man's shoulder.

She staggered towards the corridor away from the guard, almost tumbling over herself and halting abruptly. Outside, the press of Constellan Guards holding the door amassed like a tide waiting to surge into the cave, the clash of fighting almost on top of them.

Stay, Star-sister, stay. We cradle her for you. The Star's voice was clear, crisp and cold in her mind. It felt like the power of the words tugged her back toward them. She couldn't tell which Star-rock thrust the words into her mouth, but she coughed them out and they clung to her as children clutch tightly to stop a parent from leaving.

Loud, desperate screamed words suddenly spiked through the air. Sepult Disren's usually quiet voice ripped through the cavern. The guards seemed to stop, ignoring her as a strange glow permeated through the cave. *What now?*

Einya clattered back down the corridor in a whirlwind of movement towards the Stars, her shaking legs threatening to buckle beneath her. She staggered against the rough stone walls, skin tearing, still clutching her abdomen as the blood streamed over her fingers.

In the confusion, she saw Prethi had thrust a knife through his attacker's stomach and scrambled to his feet. He was sidling around towards her at the edge of the cave. She lurched forward a little further, hoping to reach him before she collapsed. It felt like the only thing holding her up was the radiating power of the Stars, guiding her like a marionette.

The Astrologer-Elect was smearing the crystals of Astamitra into the eyes of the Raskians in large quantities, one hand gripping a bowl of crumbled Star-rock.

Pearth's rapier twisted into the nape of his neck. The thrumming hum of the Constellation's bright power rose with a crescendo.

Einya's hair stood on end as the feeling of the Stars' power being tugged out of the stone and thrust into the chained Raskians bristled around the cavern.

Einya choked and gasped suddenly. The voices were back. Rasps of the Constellation's screams as their light was ripped away screeched through her ears. Doubling over and sinking to her knees, she forced her eyes upwards as they streamed with stinging blood that suddenly leaked from them.

Pulses of words from the Stars blanched through her mind. *Help us. They kill us, steal us, make us into beasts.*

Blood ran rivers down the cheeks of the Raskians and their bodies writhed, screaming in their stone jails. Sepult Disren, with his blood-stained fingers, stroked each Raskian from the edge of their hairline to the tip of their nose. With each gentle caress, the screaming silenced.

Unable to move, pain stabbing through her side, Einya looked up.

A wrangled frozen horror etched onto the closest Raskian's face, as her hair drifted like falling feathers to the ground and her fingers mangled into long stony talons before her eyes. The woman's remaining skin shifted from pallid-white to a mottled patchy grey as Einya watched from where she lay, wheezing on the floor. Einya shuddered, one thought bubbling through her mind: *Is this the difference between asking for the Star's power, and having it forced on you?*

The luring whispers of the Stars blew like wind into her ears as Einya managed to raise herself from the ground and flounder towards her cousin, her star-lit hands casting their biting light through the shadows ahead of her. A final hiss spewed from her lips and the last Raskian simultaneously as the Astrologer-Elect's touch reached the tip of their nose.

The cavern plunged into a newly-dawning silence as if the Stars had spat out one last breath with the dregs of their energy that had frittered away into the chained Raskians.

Chapter Forty-Two

Death is just another word, weaving us on our journey.
~ The Word-Weaver of Rask

After the Raskian's screams had been snuffed out, a lumbering silence shifted its heavy bulk around the cave, quashing all noise. Einya shuffled one foot in front of the other, seeing her light cast over the figure of Sepult, pressed against the wall of the cave. All around her, the warped, rib-cage bared figures that used to be Raskians hung limp against the Star-rocks. Parts of their skin had fallen away into the dust of the cavern.

Sagging briefly to her knees, Einya could see the trestles of hair carpeting the stone cave floor, and amongst it, the flesh from their fingers which had also corroded away.

Her heart burnt in painful compassion, reaching out to the nearest wretched Raskian hanging there. Her eyes blazed in rage, and she glared at Pearth, who stood looking upon her work.

"What have you done?" Einya's words stung against her cracked lips as she spat them out.

The silence breaking seemed to bring with it a tide of tumultuous action, and Einya pried herself from the floor once again. Constellan Guards were throwing their blades to the floor, Aisrenese pushing into the cavern with a group of Raskians behind them.

A warm arm scooped through hers and heaved her upright, Oenska's herbaceous scent filling Einya's senses as the older woman helped her to her feet. The Raskian woman grinned at her despite the strange situation, and Einya thought she must be marvelling in seeing her surprise. She sagged against the older woman gratefully.

"I can't hear the Stars, for the first time in months they won't speak through me. It's like they said a last farewell and left. I think they might be dead." Her voice trembled.

Oenska wrapped her up even tighter as she helped her cross the cavern towards Tollska's limp body. *Please let her be alright...* Einya grasped the woman's ankles, relieved to see her raven hair still clung to her head and to see her skin its natural colour.

"They kept her safe, the Stars I mean..." Einya rasped, looking up at the Star-rock in wonder and reaching up to Tollksa. The moment did not last long enough.

Clattering boots stamped down through the corridor and sword blades bounced off the stone walls as the fighting approached. A wave of Aisrenese warriors tore into the cave. They stood over the small handful of Constellan Guard, holding blades over them until the guards dropped any weapons they still held.

Panic shot through her, and Einya cursed her brief distraction as she saw Pearth twist a blemished iron key in the lock of the chains on the centre stone. She began pulling them free so the metal collars around the Raskians' necks were no longer pinned to the Star-rocks.

Einya grasped hold of the fragments of time this gifted her, as the stone-grey bodies of the Raskians fell to the floor. She untangled herself from Oenska, who wordlessly pressed a dagger into Einya's hands. Armed, she stumbled towards Pearth. Her teeth scraped against each other as she clenched her jaw through the pain, throwing herself at her cousin's body and grabbing her in her arms before thrusting Oenska's dagger against the woman's neck.

Einya's feet slipped across the icy cavern floor as Pearth shoved her away. Staggering back, bending her knees, she sprung back forward. The incision from the rapier in her side barely registered as Einya smashed her cousin around the head with the hilt of her dagger.

As the woman fell, Einya dug her heel into Pearth's bare skin, plunging her blade down into her cousin's side, relishing the gasping squeal it provoked.

She barely noticed the stamping of boots surround her. The Aisrenese formed themselves in an arc around the Star-rocks. Pearth struggled in Einya's grip.

"It's done, just stop." Einya gripped tighter, drawing out the dagger and placing the tip against her neck again, whispering roughly in her cousin's ear. "I won't let you go this time."

A tall Aisrenese soldier with tightly braided lavender hair stepped closer to Einya, his sword raised. "Take your blade away from her throat."

Einya glowered, unwilling to release her prey. "This is the head of the Constellan Guard, she caused all this."

The man spoke gently, his words strangely calming. "I see that. But let us do this. She'll drown in the blood from your wound before you manage to kill her with that blade. Allow me. Please."

The Aisrenese soldier placed his blade at Pearth's stomach.

"Step aside, give us that woman."

Einya didn't move, desperately clutching on to her ebbing anger. This was her revenge; no one would take it.

"This woman took everything from me. The Raskian lady embedded in that rock there is destroyed because of it. I love her, and now she's locked in stone." Einya felt her voice rip against the inside of her throat as she coughed out her words; she didn't look at the Aisrenese man but instead looked to where the feeble form of Tollska hung. The Stars were unusually silent and whispered nothing.

Einya only tore her eyes away from Tollska when warm skin brushed against her shoulder where the rags of her dress had frayed away.

Oenska's wrinkled fingers gently clasped around Einya's wrist, and the ageing lady smiled gently despite the streams of tears tumbling over her waxen cheeks. "Go to Tollska, don't let your life be marred by this. My heart aches too, but this isn't the way, as you know."

Looking back to the Aisrenese soldier, Einya raised her blade.

"She's yours, but I have a condition. Lock her in the cavern, collapse the door and the tower on top with this woman and leave her with those she killed. Let her live with what she's done."

"I did all this to save my people," Pearth rasped, squirming in Einya's tight grip, "to save our Stars from Parlenta. Good luck when they come for you."

"That we can agree on, as long as you let me check them for life first," the purple-haired man said.

Einya nodded and lowered her blade while the Aisrenese man raised his and beckoned another guard over to bind chains around Pearth's wrists. Tollska's mother wrapped her arms around Einya and supported her as she limped over to the central Star-rock, and Einya felt a warm bubbling gratitude permeate through every inch of her.

"I wish I could've helped them," Einya mumbled, struggling to keep her eyes open.

Oenska's footsteps faltered as Einya leant heavily against her, breath hissing out of her lungs. "Go to Tollska, try and…"

Einya nodded, numb, as she weakly staggered the last few feet. The glow from her hands was faint as a wind-flickered candle as she slumped against the rock.

As she stood beneath Tollska, Einya looked up and saw her familiar face beset in a stony petrified grimace.

"Let her fall to me, Stars, please," Einya whispered, a fearful tremolo in her voice. She knocked one fist against the frosty rock, pain shooting through her fingers at the impact. "*Please.*"

A rough sandpaper voice scratched through her senses at last. *Take her away, Star-sister.*

The Star-rock crumbled away, fragmenting into a gravelly-rain that clattered onto the floor and the fallen Raskians around her feet. Tollska's weight began to lurch forwards. Einya held out her arms to catch her, but she felt someone step sharply up beside her.

It was the guard who often brought her food, only he seemed to have discarded his guard clothes for a plain coat and a hollow smile that shattered her heart a little. As Tollska's slender form slipped from the embrace of the Star-stone, Malthis scooped the falling woman into both arms, holding her out to Einya.

She held out one hand, with its star-glow almost smothered out, and ran her fingers over Tollska's face. Leaning in, she rested her forehead against Tollska's and breathed in as if her inhalation would keep her lover with her even now. Oenska stood so close that Einya could feel her breath against her cheek as well, as the woman clung to her daughter's slate-like hands.

"She breathes so faintly, but she breathes." Einya's voice still trembled. At least there was some faintly kindled hope.

Around them both, the Aisrenese soldiers were lifting the bodies of the wounded and carrying them into the courtyard. The lavender-haired Aisrenese commander approached again, a soft sweet smile simmering on his lips. "Lady, will you leave here? It's best we go."

Einya looked up from where she stood, stooped over Tollska, her blue eyes bright in the sunlight. "Why are you in Gemynd?"

"We were asked to help, Lady, but you should leave."

"Tell me why you helped, please."

"We want to make sure the Stars are not misused to falsely clutch at power. Now please, leave it with us."

Einya inclined her head in a minuscule nod, and the lavender-haired man gestured towards the entrance of the cave. The procession out of the cavern was slow, both Einya and Oenska still clutching onto Tollska as they moved away. In a last private whisper to her, the Constellations twined their voices into a tuneful farewell. She walked slowly, feeling the burn of her wound getting worse. As she reached the door, their long simpering moan sputtered into a breathless gurgle in its dying embers.

As they stepped out into the courtyard, the gentle cinders of her glowing hands flickered out, the sapphire glow around her skin fading away entirely. It was there in the courtyard, in the pale winter sunlight, that Einya and Oenska cocooned themselves around Tollska as she was laid out on the stone slabs. They both whispered and called her name, the two women's hands intertwined together over Tollska's chest, which rose and fell with the faintest of breaths.

Chapter Forty-Three

Gemynd needs a strong voice to speak against the Parlentan
threat. That voice belongs to me.
~ Commander Pearth Arden

The sun brought a welcome warmth, adding to the cosiness of the heavy blanket that had been draped over Einya's shoulders. She watched everything, focusing on the smallest details of activity to avoid wincing as an Aisrenese surgeon stitched up the slice in her torso. Her free hand clutched Tollska's fingers and held them in her lap. Oenska sat opposite, similarly draped in a blanket and holding onto her daughter's wrist. Everything seemed to move slowly around them. Prethi sat close by Tollska as well.

When Einya's wound had been tended to, she slowly stood. "I'll be back in a moment."

Oenska just nodded, eyes staying on Tollska's still body.

The Astrologer-Elect sat alone, looking only at the icy cobbles. The elderly man's grey tangled hair blustered in the wind.

Stumbling over with clumsy steps towards Sepult, Einya crouched down, wincing slightly as the wax thread stitches pulled against their holes.

The man spoke before she found any words to say. "They will give me a trial, they said. I will be judged by a Council of appointed Raskians for all I have done."

Einya nodded, teeth chewing into her lower lip. "Sepult, I don't understand why. I gave you the route to peace; I gave you the information you wanted. What did you do this for; why did you follow what my…" She swallowed. "What Pearth wanted?"

When Sepult looked up at her, it was like she gazed into eyes filled with black ice, and a soul that was flickering out. "Einya, must you rip me apart even more? I see all the bodies, I see what I've done."

"I just want to know why it was worth all this…"

"She was losing control; she was losing the battle. Especially when Aisren arrived. This was a way to regain control."

"I don't understand how this gains her control, and why you would help her. Just because of blackmail?"

The man smiled, the empty smile of someone with nowhere left to store the darkest shadows of their life. "I had Luskena with a beautiful and intelligent Raskian woman who I fell for dearly. When she died, they kept Luskena in Rask. She was the last part of my shattered love in this world, and it broke my heart."

Einya ran her hand over her face, trying to rattle thoughts into a coherent list. "I don't understand. Surely you respect Raskians in some way if you loved a woman from Rask, so why persecute them?"

Sepult Disren slowly rocked his head from side to side, seeming to creak as he did so. "I walked a fine line, tried to make your cousin turn a blind eye to Luskena. Then my daughter burnt a manor down, she was seen."

"I know…"

"There was no hiding from it after that. Pearth knew too, and they took her away. Pearth threatened to kill her or ruin me. I clung to what I had, became your cousin's puppet to try and keep Luskena alive, and kept the last comforts a lonely old man has left."

Einya took a deep breath, placing one hand gently on Sepult's hand and stroked her thumb across his wrinkled skin. "I promised I would protect you. I will say all of this in your defence if it will help…"

Sepult just smiled, tearful, as he lifted his shaking hand and clutched Einya's fingers softly. "Thank you, thank you for this last kindness."

She smiled back, but it felt empty. Her eyebrows pinched together in a sympathy that throbbed within her as much as her wound did.

"Einya, you will be the Elect our settlement needs," Sepult said.

She gripped his shoulder tenderly, resisting the urge to violently shake her head. "Do you want me to find Luskena for you?"

"No. She will be dead now, like as not. I do not wish to see her that way." He took his hand away and dropped his gaze back to the floor. "I'd like to be alone now."

Einya moved her lips to speak several times before resorting to silence, standing to leave. She squeezed his hand gently before shuffling away.

Slowly walking to the cavern door, the stitches in her wound pulling uncomfortably. She turned, taking one last glance at Sepult Disren. A precise crimson line dug deeply into his pallid throat and he lay slumped upon the cobbles. His hand clutched a small knife, a crimson pool spreading around him as a look of peace laced itself into his expression and he died upon the icy stones with no one beside him.

Einya tried to say something, but all sound slipped away from her with a cavernous sadness as she saw his frosty-azure eyes still seemed to leak with tears, but no foggy breath burst from his lips. A sadness clamoured through her that she could not find words for.

Nothing more to do, she turned, hobbling back down through the corridor to find Luskena's body. She had to know for sure. It was the least she could do, for Bri and for Sepult. She limped painfully through the rows of Raskians laid out on the stones of the cave. All the bodies had cracked grey eyelids and skin blemishing from its natural colour into a pale stone hue, which seemed laced with a translucent glow. *Strange.*

Pearth was under the guard of four Aisrenese soldiers, wearing an icy disinterested expression as if she was bored instead of imprisoned. Einya didn't look toward her for long, instead turning back to the bodies. It didn't take long to find what she searched for. On the familiar form of a woman's withered body, she saw what she half-dreaded to find, folded in the ragged cloth of her dress: Bri's silver tree pendant.

Luskena's stone-like claws clutched at it as if it had been her last thought as the Star-rock magic snaked through her. Einya knelt painfully, gently running one hand over the woman's face and whispering a few words in a sort of death blessing. It took a few moments to prise the tree away from the bony fingers and lift the leather cord from around her neck. Einya clutched it close, thinking of the pain this would bring Bri. Straightening, she shuffled away and found her rapier lying on the floor and scooped it up in her spare hand, wondering how much more of this sadness she could take. The thought didn't stay for long.

A howl, piercing and shrill, lacerated through her thoughts. A strange luminescence stabbed through the chamber's darkness, accompanied by bones scraping across the stone floor. She looked around, panicked, to see a strange lumbering movement in the shadows.

Tollska was Einya's first thought, panic welling up inside her.

The Raskian bodies were twitching; one rolled over and pressed itself up onto all fours, causing the surgeons to scatter away from the writhing figures. The sixty Raskians laid out were all staggering upwards at varying speeds, bright piercing eyes with the same light that once inhabited Einya's hands bursting from within their sockets.

Not this. Einya staggered back from the gyrating, bone-grinding body of Luskena, which rose in front of her. She turned, getting ready to run as terror twisted through her.

The Aisrenese soldiers scrambled to get their weapons drawn, but the stony bodies of the fallen Raskians shifted as fast as light. One nearby beast snuffed out like a candle in one location only to snap into view behind a soldier somewhere else, digging sharp stone talons into the ripping flesh of the soldier from behind before the man could react. Einya flinched away as the soldier's body crashed to the floor in front of her.

The Aisrenese and guards alike had scattered as the fallen Raskians surged around the cavern. Only Pearth rose, slowly.

You knew. Einya's realisation boiled through her in a fresh wave of rage. *This was her plan. How did I not see this?*

Einya dashed past Pearth in her frantic sprint, desperate to get to Tollska outside, her wound still aching as she ran. A sharp smash struck against her shin, and Einya toppled over the outstretched leg of her cousin.

Pearth stood, chains clacking around her wrists. Grabbing one short shard of a broken sword from the floor, she rushed at Einya, who lay wheezing on the stone floor. She did not even manage to evade, let alone fight back.

The woman's legs squeezed around Einya's waist, Pearth dropping down and pressing her weight onto Einya's stomach so it was a struggle to move, prone on the ground. The guardswoman's heavy sword belt bashed against her wound.

"I won't let you leave. When Parlenta comes to take our Stars like I told you they would, you will suffer along with me. At least, thanks to Sepult, we will have some protection. Survival at any cost, Einya."

Gasping around the stabs of pain, Einya managed to cough out her words. "Sepult is dead because of what you made him do."

A sharp strike from Pearth's fist smashed into Einya's temple, scattering her vision with stars. She was vaguely aware of the beasts surging up the corridor out into the sunlight and felt a stab of fear for Tollska and Oenska. She had to get to them.

Gasping, Einya hooked her fingers into claws and dug them into the other woman's eyes. Einya snarled, pressing deeper, Pearth's hands flying up to her face to try to bat Einya away but she only managed to push away one hand; the other was still gripped around the guardswoman's head. Einya pressed upwards with the momentum, forcing her thumb further into Pearth's eye socket until her cousin's face slackened, gunge from her eye leaking over Einya's fingers.

Blood-rivulets clung to Pearth's damaged eye where she lay, rasping. Einya, clumsy with pain, rolled onto her feet and straightened, standing over her cousin. "Don't follow me, else I'll cut your other eye out!"

Pearth looked up, one eye half shut, her teeth slightly bared. "All I did, I did for peace, cousin. One day, you'll see."

Einya's head shook in two simple turns. Grabbing Pearth's chains, she rammed the tip of her rapier through the links into a thin crack in the stone floor so the other woman couldn't stand up.

"Your peace is no peace at all, but persecution based on a lie you'd rather believe." Einya turned, dashing away as best as she could with no more thoughts of her cousin.

There was a crescendo of noise as she staggered up the corridor. The square spiralled into madness, beasts battling soldiers in a chaotic mess of bodies, and Oenska shouted as she crouched protectively over Tollska with a blade raised. "We've got to run, Einya!"

Oenska bounced to her feet with surprising agility as Einya ran lopsidedly up to them, and between them, they hefted Tollska up.

Einya flicked her head wildly around, searching for Prethi amongst the fleeing crowds of people. *Where is he?*

Oenska shouted again. "No time, come on!"

Einya nodded, and they scrambled to start moving.

Out of the chaos, Malthis ran toward them, hollering: "Let me help you. Go to the cavern, we can try block up the door."

He lifted Tollska's legs whilst Einya and Oenska held up her torso and they quick-stepped away from the square. Scraping of swords on stone and bone on metal echoed loudly, several of the stone-beasts shifting from place to place like forks of lightning. They had to stop several times to defend themselves from beasts surging toward them. Einya blinked away the tears of pain, dredging the last of the starlight she could muster out in flickering flashes that seemed to push the beasts away from them.

What limits are there to this? Einya thought, feeling strangely powerful again. It wasn't as strong as before, but it was definitely still there. *Will their light ever truly leave me?*

They staggered onward, awkwardly moving further into the cavern. Inside there was a chaotic tumbling of bodies. As they approached, a cluster of the grey-fleshed beasts sliced their stone claws effortlessly through the chains holding Pearth. Einya saw it, looking back across the cavern. The question *how* burnt brightly in her mind; how could Pearth control them?

The answer came too quickly. Pearth held an unstoppered vial all too familiar to Einya, and she downed the entire thing. The Guardswoman's hands, mutating into a mottled grey hue, stroked the closest Star-beast between the still human-like eyes. The beasts sniffed at her, dog-like, before following the woman from the cavern, fighting as they went.

The Aisrenese man with the lavender braids shouted orders, gesturing to the soldiers to retreat out of the cave. Several soldiers scrambled to keep the stone-talons away from their necks. One woman raised a small shield to block a fast swipe and slashed her sword at the closest rock-like beast, but her arm jarred backwards as the sword ricocheted off the beast's stony flesh.

"Come on, Einya!" Oenska screamed again, more frantic now.

Einya turned, just as a glaring light snapped up out of nowhere, accompanied by the scraping rasp as a stone-fleshed beast sprung from the shadows, blocking their way. Her own light was fading, and the beast lurched closer as it did.

"Stop," the beast spoke with a phlegm-like rattle, as it lumbered toward them.

Einya managed to find her voice, just as the beast lunged. "Up the stairs to the manor."

The three of them stumbled up onto the lower steps, where the doorway gaped open just above them, but they struggled to carry Tollska up the spiral steps. The beast's stony feet scraped across the floor, slavering, sniffing, rattling through the creature's body. The lacerating grinding of the beast's talons on the walls of the cavern echoed after them tauntingly. It knew it could catch them if it wanted to, but it seemed to delight in toying with them.

"Keep going, I'll block the way!" Einya yelled, pushing them further toward the steps. "Give me your blade, I'm unarmed."

Malthis nodded and held out the hilt of his rapier toward Einya before wrapping his arms around Tollska's torso and heaving her backwards up the winding stairwell with Oenska and Einya turning to guard his retreat.

Oenska tugged a blade from her belt, and they stood shoulder to shoulder as they listened for when Malthis had opened the door and dragged Tollska through it, before slamming it shut behind them.

In a fragmented moment, a crazy thought grabbed her, and Einya tugged the last vial of Astamitra from her pocket, bit away the cork and swallowed the Star-blood. It took only a fractured second for the familiar feeling of light to sear through her body as her hands emanated undimmed starlight again.

The sensation of the Astamitra rippled through her veins like fire. She thrust her hands out as the beast pelted towards them, the fissures of light glancing off its stone-like exoskeleton.

"Go," Einya breathed out, as she raised one arm to spike her light out across the cavern in a phosphorescent arc. She began to back up the stairwell, facing downwards with her eyes scanning the darkness.

Suddenly, the stone-beast whirled into her at speed, its radiating eyes tracking light through the cavern as it scrabbled at her. It glowed a sickly-green hue, which washed over Einya as she tried to push the stony figure backwards. The flaking pebble-skin peeled away from the hairless scalp, like shingle skittering off a mountain.

Faster than her, its claw-like fingers clenched around her neck. Einya's breath grated in her throat, as the air was crushed from within her. Her own wrangled voice cried out as the sharp prongs of the beast's fingers scratched her chest, but she managed to twist enough that the slash didn't pierce straight through her.

Einya barely heard the footsteps tramping back down the stairs. A hefty shove bashed her aside. She saw Oenska slam into her, tearing the creature away. Einya struggled to coax air back into her lungs, thrusting herself forward to help the older woman.

Einya cast the stabbing glow into the darkness, just in time to see the blood-coated stone talons plunge deep into Oenska's heart. The beast dropped her to the floor as the light surging out from Einya's hands blasted into its eyes. *One last time.*

Seizing the moment, Einya cut the rapier upwards and drove it into the creature's ribcage. The point stabbed through the crumbling stone skin, its grey waxy flesh eroded apart, and tepid entrails tipped over Einya's hands. The creature's eyes, still bright as Constellations, were only inches from her own. The last piteous snarls of the beast turned into a soft wail as it sagged to the floor of the large undercroft, and Einya's hands settled into a softer glow again.

She stood up, feet slipping in the blood creeping across the stones. Her spare hand fumbled against the uneven rocky wall, finally finding it and supporting herself as she rested against it.

Only then did she look down at the gash across her chest: four glistening, sharp-raked scratches. Her breath rasped, vision oscillating in and out of focus. Einya tried to find one small detail in the cavernous room as her mind lost its clarity and everything blurred. She dropped to her knees and crawled to Oenska's side. Despite everything, the woman was laughing, her eyes rich with warmth as she feebly lifted one hand to Einya's blood-stained cheek.

"I know," Oenska gasped out between wrangled chuckles. "That you will make her happy, and for that, I'm eternally grateful. I only wish I could have spoken to her again, and that we all could've eaten cake together again on the shores of the forest river, just like we used to do."

Einya gripped Oenska's hand tightly, trying desperately to press the last dregs of starlight into the woman's wound, hoping it might work like that too. It didn't. She leant down and kissed the dying woman's forehead just as the last breath rasped from Oenska's broken body.

Chapter Forty-Four

The aftermath was quiet, I wish it had remained so.
~ Einya Arden

Einya's legs trembled as she trudged up the stairs in the silent aftermath. In the towering hall of the manor, Malthis had knelt, his knotted black hair falling over his face as he looked down at Tollska, whose head rested against his shoulder. He held her up as best as possible, only lifting his head as Einya pushed through the small door from the cavern.

She caught a glimpse of herself flitting into the large mirror in the hall. Her earth-like complexion was splattered in blood and she felt her jaw still locked together.

Malthis' pallid face looked up at her, his eyes wet like morning dew. "What now? Do we help the other people?"

She ran her tongue over her mud-cracked lips until they were no longer stinging. No time for mourning now; they needed to move. "No, I need to get Tollska somewhere safe. We eat something, and then we need to get away from here. Look after her whilst I get some food."

"Away to where?"

"I don't know. Out of Gemynd, out of Rask."

"I've never gone that far—"

Einya cut him off. "I didn't expect you to come, but I have to get her out of all this."

Malthis nodded. "What about the woman with the grey and purple hair?"

Einya tried to spit out some words, but in the end could only shake her head. "Her name was Oenska."

She looked away, staggering through a door off the main hall, and eventually weaved her way through the small warren of rooms to the kitchen. Setting about the two tasks she focused herself on to keep herself moving, she first grabbed a cloth from the side and dampened it in a large basin of water on the side. Hissing as she cleaned the shallow rips across her torso, she clamped her teeth on the tip of her tongue to keep from crying out.

After tying some rags around her chest, she emptied a hessian sack of its potatoes and they careened away across the stone slabs. Into the sack she stuffed bread, cold meats wrapped in linen, pies, a few bottles of juice and a dozen apples. Throwing it over one shoulder, she painfully dragged herself back to the hall.

"We need to move. I don't think we'll manage well if one of the stone Raskians finds us now," she informed Malthis as she entered.

Malthis had laid Tollska back down on the floor, bunching his cloak up under the Raskian woman's head. "I have an idea. Will you help me bring Oenska up here? Then, when we're ready and by the two big doors, I'll get one of the carriages in the square and we'll put them in the back. I'll go with you, get you out of Rask."

Einya nodded. "Thank you, Malthis."

Malthis smiled faintly and unbuttoned his velvet overcoat and threw it to the floor. He then took a torch that blazed low from a bracket on the wall and headed down the stairs, Einya following behind with one hand resting on the man's shoulder in the darkness.

At the base of the stairs, they set down the torch and awkwardly wrapped their arms around Oenska. Carrying the body up felt to Einya like swimming against a tidal current.

Einya's cuts and wound stung viciously by the time they laid Oenska down on the stone slabs beside Tollska, but she focused only on her tears at seeing the two marble-like figures of mother and daughter side by side. She felt faint, but the cold air at least kept her awake.

Time sloped away quickly, and she only noticed her mind had drifted when Malthis gently touched her elbow and smiled. "I went and got the carriage... if you're ready? The square is empty, no beasts—thankfully. The Raskians must have followed the Aisren soldiers, and the beasts after them."

"Some luck at last." Einya managed to smile a little. "Let's go."

Lifting Tollska and Oenska was heavy work, and as they settled behind the horses, Einya was rasping and wheezing as if the hands of the beast were still around her neck. Malthis clutched her shoulder briefly to steady her, and then clicked his tongue at the large shire horses until they shuffled onwards out of the eerily empty square. Einya settled herself in the back, holding Tollska close to her and murmuring to her softly.

As they trundled closer to the promontory, Einya looked out the side of the carriage as the silence of the streets was ripped away by frantic, throat-grating shouts. The promontory was carpeted with bodies, and the stone-skinned beasts were scattering Gemyndians and Raskians alike with effortless strikes. Their rock claws were tearing into flesh, leaving twitching men, women and children on the cobbles. The carriage lurched as Malthis hurried the horses on, and the wheels clattered unsteadily onwards. Einya closed her eyes briefly, forcing away the guilt of leaving these people. But what could she do, barely staying awake as it was? Dregs of adrenaline and starlight was all she had.

Upon the promontory, Aisrenese soldiers slashed and pierced the beasts with their curved blades, most blows skittering off the stone-hardened skin but the occasional blade pierced through. Close by, a small unit had pulled doors out of their frames and were forming a wall with them propped against carts in the street. Gemyndian citizens, in all their fine gowns and flower-stitched shoes, were scrabbling to get through before the barrier closed the way to them.

"The carriage won't fit through." Malthis' voice quivered with panic. Einya gently eased Tollska down to the floor and staggered forward, gripping the splintered frame of the carriage to keep herself steady. "We'll have to go to another; turn around before we get too close. We'll have to go faster and keep away from the creatures."

Einya saw the fear frozen in the young man's eyes as he looked around at her briefly. "I don't understand why the Constellan Guard aren't here helping."

"Because they're under the control of my despotic cousin."

"Why would Commander Arden leave us to all this…"

"Focus, we can talk about this later. Turn the carriage."

Einya crouched back down by Tollska as the clatter of the vehicle sped into a cantering pace toward the northernmost promontory. Her heart tripped as she settled down and stroked Tollska's flaring hot forehead. How would she explain this all to her?

Einya shut her eyes and let her mind drift into nothingness for a short blissful respite from her thoughts, but instantly snapped awake and looked up again when Malthis called out to her that the north promontory was clear. She hauled herself up to the open front of the carriage again, her legs vibrating beneath her as she moved.

Malthis tugged the reins so the horses tentatively tiptoed their way down the sloping stone bridge, beneath turrets of smoke still spiralling from the burning settlement. As they eventually reached the bottom, Einya saw the stacked-up carriages and debris of a barricade still in place. Pointed across were several long pikes.

"Let me deal with this." Einya squeezed Malthis' arm and clambered awkwardly over into the seat next to him, taking a quick glance back to make sure Tollska was secure.

As they approached, a man stepped out onto the platform above the barricade. "You're not welcome here, Gemyndians."

Einya stood, towering over the barricade high on the carriage. "I am Einya Arden, loved by Oenska and Tollska of Rask. I have them in this carriage, I'm taking them to safety."

The man on the barricade, old and stooped, didn't lower the rusty matchlock despite his trembling hands. He clearly wasn't comfortable with it, having probably picked it up from a guard. "Prove it. You might as not just have soldiers back there."

Einya jumped from the carriage, raised her hands above her head and ignored the ripping pain as she did so. "Come look, I will stand away while you do. Oenska is dead, her daughter injured. I wish to save one and burn the other."

As the crooked man lowered the matchlock, he looked around. "Beska, you hear that? Oenska, dead." The man, accompanied by the woman Einya guessed to be Beska, squeezed their way out of the wooden barricade and down the steps. Each step they took, they winced in pain.

Einya lowered her hands. "Let me help you, please."

A tense silence followed, and eventually Beska nodded and Einya slipped one arm through hers, so the elderly woman could use her as a crutch. The three of them slowly shuffled to the rear of the cart, and Einya pulled the door open with her free hand. The two figures, laid out in the back, had not moved at all in the carriage's gentle descent from Gemynd, and both looked peaceful.

The old man strangled a few soft sobs as he found the faces of the two women. "I ain't never seen so many broken lives as caused by this. Oenska was such a bright flame, like I never knew any other. I curse the day that her daughter was given the task of being sacrificial for our cause. Such radiant lights, both of them."

Einya reached out and clutched the man's wrist tenderly. "Still bright. Tollska will live if you let me pass. And Oenska's flame will burn with her, and in my love for them."

"Pass by, then," the woman croaked, her eyes dribbling with tears. "Look after them."

"I will." Einya swallowed. "There's something else. Something went wrong in Gemynd, there are beasts... I can't explain them any other way. Made from an accident with the Stars up there. They'll come if we don't block this up properly."

The man shook his head. "Block it? We have a barricade."

"It won't be enough. Can you get someone to bring down the stones of the bridge? Empty the houses beneath and collapse the lower part of the promontory."

"Is this a trick?"

Einya shook her head and unwrapped the folds of her dress to show the elderly couple the claw scratches across her skin. "I wish I was lying."

Beska reached one gnarled finger out to trace the claw marks, beckoning to a young man nearby. "We'll move the barricade and let you through, then do as you suggest. Jek, go get some folks to do that."

"Thank you." Einya pulled herself back up to the front of the carriage, sat down and slumped slightly against Malthis.

Rask had become a graveyard of the simmering husks of burnt-out buildings. Inside, people still huddled together with children, families clustered together trying to keep warm in the biting winter wind.

"It tears me down to see anyone live like this," Einya muttered.

"I never really saw it, not like this," Malthis whispered. "I always thought it was better than this."

"We all did. We all liked to look the other way."

A small cluster of men and women hustled out from within the nearby hovels, pushing the carts from the barricade aside to let the carriage pass. Then, carrying chisels, lump hammers and an assortment of rusting tools, the Raskians went about chipping away the stones of the promontory as the red sunset soaked through the streets of Rask.

Chapter Forty-Five

*The empty days of Rask are our free days, let's make the most of
them and mourn.*
~ The Word-Weaver of Rask

The carriage clattered roughly off the edge of the last
cobblestones in Rask, down a small drop onto the ridged earth of
the forest road. It led past cropped fields, which had been left
fallow over the winter months. Einya re-joined Tollska in the back
of the carriage, as she had constantly worried that Tollska would
wake and see Oenska without her there to explain everything.

Eventually, they reached the banks of the River Rask,
which hid beneath the canopy of trees and wove its way to Aisren
before tumbling over the edge of a cliff into the sea. Stopping the
carriage, Malthis went off to search for wood to build a fire.

Einya, meanwhile, cobbled together a makeshift bed from
some sheets and clothing they'd taken from an abandoned house at
the edge of Rask. She stacked them on top of each other in a rough

approximation of a mattress and tucked Tollska underneath the thickest coat she could find.

Whilst Malthis sat kindling an ember into a flame, Einya gathered some moss and fallen willow to weave into a bier. As she twisted the wood together, it rubbed against her hands until the skin on her palms was raw, but she didn't stop until a small dais was raised by the churning river.

Between her and Malthis, they awkwardly lifted Oenska from the cart, and onto the willow bed. Einya placed a handful of winter heather and snowdrops at her breast, before retreating to the fire to rub her stinging hands together and try to steal some warmth from its blaze.

"What now?" Malthis stared across the flames at her, his jaw locked together, and shoulders hunched up tightly.

Einya's eyes were lost in searching Tollska's still form for any twitches of life. "We wait until Tollska wakes."

"And then what?"

Einya smiled, plunging her hand into the tattered pocket of her gown. Her heart glowed a little with the joy of clutching hold of the card she'd come to think of as her only link with Bri, pulling it out so the light of the fire flickered against the pale letters.

"Then I will go find my brother. You can stay here, if you like."

"I can't go back to Gemynd," Malthis spluttered out, after several attempts at speaking.

"Why not? The Guard are still there, you still have a life there."

"Not if Pearth knows we helped Raskians run, we'll both be outlaws."

"I already am, I imagine. You don't have to be. Tell them I made you."

Malthis tousled the flames with a long stick until they spat and fizzled in the darkening evening. His eyebrows seemed glued together where his frown met across the bridge of his nose. The fire's sputtering and the tormented churning of the river entwined with the evensong birds in the forest. It was almost peaceful. *Almost.* Einya felt like peace would never find her again.

"Lady Arden—"

"Call me Einya, please."

Malthis seemed to wring his hands in a tight grip, lips pressed together before he spoke. "Einya, I'm not sure I want to go back. Did you see how Pearth looked, with a strange sort of ghostly glow behind her eyes? It was like looking at someone hollowed out…"

"Like a burnt-out shell of a lantern. Yes, I saw. I think she's been taking Astamitra, like you saw me do… but with a darker purpose."

"I know it's bad to be scared, but I don't want to be part of that."

"Then come with us."

"To where?" Malthis's voice rippled with uncertainty.

Einya looked from Malthis to the folded card in her hands. She struggled to flick open the wax seal, her hands riven with little jolts and trembles as she finally opened the letter.

She grinned at the guard, trying to press all uncertainties about the journey out of her expression. "To the settlement of Aisren. Mysterious as ever, my brother. We'll just have to follow the river."

"But what about all the people in Gemynd?"

"I have thought about the betterment of others all my life, at the expense of myself. One day, I'm sure I will again; but for now, I need to tend to what is closest to me," Einya mumbled, trying to ignore a fresh stab of guilt.

Malthis had opened his mouth to reply when a choked stabbing cough from the carriage caused Einya to leap upwards and run towards the sound.

She clambered through the doors into the half-light to see shrill hyperventilating breaths in a grey frosty mist puffing from Tollska's lips.

Einya scrambled towards her on hands and knees, her boots snagging against the clothes thrown across the floor.

Reaching Tollska, Einya didn't hesitate. She wrapped her arms and legs around the woman from behind, holding tenderly but securely with both. Against Tollska's frosty and trembling body, Einya felt warmth ebbing from her into Tollska. "I'm here, Tollska, it's me, I'm here."

Einya held tighter then as Tollska clutched at her, the Raskian woman's hands twisting so tightly into Einya's clothes that they might have been fused together in the darkness.

Eventually, after Tollska's lips scraped and ripped out various words in incoherent babbling whilst Einya stroked her hair, she finally said: "I remember everything, I remember it all. I could see everything, even as I was frozen in the stone."

Einya leant over and kissed her cheeks, her forehead, her eyelids and curled tenderly around her, letting the woman sob and howl, fists beating on the carriage floor. After a while she sagged into a quiet reverie, clinging tightly to Einya.

It was close to midnight when Tollska finally asked to see Oenska, and Einya patiently and gently helped Tollska struggle her way out from under the piled-up clothes. The long grass brushed their legs as they stepped down from the carriage, the moss soft beneath their feet as they walked with Tollska leaning heavily against Einya.

They slumped down together in the long grass and winter-wildflowers by Oenska's bier, with the luminescent moon casting its glow across the river and hiding shyly behind the veil of clouds. They sat by the willow deathbed until dawn crept up with a dewdrop laced breeze that brushed away the shadows of the night.

Chapter Forty-Six

The last word of life is often the most significant.
~ The Word-Weaver of Rask

The time that followed in the forest smudged together in Tollska's mind as she let herself lace her life around Einya again. It wasn't easy, not at first. Everything felt disjointed, and the sense of loss and sadness lingered for days.

Even so, Einya spent the days talking non-stop with Tollska, which she was grateful for. The Gemyndian woman she'd once called lover artfully tilted their conversations towards happier times, whilst she made stews or stoked the fire.

Tollska had looked regularly at her skin, which still had a grey glow dappling it in various places. She'd tuck her hands away quickly into the cloak to hide them, preferring not to think about it.

On one morning, when Tollska had a little more energy, she'd playfully nudged Einya in the ribs repeatedly to make her laugh with her familiar rising cadence. In the trees, it felt safer, at least for now.

"Let's go walk amongst the trees, like we used to," she suggested.

Einya had helped her walk deeper into the woods. They walked with the ferns stroking their legs as they stepped forward little by little, breathing in the musky cyclamen pollen woven into the breeze. Tollska had taken up a pointed stick in one hand and, with the other looped through Einya's arm, lifted disintegrating bark off the forest floor in search of mushrooms hiding beneath.

They returned when the tips of Tollska's fingers had turned a little blue, and they both huddled in front of the fire.

"I never loved her, you know," Tollska whispered as she watched the flames wrap themselves around the logs, and she turned with her eyes flicking left to right as she watched every scrap of Einya's reaction. She eventually untangled her words from her twisted up thoughts. "It was all politics, so I could be in Gemynd, so I could know when we needed to act."

Einya reached one hand over to Tollska's and knotted their fingers together. "I wish you had told me."

"I should have. Please, don't be angry. I didn't expect it to get this out of control. I can't lose you as well." Tollska flinched slightly then, as Einya's flurry of movement took her by surprise when she twisted her whole body so Tollska could see every expression written in her faded eyes.

"I could never, ever be angry with you."

Tollska choked out an unbidden sigh, and she relaxed a little as Einya nuzzled against her cheek and rested her forehead there.

"I am purely, and will only ever be, thrilled that I have you back," Einya whispered.

Tollska held on tighter then. "I'll stay by you. I promise you that, shining Einya."

"Even if it means leaving Rask?"

"There's nothing left for me there. Will you ever want to return to Gemynd?"

"Now I know what our ways were built on, I can't look back there. Not now, maybe never."

"We should help them; the fighting continues."

"What can we do that Aisren can't? For once, let's look to ourselves, Tollska."

"Always look forward, we say in Rask." A grin skimmed across Tollska's lips, but it faded quickly. "What about Pearth; what if she keeps expanding her clutch on Rask? Where does it end?"

Tollska watched as Einya snorted bitterly and shook her head. "Pearth will eventually destroy herself with ambition. Truthfully, I'm torn and still want to help people, but we will have to trust Aisren's soldiers to manage her. My priority is you, and to find us a life where we can be free."

Tollska stroked her thumb over Einya's hand, the corner of a smile forming gently. "So, we'll be wayward wanderers together come the morning?"

Einya nodded. "If you're ready. You'll need more comfort and healing than I can offer with a battered carriage and some tattered clothes. I hope we'll find that in Aisren, Bri might be there to help us if everything is well."

"Got it all planned out, eh, Arden?" Tollska whispered, feeling her eyes droop a little as the warmth of the fire seeped further into her frosty skin.

"Always for you, Tollska."

Tollska felt the other woman gently grip her chin, and she let Einya tilt her head until she rested comfortably against her shoulder. The last thing Tollska saw as she drifted off to sleep was Einya's grin and the hot tears raining down from her eyes; they trickled onto her cheeks as she fell into a contented slumber in Einya's arms.

Goldfinches layered their songs over one another's as the sunlight filtered away over the river, the little birds' yellow flushes flitting in and out of the foliage. Einya stared intently into the fire, hoping the flickering flames would keep her awake as she held Tollska upright against her. Einya's long hair hung loose in waves around her and Tollska's shoulders as they rested against each other.

Malthis had sagged to one side where he sat next to the fire, and Einya took up Tollska's mushroom stick from the frosty-leaf floor. She gently prodded him. "Get some sleep in the carriage, Malth. I'll stay awake here."

She stoked the fire throughout the night and watched as the ice-white sun struggled to climb over the horizon amongst a gentle descent of snow.

In the morning, when everyone was awake, Einya toasted the last of the mushrooms on twigs poked into the dying embers of the flames. They awkwardly ate these stuffed into the crumbling stale rolls Einya had taken from the settlement, washing away the crusted fragments of bread from their throats with a little water from the river.

Then, crouched at the river's edge by the bier, Einya coaxed the last of the embers into a small flame that she kept stoked with her dwindling pile of twigs. Outside the small circle of fire, filigree frost wove over the leaves of the woodland floor. Across the river, the Raskian farming fields were dappled with morning snow save for where scrub-plants poked through and reached toward the sun.

A little distance away, Tollska stood with her hand entwined in Oenska's hair.

"Time to set our feet on a different path, Ma. Blow free with the wind, wherever it takes you," she whispered to her mother.

Einya reached up with one hand, clutching the tips of Tollska's fingers with a tender squeeze. "Are you sure you're ready? We can wait a bit longer if you need."

"Just another spike in the road, Einya. It wouldn't stop her, and it won't stop me."

Einya let her hand tumble back to the forest floor, feeling admiration warm her heart. "Even in the harshest of storms, you never seem to be struck by lightning." Einya looked up as she felt the gentle fumble of fingers running through the coarse strands of her hair, Tollska's hand twisting through them one by one.

Tollska's asymmetrical smile, curved upwards only on one side, glowed as much as the Stars that Einya still saw spotted in her vision. "It's just about making sure you don't split down the middle when the lightning strikes. You are stronger than you think."

The three of them slid the bier off the rustling russet leaves and onto the river. Malthis held onto the edge as the wooden frame strained against his grip in the current.

"Pass me up that flame, sweet starlight," Tollska asked.

Einya smiled softly. It'd been a long time since Tollska had called her that. She took a thin branch, burnt the tip in the lone flame until it sparked onto the new wood and spread onto the branch. Passing it to Tollska, Einya stood and wrapped one arm around the woman's waist. A warm glow radiated through her as if the Stars were present again but this time less invasive and otherworldly.

Tollska set the torch to the wood and the flames took quickly, clinging to the dry moss that snaked around the pyre. Einya felt her eyes twinge as Tollska's emerald eyes welled up with tears, which fell into the flames and hissed away into the dewy air. Einya gently rubbed the remaining glints of tears away with the hem of her sleeve and kissed her eyelids tenderly. "She's sailing over the breeze, away to fantastic adventures."

"To a bright world she never found here."

"She found brightness wherever she went, Tollska."

Einya felt Tollska cling a little tighter, then, as the woman choked out a final "goodbye."

A trembling twist of purple smoke simmered out of the pyre in that final moment before Malthis let go of the straining bier and it floated down the river amongst the fallen leaves drifting there.

Her heart struck hard against her chest, as if two flecks of flint were being bashed together to spark the glow of determination she felt as Tollska turned away and walked back to the carriage.

"I will knit happiness into every aspect of her life, for as long as I can. Let my love journey with you, Oenska," Einya mumbled, kissing her fingers and holding them out after the drifting bier.

The lavender wisp danced through the rest of the grey smoke before twisting away into the distance as the bier floated out of sight. The last plumes of smoke wafted between the fluttering snowflakes until Einya couldn't see the flash of colour amongst them any longer. Her boots pressed into the grey-frosted leaves as she trudged away to the carriage.

Chapter Forty-Seven

*Our three settlements were always too close; they would always
threaten to overlap.*
~ Breyneda of Aisren

Bri had waited at the forest opening for a month after the
soldiers had left for Gemynd. Today, he rested his legs against the
crumbling stone and felt the ivy brush against them as if they were
claiming him as well as the structure. Breyneda sat beside him,
gently whittling a small frog out of a piece of fallen wood.

She smiled across at him. "You keep your words unusually
locked in, Briarth Arden."

His golden eyes roved away from the road winding into the
distance. "I begin to doubt that she got away," he mumbled, tightly
gripping his arms around his chest.

Breyneda reached one hand over and tilted his chin up, and
Bri couldn't help but smirk a little then. "She may already be here,
Bri. Or will be very soon. Let us go look again."

"Where would she be, though? She would find me and tell me how much she dreamed of somewhere this filled up with nature. It'd be the first thing she'd do."

"Let us look anyway, and then get you warmed through a little. The heated wines should be brewing by now."

Bri smiled, rising to his feet. He and Breyneda stepped lightly amongst the leaves that spiralled around the dilapidated archway, hopping easily down the steps to the woodland floor. Abutting the gate were thick-trunked evergreen trees, mostly towering pines, that stretched deep into the heart of Aisren beyond the gate.

As much as he had happily etched the sight of Aisren into his mind, the foliage-framed windows and the vines plunging over every scrap of stone they could find always ripped the breath from his lungs and filled him with awe. The Aisrenese called it the Reclamation—when they had stepped away from the stone world and let the leaves return—but Bri hadn't found out much more than this.

Breyneda led him through the winding root-crossed paths, stopping at all the places they usually looked for Einya and some of the ones they didn't. The forest kept only its usual inhabitants. They eventually settled under a small canopy of trees where a grinning man was trading heated elderberry wine, Breyneda procuring two steaming clay cups by trading her little carved frog for them.

As Bri wrapped his hands around the cup and felt the heat pricking back into his hands, he looked over to where Breyneda sat, her curled brown hair twisting up at the ends like ivy reaching to cling to a wall.

"I still can't quite get my head around this place, even though I've been here for maybe a month? But I lose track," he spoke.

Breyneda grinned, her earth-coloured eyes dappled in the evening sun breaking through the canopy as it dropped low behind the trees. "This was always meant to be the way."

They both sipped at the fragrant wine, hearing the evensong of birds chime like church bells telling the hour.

"What happened with the Reclamation?" he asked. "You've spoken of it before, but never told how it came about."

"Curious, aren't you?"

"Always, it's my most endearing and annoying quality."

"Like a cat." She grinned again, leaned over and gently rubbed behind his ear.

"Exactly that," he mumbled, nudging her hand with the side of his head. It felt strange, letting someone else into his heart, but he couldn't hold himself back. It wasn't in his nature.

Breyneda stood, the folds of her skirt tumbling back around her knees as she did so. "Come on then, let me show you the answer to your curiosity."

Bri drained away the last of the wine, setting his cup down on the trader's table before shuffling into the thick undergrowth after his companion. They didn't walk far, and Bri was surprised he hadn't seen this little path off into the woods before as he followed the skipping steps of Breyneda.

A grove stretched out before them with cornflowers and lavender twined around each other, filling almost the entirety of the space between the trees. In the centre of the wildflower meadow, a large but barely visible rock orb sat. It could scarcely be seen underneath the clinging vines and purple climbing flowers weaving over the entirety of the stone's surface, little ferns and alpines half-hidden away in the pocks of the rock.

Breyneda had slipped her boots off at the side of the glade and now walked softly through the flowers until she had wound her hand in the vines around the rock. Looking back to him, she smiled, and he felt his heart trembling against his ribcage at the enchanted beauty of the sun-soaked leaves creating their own little paths wherever they could reach.

"This is our Star," Breyneda whispered, but the words still caught up with him in the lavender-scented breeze. "This was how the Reclamation began."

He looked, and the vines seemed to be sprouting from the Star with an oak-leaf hued glow gently fading in and out of focus around the roots. "How?"

"There was no more need for coins; we saw its horrors when Parlenta offered us gold for our wood and our Star. We told them no, and they put many of us to the blade. The Star forced them out, blended its light with the trees. Now, the woodland protects us."

Bri looked back at the leaf-laden Star, his jaw still hanging loosely open. "My sister will love it here, if she gets to see it."

Breyneda retraced her steps back through the undergrowth towards him and clutched his hand. "She will."

Bri leant his head against his companion's; he felt as if their long hair twined together as the flowers and ivy had curled around each other in the glade. A bright, slightly mournful, warbling birdsong trembled through the trees, which Bri was sure emanated from the vine-clad Star.

Chapter Forty-Eight

Happiness is often best found after strife.
~ Breyneda of Aisren

Winter wind hammered the carriage, frosty gusts battering in through the flimsy windowpanes. Einya had gratefully stepped away from the reins, letting Malthis guide the horses for a while, and she had gone to huddle next to Tollska, her hands trembling with blue frost clinging to them. She felt ill, and the cuts in her chest didn't seem to be closing as fast as she had expected. It had been nearly two weeks of the carriage slowly being dragged through the undergrowth of the forest towards Aisren, and Einya had roughly tried to guide them for a while but lost track somewhere along the way when the road had veered away from the river.

Now, buried under a few thick coats, she felt like her eyelids were carved of stone and she weakly clung to Tollska's side. Tollska pressed the back of her palm against Einya's clammy forehead, and Einya was only faintly aware of that and the fact that her wounds still ached. The rumble and jolting of the carriage did little to help this.

Malthis paused the carriage occasionally to light a fire and toast the stale bread clumsily, to try and make it palatable. With much cajoling, Einya managed to stumble her way out of the carriage to sit by the fire and nibble at the toasted chunks of bread. She shivered, feeling as if a river was running down her face.

Yet, for all this, she was grateful whilst Tollska chattered nervously away across from her.

"Not long left," she said. "And imagine what adventures we'll have then, when Briarth shows us all the wonders he's discovered, just like when you were young."

Einya could only bring herself to smile and chuckle a little, which then collapsed away into wet hacking coughs, while Tollska and Malthis shared increasingly fretful looks.

Thankfully, she didn't have to think about that for much longer when they helped her back to the carriage, a little warmer for eating. Einya sagged back into the pile of old clothes, eyelids dropping shut into a thick and heavy sleep. It was fitful and the Stars seemed ever-present in her dreams, reaching out to her and engulfing her in stone and starlight.

When she woke, it felt like a strangely warped amount of time had eluded her whilst she slept. A chromatic chattering of birdsong crept into her ears.

There was no movement and no fretful conversations between Malthis and Tollska that she remembered from the past few days. Instead, the only sounds were the morning chorus and the crackle of a fire, spattering away next to her as dry leaves fizzled into pleasant-smelling smoke. Beneath her, soft moss cradled her back better than any grand mattress she remembered, and a soothing scent of lavender mingled with the sweet scent of roasting chestnuts.

When she finally managed to prise open her eyes, the sky shining with bright Stars hung above her, cloaked partially by the clouds. Near her head, a tiny wren trembled its wings as it settled by a cornflower and pecked at a little cluster of seeds. It jittered about playfully until Einya reached one hand slowly towards and it hopped away to a nearby flower.

"Decided to wake up then?"

Einya rolled her head quickly over to the other side at the familiar buttery-soft voice and felt a little light-headed. Bri sat there, close enough to reach out to, plaiting together dried flowers that had fallen to the ground. He set them quickly aside as Einya tried to struggle upright, placing a firm hand on the small of her back to steady her as she sat up.

Grinning, a twitter of laughter welling up within her, she tried for some words whilst her gaze was torn between her brother and the woodland. "You found me and took me to the trees. I've never seen trees so large... is it real?"

"What else would it be?" Bri smirked and eased himself closer, draping one arm over her shoulder so they nestled next to each other. "This is Aisren, they revere trees over all else."

Einya frowned, surprised, yet relieved. "They don't follow the Stars?"

"Not in the same way Gemynd does."

Bri explained the Reclamation, and with characteristically flowery words, he described the vines flowing out of the Star to grow the wood and wrap the stone houses of Aisren in verdant cladding.

Einya felt like her heart was laced with new wonder, like a fresh and untasted air had filled her up with undiminishing energy.

She toyed with the tip of a climber's vine that had wrapped itself over her leg, tumbling through different thoughts and questions.

"The Stars choose where to place their glow, then..." she said at last.

Bri nodded a little. "Breyneda says you and Tollska still have a little within you."

"Breyneda?"

"The architect of the Reclamation, if she can be called that."

"Aisren's leader?"

"They don't really have a leader, but if they did it would be her. You'll meet her and like her, I've no doubt."

Einya looked around the glade then, eyes a little wide. "Where's Tollska? Is she still afflicted with the Star? Is she well?"

"She is, sis; we've taken turns sitting with you. You've been here a few days. She still has a little of the grey glow to her skin, but that should fade, apparently. Maybe your eyes will get their colour back too..."

"Do we know that?"

"Well, not precisely, but she's already looking healthier. Peace, Einya, all is well. Tollska tells me you tried to kill our cousin?"

Einya nodded. "She was sacrificing Raskians, and she dragged us all with her into her darkness. It had to end. I drank undiluted blood of the Stars, and..."

Bri waved one hand and Einya's words faded. "Tollska and Malthis told me, between them. You don't need to repeat it if you don't want to."

Einya just nodded, grateful, but everything she had thought to say still burned on her tongue. "There was still fighting when we left..."

"Is it over, then? No one in Aisren has heard back from the rangers they sent to help."

"It still continues, perhaps. In truth, I don't know. Pearth had somehow made beasts using the Stars."

"There's a power to the Stars we still don't understand... Parlenta is further along than Gemynd ever was. I saw that first-hand. What were they like, can I ask?"

Einya tried a few times to explain what had become of the Raskians that had been imprisoned in the Star cavern, but eventually, she shook her head and pointed instead with a trembling hand to the claw mark raked across her chest, which had been smeared with a green poultice.

"They were made from the Stars' energy," was all she managed to mumble.

Einya saw Bri's smile was wrapped in a sadness for everything he couldn't understand but could only guess at. He gripped her fingers gently and didn't ask anything more.

"I'm sorry I was not there for you." He brushed one tiny drip of a tear away from the corner of Einya's eye. She felt warmth bubble within her as she smiled back at him. It was good to be back close to Bri.

He stood, offering his hand to Einya and swiping away a tear from his eye. "Let's go find Tollska, I'm sure you want to see her."

They walked through the trees, admiring all the leaves glistening in their mid-morning dew coats. Winding through little mossy paths dotted with lilac flowers, Bri led them both to a canopy by a river, next to a quaint building crowned with ivy.

The small oak door to the hut had meandering vine marks over it. "They have to take the vines from the doors or lose access entirely, unfortunately! But they always just move them, so they cling on elsewhere."

Einya's lips were slightly parted as she gawped at the perfection of this place; the canopy outside the hut was a piece of canvas suspended on a wooden frame with wisteria twining around it and small oil lanterns woven between the hanging flowers. It seemed everything flowered here, even when it would normally be out of season.

Einya reached up to brush her fingers over the small purple flowers hanging over the door. "I hope they'll let me stay here," she whispered.

Bri tugged the door open. Curled up on a knitted pouf was Tollska, Malthis and a radiant woman she didn't recognise. It looked like a forest-witch's caravan in here, with little trinkets like fallen acorns or painted driftwood hanging from every part of the walls. The scent of heated cider hung with a sweet tang in the air, but to Einya, all of this formed part of a beautiful tapestry backdrop to the sight of Tollska, who sat with her legs tucked underneath her.

She was thinner than Einya remembered, and her skin was still mottled grey, but there was something warm and free in the woman's demeanour and her bright green eyes and plaited hair with leaves woven into it.

Einya struggled for words, feeling a furnace burning within her as she stepped into the little room. She was faintly aware of Bri ushering the others out, and the childish giddy whispers they shared as they left together.

"Tollska, I'm so sorry for all that…" Einya began, but her voice quickly trailed off.

Tollska was still smiling as she held one hand up to her own lips, pressing a finger against them. "Don't speak, close the door."

Einya fumbled behind her for the handle and tugged it shut whilst keeping her eyes on Tollska.

Tollska shifted her weight to the side and gently dug her hand into her pocket. The woman's eyes glowed with natural warmth, beautiful smile lines framing them. A small leaf-package sat cocooned in the kneeling woman's hands.

Nestled in Tollska's fingers, between the leaves, was an ornately carved wooden ring with an emerald stone set within it. "Einya, will you wed me in a starlit glen and stay with me in this paradise?"

Einya's heart thrummed with joy as she knelt carefully down on the creaking wooden floor. Could it really be, after all this? Words didn't form, but she nodded vigorously, grinning, with tears running rivers down her face as Tollska smiled and slipped the smooth ring onto her finger.

In the little hut, they curled up together, feeling the warmth of the winter sun dapple their skin and gently soak away the grey stone hue from their lives.

Chapter Forty-Nine

The Reclamation will guard us from the ravenous eyes of other settlements.
~ Breyneda of Aisren

A week later, Einya had found her way into most of the hidden woodland paths that wound through Aisren. She'd found a new warren or ivy-clad hideaway every day and had quickly grown to love the simple life of the forest. Bri had given her some notion of how the barter system worked here, and she had found a few ways to trade little trinkets she made or blessings on weddings and celebrations in exchange for food.

She found that, although the barter system nominally existed, there was no set value to any of the goods traded, and everyone always made sure those who had not traded something still ate and had all they needed. Everyone seemed confident that the kindness would be repaid on a different day, and there was a general ease about the whole system.

Breyneda, she found, was the radiant woman who'd been in the hut. Bri had quickly introduced Einya to her, and the two of them had shown Einya around all the places they thought she would love before settling in the evening to drink hot wine and eat sweet meats.

Einya's gladness at her brother's clear happiness with Breyneda wove quickly through her, and she found a love for the woman as well. Her warmth and unfiltered kindness were evidently the backbone of Aisren, and it was easy to think of her as a sister.

Instead of saying anything to Bri about Luskena, Einya just silently slipped the woman's necklace she carried with her to Bri one evening. She clasped his hand as she did and Bri just nodded, clutched the pendant to his lips and briefly kissed it.

"She's gone?" he whispered.

"Gone," Einya said and watched as he cast the pendant into the river, whispering his goodbye.

"I loved her with everything I had, so thank you for letting me move on."

Einya just nodded and pulled her brother closer to her so he could rest against her as they watched the sun set over the water together.

One evening, some days later, when Tollska was away with Bri making some plans for the wedding they wouldn't tell her about, Einya sat with Breyneda. They dangled their feet in the stream, the current rippling around their toes. The curious fox that usually followed Bri around squirmed playfully in the long grass nearby. As with everything here, the water was warm and felt more like a summery stream than a frosty winter one. They spoke about anything and everything, their conversation easily flowing. One question burnt strongly on Einya's lips, and she finally forced herself to ask it.

"Breyneda, can I ask, why let me stay here? I go against all you believe in, as an Astrologer from Gemynd."

Breyneda smiled. "Those are just words, and though the Stars still cling to you, they can leave you and disperse their energy if you let them."

"I want them gone, but I don't know how."

"I'll show you if you like. It's how the Reclamation happened, after all," Breyneda offered.

"Why haven't you made me disperse them, if it's against what you stand for?"

Breyneda reached one hand out and brushed one finger over Einya's hand. "It's not quite like that; it's a little more complex. You keep the glow if you need the glow; it goes where it is needed."

"It chooses?"

"Sort of, I suppose. But some things are better as a mystery!" She grinned. "I think that maybe you'll need it one day."

"And Tollska?"

"Well, she didn't take it willingly by the sounds of it—but, yes, maybe."

"Can she get rid of it?"

"If she wishes, yes."

"How do you know all this?" Einya wondered aloud.

Breyneda looked out over the river, a wistful look drifting over her face. "I am the descendant of the Astrologer-Elect who was forced away from Gemynd for her support of Rask, all those years ago. We've kept the knowledge ever since, in case we needed to stop Gemynd doing it again."

"Or Parlenta."

"Indeed."

Einya soaked the information in and found her questions fled her. "I need to think about this, but for now I want to forget Gemynd. I may ask you again, one day, if that's alright?"

Breyneda smiled at her, warmth radiating through her expression. "Whenever you wish."

The following night, Einya stood within a moonlit glade, a garland of lavender plaited by Bri twisted through the braids in her hair. Tollska's hands were wound around her own, and they clung tightly to avoid slipping apart again. Lanterns hung from the trees, their wicks burning low. Glints of starlight speckled the underside of fallen logs beneath the canopy where glow worms hung their threads.

As Breyneda wrapped their hands in cloth and sang to the trees for the union, the eternal birdsong chorus chimed along with her, and there in the glade, Tollska and Einya were bound as one. The remnant glow in their hands glistened as they tenderly held onto each other. Einya felt her heart throb with an easy happiness. This is where I am meant to be, this is who I am meant to be. She thought, smiling warmly as she and Tollska gazed at each other.

"Einya…" Tollska whispered as the ceremony dissolved into celebrations.

"Yes?"

"There's some blue back in your eyes."

"You are the colour in my life," Einya whispered.

"I always will be."

The feasting lasted late into the night, with rich tapestries of food spread on wicker baskets across the moonlit forest floor. Einya and Tollska allowed themselves to be absorbed into the festivities, both grinning widely. Rose petals were steeped in boiling water, then mixed with an array of floral-scented alcoholic elixirs. The dancing and music lapsed over into the morning when the scarlet sun burst its way through the trees.

Bri stood beyond the wood line as the day emerged, sombrely sipping on the cold remnants of his wine. Beyond the distant Raskian trees, an ash cloud of smoke drifted towards Aisren. Only Bri saw it and caught its charcoal scent, knowing it would one day beckon them back. He dreaded that day.

He returned to the smiles and laughter of the celebrations, forcing his lips into a grin. He said nothing, even as the smoke still stung inside his nose.

Epilogue

We may run from the words of our past, but they always stay with us.
~ The Word Weaver of Rask

A few days later, Bri found Einya in a glow-worm lit glade, nestled between the outstretched roots of a fallen tree. He settled beside her, their shoulders brushing closely. *It is time.* He sighed.

After a long silence, he spoke. "I'm leaving, and it will be the only thing I've done right in these past months. Trust me."

Einya turned to face him, a strangely unreadable look in her eyes. "No notes this time?"

"No notes, just trust."

"I'll come with you…"

He shook his head. "No, you should live in peace. I've something to make right. There's something I need to tell you… I got this so wrong, Einya. What our cousin did was wrong, but it was me who told the Parlentan Queen that Rask needed help. I told her we were weak, and that the civil war raged, and because of that, I think she'll take our home if what Tollska says is right. Tollska told me a messenger came to demand the Stars. Our cousin is still there, fighting for our settlement…"

"What are you saying?"

"I need to go back to help."

"So, you're on our cousin's side now? After all she did to us?"

"Parlenta tried to control me using their Star, Einya. I was lucky I didn't become one of the beasts you saw… I must stop that happening to our family, our people. There might still be light left in Gemynd's Stars…"

The fox skittered around their legs as Einya shook her head. "I don't know how to follow your whims, Bri… please, stay."

Bri smiled, clutching his sister's hand. "I'm on freedom's side, Einya, if sides even exist in this world anymore. I'll make sure no one is enthralled like they tried to do to me. If it wasn't for Quandary, then…"

Bri felt his heart tremble at the single tear that tumbled down Einya's cheek as she spoke. "Bri, you're still vulnerable. Even if…"

"I have an idea, it will work. Trust me. My heart is bound here, like yours is. If it goes wrong, I'll have Quandary with me and Breyneda in my heart. I will do the right thing, but I'll act with caution this time," he assured her.

"You've changed, Bri."

The little fox had flumped next to Einya. He'd begun to nestle up to her but had pricked his ears up at his name. Bri smirked as Einya rested one hand uneasily on the fox's head and he *peruffed* gently at her touch.

"Look after him, little fox," Einya whispered.

It was a day later when Bri left, dressed back in the gold-white tattered doublet he'd worn when he had arrived in Aisren. He carried a large haversack upon his back, which Quandary had obligingly hidden within as if it was part of some great game. The fox now had the canvas lid of the pack balanced on his head like a hat, so he could duck back within the large bag if needed.

Bri thought he must be imagining this level of awareness in Quandary and had to remind himself this was a Star, not just a fox.

It took him three days riding swiftly to reach Rask. He hadn't stopped except to eat small morsels of pie and fruit, and then journey on again. In the foothills of the farms, he finally slowed. Tall pillars of smoke still spiked up from the housing districts of the lower edge of the settlement.

In the battered, dilapidated streets where the guiding words that were painted on the sides of buildings had faded, amongst the blood splatter across the white facades, he walked with the horse clopping along behind him. He tethered the steed at the corner of the cottage he'd spent many days printing pamphlets inside.

Leaning against the back of the hovel, he took from his pocket a large flask that stunk with the paint-like stench of overly strong brandy. He unstoppered it and in three long, calculated glugs, he drank it all down.

"Quandary, time to keep quiet like we spoke about. Time for the plan. You'll know how to find me?"

One chirrup-like gekker answered him, and he smiled. Then, taking his warm boots from his feet, he stashed them in the cottage. Barefooted, he stumbled off into the streets.

It didn't take long. He found a crowd of Parlentan soldiers stood by a tavern, and he staggered up to them. They were passing bottles around between them. They were drunk, that was good—it would make this easier. He sagged to his knees, voice slurring all his syllables into one as he spoke. "Please, I need the Queen. I must..."

"Who are you? How did you come here?" one guard spat.

"I followed her, she is everything to me, I need the light she gifted me. I am hollow without her," Bri mumbled, hoping he seemed ragged enough and that he'd said the right thing. He kept his eyes downcast, curled in on himself to appear desperate.

"He's one of the experiments...gotta be," the same guard spoke.

"How did he get to be here?" another said.

"He followed. Didn't you hear? We'll take him to the Queen."

Bri didn't object and let himself be taken. They dragged him, heels bashing, through the streets. Laughing, they too having drunk too much. Vague mutterings and bright lights of street lanterns wavered through his thoughts, his head spinning slightly.

The base of a promontory was where they dropped him. Beyond scattered remnants of barricades, a large stone barrier stood in the distance, erected in a wall-like structure between Rask and Gemynd. He tried not to look that far ahead but tried to stare doe-eyed at the woman before him. It wasn't so hard. She was clad in a magnificent gem-encrusted dress, but this time it had plates of jewel-embellished armour over it. Her imperious look seemed somehow splendid as she turned, and Bri swallowed. *Be strong. I hope I haven't misjudged myself ...*

"My Queen, he begged to see you," one of the soldiers announced.

Bri held his head up limply where he knelt, and then bent in a bow until the skin of his forehead brushed the tip of her shoe. The Queen's bone-like hand lifted his jaw, her eyes digging deep into his.

"My little experiment. Unexpected." Her eyes glowed, colourless but bright.

"I've been lost without…"

"Hush, hush."

She reached one hand out, thumb grazing the tip of his hairline. Silk-like, the stroke of her thumb slid over the fine hairs above his nose and down to the tip. He quivered at her touch, feeling unexpectedly flushed.

A brief glint of almond shone through her grey eyes, which shone brightly in the firelight of the lanterns as she smiled magnificently. Bri reached one hand out to clutch her slender, ring-clad fingers and pressed them to his lips.

To be continued...

Acknowledgements

My eternal gratitude to my wonderful friends Liz and Sally, who read the entire manuscript and encouraged me to keep writing when uncertainty struck.

To my crazy best friend Ana: thank you for psychoanalysing my characters and being the spark for much of my creativity for as long as I can remember.

To Mum, who would have been so pleased to see her daughter become a published author. To Dad, who always believed I could.

Lastly my everlasting love to Paul for being supportive, patient, encouraging and fun.

About The Author

Alexandra was raised on fairy tales, folklore and legends. She followed adventures at every turn: exploring the old parts of London, taking part in medieval re-enactments, and writing in every spare moment.

When not writing, Alexandra has a wanderlust for exploring new places, roaming the countryside and taking part in Live Action Fantasy Role Play. (Meaning she's often covered in mud, grass and leaves.) Her passion for exploring new worlds drives her creative endeavours.

https://twitter.com/ABeaumontWriter
https://www.instagram.com/ABeaumontWrites/
https://www.facebook.com/ABeaumontWrites/
https://abeaumont75.wixsite.com/home

A Gurt Dog Press
Publication

2021

Printed in Great Britain
by Amazon